ANCESTRAL SIN

Maureen Devlin

With love to all my friends and family.
We will see each other again.

Chapter 1

Detective Inspector Tom Ashton stretched, luxuri-
ating in the fact that it was early on a Friday
morning and he had the day off. Even better he wasn't
alone.

Wrapping his right arm around Lily's warm, soft
waist, he let his head sink towards the fragrant nape
of her neck. It was hard to believe they'd only known
each other a short time. She smelt so familiar.

He kissed her shoulder. He kissed her again, hoping
to rouse her from sleep but the only reaction he got
was a small sigh. He raised his head up a couple of
inches to peer at the clock. To be fair, 5.45am possibly
was a little early for a repeat of last night's activity.
He'd give it another half an hour.

"Wha?!" The beeping of his mobile phone woke
him so suddenly that his whole body shot into flight
mode. Heart racing, his legs were over the edge of the
bed before he realised what he was doing. He peered
at the screen and saw that the caller was Dean
Wilson. He'd been asleep for just over the planned

thirty minutes. A conversation with his friend and colleague was not what he had in mind right now.

"This had better be good," he hissed, slipping out of the bedroom so as not to disturb Lily. She hadn't stirred.

"It isn't," came the reply. "It's the worst. Get down here. Long stay car park by Terminal 3."

Tom stared for a moment at the silent phone. Dean ringing him at inconvenient moments wasn't unusual, but his voice sounded weird. Tight and small; which for a bodybuilding, ex inner-city school teacher was very unusual indeed. He hadn't sounded angry. He'd sounded frightened.

Tom wound down the window of his aging maroon BMW. A kind breeze wove around the inside of the car as he sped towards the main arterial road south. Traffic was building on the opposite carriageway but it was still light travelling away from the city and he was soon joining the M56, heading for Manchester International Airport.

What the hell had freaked Dean out? The guy was as tough as they come. Tom had only seen his colleague crumble once in all the time he'd known him – crushed almost to defeat by false charges of sexual assault and racism. But that was personal. On a case? Never.

He reached the entrance to the car park a little under fifteen minutes later. A slim female officer was standing firmly behind a sign stating that the car park was closed while clearly trying to appease a stressed traveller. Tom edged his car onto the pavement and around the stricken man's Mercedes, ignoring the yell of protest. Tom quickly rolled down his window and held out his ID card.

A second young airport constable was waiting by the ticket booth, flanked by a plump, sweating man in tight grey shirt and black trousers and a large German Shepherd dog. Tom raised an eyebrow in query.

"DS Wilson is at the site, sir. Bottom left corner."

Tom nodded as the barrier lifted to allow him through.

Dean wasn't alone. With him were two airport officers and two men wearing the distinctive jackets of the Explosives and Ordnance Division. A bomb? They all turned as he approached, staying silent as he got out of the car. Tom's eyes flicked over to the small robot standing to attention near the rear of a small red Fiesta. What the hell was going on? Dean's face was the colour of chalk and his lips were clamped tight shut.

Tom introduced himself, firmly establishing control as the senior investigating officer.

"Dean?"

"A body." Dean rubbed his face vigorously. "Or at least, part of one. Told you it was the worst."

Tom scanned the faces of the other officers.

"Who called this in?"

The larger of the two spoke first.

"Attendant noticed something odd about this car, sir. Brings his dog sometimes to keep him company. Was walking it when the dog went ballistic, sniffing around the boot of this one. The guy saw a wire dangling from underneath; just didn't like the look of it so called us. Check showed it'd been stolen a few months ago. We did a Ballinger test. Positive, so we alerted the EOD and they sent 'Charlie' in. "He nodded towards the robot, then swallowed hard. "No explosives."

Tom could see the officer was shaken but his brief resume was enough for now.

"I'll need more from you all later," he said, turning to look back at Dean. "Let's see it then."

Dean hesitated, just for a second. Tom narrowed his eyes.

"What gives?"

"Just – prepare yourself."

Tom raised his eyebrows. This could hardly be worse than the state of the young rent boy squashed in a wheelie bin just before Christmas and left to the rats.

"The boot, Dean," Tom spoke quietly, reaching into his pocket for a pair of latex gloves.

Dean clicked it open. Inside was a large cheap black canvas sports bag. Tom put on the gloves before leaning in and gently taking hold of the metal zipper. He took a deep breath.

"You fasten this up?"

"Yep. Couldn't leave it open. Not right."

Tom turned his head and saw that Dean was facing away from the car, his jawline clenched and his arms fastened tightly across his chest. Tom looked back into the boot and opened the bag.

"Dear God."

The little bundle was unmistakably the remains of a child, and yet hardly human. For a moment, Tom couldn't think of what it did look like – his brain wanting to reject the idea that this was someone's son or daughter. He saw green and white stained fabric. He saw the places where arms, legs and head should be. Fury gripped him; then he caught the smell. Faintly metallic, rich but cloying. Like an old-fashioned butcher's shop.

"The SOCOs on their way?" Tom asked as he forced himself to keep looking at the contents of the bag.

"Yep. Delayed over in Rochdale."

Tom nodded, trying to keep his mind on the tasks they needed to do.

"Get the place sealed properly. Car park closed until further notice. Get what info you can from the attendant. I'll contact the pathologist."

Tom gently eased one leg of the shorts away from the torso with a gloved finger. He zipped the bag back up with as much care as he could before closing the car boot, resting his hand on it until it gave a slight click. Acid poured into his empty stomach and he swallowed hard to control the bile that rose in his throat.

He wrenched off the gloves and pushed them into the plastic bag Dean was holding open for him. His mind was racing with questions. Who was he? How old? How long had the car been here? Who the fuck does that to a child? Why?

In less than an hour the area was swarming with activity. Three SOCOs, in white protective suits, quietly and painstakingly examined the inside and outside of the car. A photographer stood slightly to one side, recording the scene. He must have taken twenty images of the bag in the boot; its position – zip open and zip closed and at least as many more of the grisly contents. Zoom in, zoom out. Tom felt faintly sick.

Ray Stephenson stood waiting nearby for the cameraman to finish. He was also in protective gear, his hands gloved and ready. Tom liked the young pathologist a lot, but he wondered again how he dealt with the daily companion of death. He'd need all his clinical detachment for this one. Especially given the age of his own two sons.

"All done, sir."

Tom nodded as the photographer moved away. He watched as the pathologist approached the car and leaned into the boot. As he walked up to join him, Tom saw the doctor's shoulders rise as he drew a very deep breath.

They stood in silence. Tom waited as his colleague pushed the sides of the open bag apart as far as they would go. The harsh arc light all but erased the weak spring morning sunlight, throwing a shadow around the car but bringing the gruesome find into sharp relief.

"Jesus, Tom. What bastards..." Stephenson's voice trembled slightly, then he coughed, took another deep breath and when he spoke again, it was in a detached, professional monotone.

"I'd say he was between three and four years old. Without the teeth, it's going to be difficult." He eased up the little vest. "Mixed race." He peered in more closely.

"At first glance, I'd say the head and limbs were hacked off with a saw but I'll know more when I get him back to the morgue. Not much blood so I suspect he was drained of that before he was put in the bag. When did you say the car was parked?" His fingers pushed the vest further up and he gently kneaded the boy's stomach. The skin was a ghastly shade of beige.

"Not sure. Dean's going to have to go through the CCTV. Car park issues a ticket that the driver takes away. Could be days."

Stephenson nodded.

"The cool weather's minimised the decomposition but I would say he's been dead at least forty-eight hours."

The briefing room near the canteen was small and coffee-scented. Tom wanted to share what information he had with the team away from distractions of the open plan CID office. There was a space in the corner by the window they'd section off as a quasi-incident room; keep everything in one place. Right now, he needed to gather his thoughts, to help him treat the briefing like a training session.

He'd bought a huge black coffee at the airport after finishing his interviews with the officers involved and alerting the divisional head. Getting it back to the office had been a challenge; he'd ended up wedging the cup amongst the clutter in his boot. At least now the stuff was cool enough to drink. Holding the paper cup that was almost a bucket, he wondered whether he was putting too much trust in his forty-two-year-old bladder.

DS Ryan was the first to arrive. She'd been with Manchester CID for just over two years and Tom rated her. She was competent and thorough and her regular spats with Dean brought out the best in both of them. She was even easier to work with now that she'd finally given up the chewing gum and constant snacking that she'd needed to quit smoking. Her short dark hair looked damp.

"Afternoon, sir," she breezed. "That stuff'll kill you," she added, eyeing the container in Tom's hand.

He groaned. "Don't tell me you're off caffeine now."

Ryan gave up alcohol in another detox drive but it hadn't lasted. She always tried to make him feel guilty and it generally annoyed him, but right now he was glad of the trivial banter.

"This is my second of the day," he lied just to see her wince. "Still on that herb tea that smells of cat piss?"

"It's nettle," she retorted. "And I'll bet my liver is in better nick than yours."

"No chance. Saw you in the wine bar last week. Nothing herbal going down then."

Ryan held up her hands.

"You've got me," she said and smiled.

"Reckon we'll all be sinking a few before this is over," Tom said, half under his breath.

Ryan looked at him, her smile fading.

Five minutes later, he rapped his knuckles on the table to get everyone's attention. There were eight of them in the room. All conscientious officers but Ryan, Dean and DC Elliott were the brightest of the bunch by a mile. Intuitive detectives with sharp minds and equally sharp instincts. Only the newest member of the team, DC Joe Talbot, was a parent.

Dean was standing at the back of the room, leaning against the wall. Tom wasn't fooled by the relaxed pose. Dean knew most of what was coming. He'd earlier confessed to Tom that he was filled with such rage for whoever had done this, he was worried about how he'd control himself if they found the killer. Tom figured he wasn't the only one.

"We've got a dead child," he began, then ran quickly through the events leading up to the call to CID.

"Just to remind you, we don't know when the vehicle was left but it's now been nearly ten hours since the car park guy alerted the airport police thinking he'd found a bomb."

Elliott raised his hand.

"How come the positive Barringer?"

"Forensics are at the site now. Could be drug traces but apparently the test strip can react to hydrogen peroxide – bleach. But not the household stuff, has to be stronger. Like they use in hairdressers. The airport guys have had a few false alarms because of that."

Tom took a long drink of coffee. Then he described the boy, his injuries and the early deductions of the pathologist. The room was quiet, as everyone absorbed the horror behind his words.

"I hardly need to tell you that this case is our priority," he said. "I want Dean and Ryan to lead on trying to find the driver. The rest of you start by checking missing persons. Someone must be wondering where this boy is."

He took more coffee.

He waited, hoping someone would raise the possibility.

It was Ryan.

"Do you think this might be sacrificial?" she said. "Like the Torso in the Thames?"

Tom nodded.

"That's why before we brief the press," he said, "I'm going to talk to the Met."

Chapter 2

Tom was getting increasingly frustrated. It was nearly five o'clock in the evening and he still hadn't been able to connect with anyone who had worked on the Adam case. The female CID officer he did speak to tried to be helpful.

"They're all out just now," she said, "but I can try their mobiles and get someone to call you?"

For heaven's sake.

"Please."

While he waited, he logged into the internet to search for any reports on the London case. Each force had its own secure internal site which meant that the Met's files were out of reach. He was reading the old coverage on the BBC website when his phone rang.

"DI Tom Ashton."

"This is DS Charles Seymour." The voice was deep and rich. "Understand you need to have a chat?"

Less than five minutes after Tom put the phone down, Charles Seymour rang again.

"Rather than me just send you those reports, I think it would be more useful for you to meet with the whole team," he said, without preamble. "Figure you want to get as much as you can, as quickly as you can. I've arranged for you to join our regular briefing on Monday morning at nine. Okay?"

By the time the train pulled into Euston, Tom was already in danger of being late for his meeting at Scotland Yard. He rang to let them know but the familiar acid was creeping up his gullet. His New Year's resolution of just under three months ago, not to get wound up about things he couldn't control, lasted about a week. He hated being late almost as much as people holding him up. He ran to the Underground and was soon swaying with the motion of the tube train, a hundred feet under the London streets.

He wasn't sure how he felt about seeing Yvonne Grey. The last time they'd spoken was just before his boss Frank Dawson came back to work after a horrific accident that destroyed his family and nearly killed him. Grey had been the acting Detective Chief Inspector in Frank's absence. It hadn't been an overwhelming success.

He reached the steps of the headquarters of the London Metropolitan Police Force just after nine twenty on Monday March 17th.

"Morning Tom."

"Ma'am." Tom couldn't bring himself to reply informally. The three other officers in the room would take it as respect for her new position as Detective Chief Inspector. Yvonne Grey knew he was confirming the boundaries of their relationship. The three others in the room were DS Seymour, DS Mike Johnson and DC Carol Law.

He looked directly at Yvonne, silently demanding control. She nodded.

"I appreciate your time," he began. "You're all here because of your close involvement with the 'Torso in the Thames' case. We think we might have something like it in Manchester."

"What've you got so far?" DS Mike Johnson asked.

Tom summarised when, where and how the body was found. As he finished, he passed out copies of photographs taken of the car, the bag and the child.

The room was silent as the two men and two women concentrated on the pictures.

DC Carol Law, sitting on Tom's right, drew in a long breath and then noisily exhaled.

"The bastards."

"Plural?" Tom said.

"Quite possibly." DS Charles Seymour answered. A handsome black man with long, slim hands, he was lounging back in his chair as he spoke. "If this is a sacrificial killing, there would have been a ceremony. A group thing. Also, possible there was somebody there that the child felt safe with."

Tom swallowed. Christ.

"Could the child have been killed by one person after he'd been drugged and not struggling?"

"Maybe, but all the research work we did on Adam's murder led us to believe there is almost a sort of template, things you have to have in place, number of attendees at the killing, that sort of thing. It's probable that the ritual would be particular to the one in control of it. But you're right to keep an open mind. We're all new to this type of incident."

DS Seymour's delivery was so detached, so seemingly indifferent to the topic of the discussion that Tom took a moment to look at the expressions of the others. Only Yvonne Grey was looking uncomfortable. The other two, who'd been part of the Thames investigation, seemed just as relaxed as Seymour. That's what must happen to you, thought Tom. When you've looked directly at the work of the devil.

It was a long, intense, informative and depressing day. Tom left London with his notebook and head full of ideas and contacts. They could think about following London and offer a large reward for information; certainly bring the press on board; try and engage the local population. They had a lot of work to do now, to try and understand the possible background to the child's death. He pushed his ticket into the Underground barrier, his shoulders feeling the pressure of a wave of commuters. Surely people would come forward without having to give them money? This was a child for God's sake.

Don't be thick, Tom, he thought as someone behind him gave him a shove in the kidneys for moving too slowly. You're expecting decency where it might not exist.

As soon as he emerged up onto the Euston concourse he switched on his phone. A text message was waiting. From Lily.

"Sorry can't do tonight – got a leaving do. Thought told you. How about tomorrow? L x".

He pressed her number.

"Hi, it's me."

"Hello, you. Did you get my message?"

"I did," he tried not to sound grumpy. "I'd forgotten – just wanted to see you." He could hear water running in the background and tried not to think of her sinking into a warm, deep bubble-bath.

"Bad day?"

"Something like that." He undid his tie and shirt top button. "Actually, it's been grim. Hours talking about the shitty things that shitty people do in the name of fuck knows what…" He stopped in mid flow as he saw a woman look at him with distaste. She had no idea.

Lily was quiet.

"Lily?"

"Erm, I'm not sure what to say, Tom. Sounds like you maybe need to talk to Dean or someone?"

He sighed. She was right. He shouldn't be laying this at her door.

"Where are you off to tonight?" He kept his voice light, wanting to keep the conversation going. There was another pause before Lily answered.

"Just to Pizza Express near St Ann's Square. Meeting for a drink in that posh place across the road first. Can't remember the name but we knew not everyone could afford to eat there as well."

Tom knew the place. He couldn't afford it either. And he suddenly realised that it was just as well he was hundreds of miles away, otherwise he might crash the party just so he could make himself feel better. Hardly fair.

He strode across to a booth selling greetings cards and rested his back against the wall in an effort to keep out of the way of the purposeful rail travelling public. He glanced up at the departure board for the Manchester train. Platform 5. Lily was talking again.

"I'm going to have to go in a mo, Tom. I want to have a soak. Call you back in a while if you like?"

"No, it's okay. Train's in. You have a good time and I'll see you tomorrow."

"Okay. Talk to Dean, okay?" Then she was gone before he had time to reply.

It was almost eight o'clock when the train pulled into Piccadilly Station. Bright and gleaming, it was a testament to the town planners and designers and a long way from the dingy Victorian monstrosity that Tom saw when he came for his transfer interview seven years ago. Now the place had an air of expectation, of vibrancy and possibility. Manchester was a true destination and Tom really couldn't see why anyone would want to leave it and particularly not for London. The capital was a place he was happy to visit, and equally happy to leave.

He deliberately closed his mind to work and concentrated instead on the contents of his fridge. Did he need to pop into the supermarket by the station exit? Not that there was likely to be much choice there. He could go via China Town and pick up some fresh ginger and…

"Get yer fuckin' hands off of me!"

A woman's screech cut into his thoughts of stir fry. Tom, and just about everyone else, looked round to see two uniformed policemen grappling with a slight, red-haired woman who seemed to be winning on points. One officer was trying to pin her flailing arms to her side and the other was dodging away from furious kicks while trying to reason with her.

"Now, calm down. Calm down. We just need to talk to you – somewhere quiet. Behave now."

"Help!" She yelled. "I'm being attacked here – fuckin' bastards!"

"Shameful."

Tom turned to his left where an elderly man was watching the scene.

"Pardon?"

"Drunk," the older man replied. "Saw her coming out of the bar up there." He nodded up to the Yates

Wine Lodge on the upper floor. "Asked to leave, I think. Sad in a young person though, don't you think?"

"'Aven't done nuthin'," the woman was shouting now. "Leave me alone!"

She looked like a child, refusing to go one more step. She was trying to sit down, her legs loose and her feet splayed. The policeman struggling to hold her had his arms under her armpits, valiantly avoiding any contact with her breasts. Tom wondered for a moment whether to help but the second guy took the plunge and grabbed one of her arms and had it over his shoulder in one swift movement. His colleague followed suit and between them, began to drag the unwilling woman towards the exit.

As they passed close by, Tom caught a glimpse of her face as her head lolled to one side. What on earth had happened in her life so that she had to seek such a public oblivion?

He picked up his BMW from the overflow car park and headed south. The traffic was light, and – a rare occurrence – he managed to get a parking space outside his Victorian terraced house. Built over a decade before mass production of the motorcar, it boasted two decent sized bedrooms, a small back yard, no garage and a front doorstep that led directly onto the pavement. The district had come into its own since he moved in and was becoming more desirable for the 'young professional'; all with at least one car per household which meant he often had to leave his car some distance away. As he put the key in his dark green door, he was greeted by a long howl at shin level.

"Hi buddy," Tom stooped to stroke the lithe, black figure. It was a similar time of day, not long after Tom had moved in, that Jack appeared from nowhere and strutted into the house, tail up, as if annoyed to be kept waiting. He'd been there ever since, despite numerous early attempts to re-house him. Looking back, Tom was grateful for the company. It was the first time he'd really lived alone since he left home to join the army, soon followed by marriage.

The cat upped the volume.

"What are you after? Bit peckish?"

Tom knew full well that Alice, his elderly neighbour, would have already fed him, but he let himself be led towards the kitchen. Jack checked his progress with every other step.

The light on his answering machine was flashing. Tom pressed the button as he passed the phone and listened as he reached for the corkscrew. In spite of the floorshow at the station he needed a drink. The first was his mother.

"Hello? Are you there? Oh…" End of message.

He'd call her back later even though there was only an evens chance of her knowing why she'd called in the first place. The machine clicked on to the next message.

"Alex? I need to talk to you about your father's birthday. Call me back please."

The voice was stronger this time but that made it even worse. Tom's brother Alex was back in Seattle and his father had been dead for years. Her creeping oblivion wasn't sought. She had no choice.

He poured the Shiraz, hardly waiting to sniff the bouquet before slurping down a mouthful. Experience taught him not to overreact; not to call back immediately and try and reason with her, explain how things were now. If she wasn't aware of what nonsense she was talking, then she didn't get upset. He didn't know if it was working. Even though his mother's doctor had made it clear that Alzheimer's wasn't a death sentence in itself, it felt like it. She was gently and slowly disappearing like an ice sculpture warmed by a weak winter sun.

Tom rubbed his eyes. He was as alarmed as she was but for different reasons. He just didn't know if he was up to the challenge. Not on his own.

Jack jumped up onto the worktop, stretched his front paws up Tom's chest and eyeballed him. In spite of the day and his mother, Tom laughed.

"All you have to worry about, eh boy?" He tickled Jack's ears. "The next meal." He lifted the cat up and gave him a rare hug before plopping him gently onto the floor. "Tuna for you. Steak for me."

He crushed some fresh peppercorns. Then he laid the meat on a wooden board and began to tenderise it, turning it, hitting it with the mallet until it was half the size again and thinner. He built up a rhythm that reverberated in his head; pounding like a giant metronome. The oil was beginning to haze and the wine was easing his muscles when an image came unbidden into his head. He looked at the flesh in his hand and felt suddenly, violently sick.

Shaking, he put the steak back on the chopping board and turned quickly to the sink to wash all traces from his hands. He then let cold water flood over his lower arms before throwing the freezing water on his face. Christ.

It took ten minutes of steady breathing and another glass of wine before he felt anything like normal. He'd have to ask one of the London team. Did they ever react like this? He wasn't going to be any damn use if he was going soft. Empathy, yes, up to a point. Not to the point of incapacity. Remember, Tom, he told himself. Remember you're looking for the bastards behind all this.

The phone rang. Tom grabbed at the receiver, happy to talk to anyone.

"So, how was the old trout?" Dean was in a bar somewhere by the sound of it. Yvonne Grey was not one of his favourite people. Tom thankfully allowed himself a small smile.

"Grab a vegetable biryani for me on your way round and I'll tell you."

"Lazy sod. Alright. See you in a bit."

She tried to stop the world spinning. If she kept her eyes on the dark stain on the wall opposite then she was okay. If she closed them, everything tilted upwards and she knew she was going to be sick. Karen Abbott tried to re-focus on the wall. It'll pass, she told herself. It'll pass. She wrapped her arms around her unhappy belly as if trying to hold everything in.

It was too bright. Even the air seemed sharpened by the light as it pushed its way into her lungs. She wanted to go home. She just wished she knew where it was.

A sharp bang sounded to her left, but she made no move to acknowledge it. She had to keep her head still. A voice, not unkind, came through the observation flap in the reinforced metal door.

"Are you ready to talk to us yet? There's a nice cup of tea ready for you."

She wanted to scream at the man. To tell him to leave her alone, to tell him that she didn't want a fucking cup of tea, that she wanted her life back, but she didn't. She gathered the last of her strength and nodded. Very gently.

"I'll take that as a yes then," he said. "We'll have no nonsense when I open this door – okay?"

Again, she nodded. She wondered what time it was. And what day.

Apparently, it was Tuesday March 18th. Three whole days of her life had passed this time. The tea was hot and sweet. Her hand shook as she raised the cup to her lips but she wasn't nervous. The worst had already happened. Patrick had been taken away again. She was tired to the point beyond exhaustion and she couldn't remember when she had last eaten. Her stomach growled as if insulted at the meagre liquid offering.

"Any chance of some toast?" she whispered. The man sighed and signalled to someone behind her. She'd forgotten his name already. She thought it was Brown or Green – a colour anyway. A tear of gratitude trickled towards her chin.

"Right." His voice was firm now and she tried to gather her mind.

"Let's start with the basics, shall we? Name?"

"Karen Abbott."

"And where do you live, Karen?"

Another tear broke free but she squared her shoulders and looked at him straight in the face. She gave a house number and street name. As he wrote it down, a plate was put in front of her with two slices of dark brown toast. She picked up a piece and dragged a corner off with her teeth. It was almost the best thing she had ever tasted. She had to get out of here.

"I'm sorry," she said.

He was quite sympathetic really. Whether he believed her lies or not didn't really matter. She thought the combination of a dying father and the recent breakdown of her marriage was enough to explain why she'd gone off the rails and got roaring drunk. Even the choice of Piccadilly Station rang true. She was lost. Nowhere to go. Her life was in tatters and it was all bloody Annie Colgan's fault.

Sergeant Green (not Brown, as he'd gently reminded her) was going to let her off with a caution but she needed to promise him that she would get some help. Karen nodded. She'd say anything to get away. Obviously he thought she would be true to her word, pressing a pile of leaflets into her hand before she left. One had details of a counselling service on it.

She forgot she was still holding the leaflets until she got to the door of the off-licence near the refuge. Karen threw them all away.

Chapter 3

Detective Chief Inspector Frank Dawson was standing at the top of the stairs. His uniform hung off his thin frame – he was still struggling to put back on the weight he'd lost along with almost everything else in his life but his eyes were very much alive. Tom was glad to see him.

Frank's face broke into a smile, his prominent teeth looking even more alarming, emerging from his shrunken cheeks. Tom thought Frank probably knew his nickname was 'The Rodent', but hoped he also re-cognised the admiration and respect behind the jibe.

"Morning, Tom. Useful trip yesterday?"

"Morning, sir." Tom took a deep breath, wanting to off-load some of the trouble he was feeling but quickly decided now wasn't the time or place. "Got a lot of background and ideas for how we might tackle this one. Very useful. Are you joining the briefing?"

Frank clearly wasn't fooled. He gave Tom a com-passionate glance and patted him on the shoulder.

"Everyone gets one case in their career that stays with them for ever," he said quietly. "Training people on how to deal with depravity isn't something we're very good at – you have to be affected by it to feel it. You'll be fine. As will your team. Come and talk to me later."

Tom opened the door of the CID office. Most of the team were already in, even though it was only just after eight o'clock. He strode towards the case corner (as everyone called the area set aside for details of the investigation), telling everyone to join him as soon as Elliott arrived.

"He's just gone across the road for coffees while we waited," said Ryan. "Saw you with the Rodent. I ordered you a large black."

Tom was grateful. For the support as well as the drink.

It was a bit of a squeeze, but no-one complained. Some stood, some managed to find a chair. Others, like Dean, perched on the edge of a desk. It was warm.

"I'm going to take you through some of the intel I got from Scotland Yard yesterday. It might give us more of an idea of what we're dealing with here, and help us to look for answers in the right places." Tom was unhurried, determined to deliver this stuff objectively. He took a gulp of coffee.

"You all remember the Torso in the Thames case?" Various nods and the occasional mutter told him they'd already got up to speed.

"Looks like we're dealing with something similar here. Voodoo, sacrifice, call it what you will. This child – and I propose we give him a name this morning – was ritually killed. We need to find out why. What was the reason, the need? Who was responsible? Who and where are his parents? Is this part of a bigger situation or a one-off?" He paused.

"This is what I learned about what happened to Adam, the Thames boy." He sat on the window ledge and told them about the drugs found in the child's body. That his eyes were removed because they represented independence. That his limbs were cut off because they symbolise mobility and creativity.

More coffee.

Ryan, as ever, was taking notes. Dean was staring at Tom with fierce intensity, daring him not to miss any detail that might help them. DC Talbot, head down, was studiously examining his fingernails.

"His head…" Tom paused as he looked around the faces of his colleagues. Some impassive, some showing disgust, most overlaid by a veil of disbelief. "…intelligence." He let the thought sink in before he finished the gruesome list.

"The boy's blood would have been tasted for purity; maybe drunk in quantity or used in specific rites. His penis, representing ongoing life, was probably stored in a white spirit to be buried later for good luck."

Tom explained that the Met detectives had learned most of this in an interview with a voodoo priest, and research on the role of witchcraft in the culture of places such as Haiti and parts of Africa and South America. A world that seemed ludicrous to acknowledge as they sat and stood; squashed together in a cream painted room with the Manchester skyline occasionally visible through the undulating vertical blinds.

He took a gulp of coffee which was cold and bitter.

"Our child is different. You've all seen the path report. We need to understand the significance of the scoring around the nipples and navel. It could be a signature, decided upon by whoever was controlling the ritual. And the killers left him with a muslin bag of small stones sprinkled in lavender oil for company. This must mean something."

A grunt from the back of the room told him that Dean had a view but wasn't about to share it.

Ryan gave a small cough before she spoke.

"Our victim was mixed-race. Was there any view on that?"

Tom nodded. "Not unusual. But there will be a clear reason why he was chosen."

"Chosen?! Christ!" Elliott's face was red with indignation. "Makes it sound like a fuckin' honour."

Tom waved his hands to acknowledge the point, but also to calm the atmosphere down. "I know how you feel but this is the language of the situation. You're all going to have to suspend your views and beliefs in order to try and understand what happened here. And to get justice for the boy."

"We need to give him a name," Dean's voiced boomed. "Otherwise, it's like we're giving him no respect. Who knows the Bible?"

After a moment's silence, a muttering broke out as people tried out names they remembered from school or intermittent church attendance.

"Adam was named as the First Son, wasn't he?" asked Ryan. "What was his son called?"

"Seth, I think." Elliott offered, full of surprises.

"Can't have that," someone said. "That's an old man's name."

More collective thinking.

"Abel," said Dean suddenly. "He was killed by his brother, wasn't he?"

"Let's not get too symbolic," Tom advised. "This is a four-year-old boy. We just need to approach this with kindness and to agree quickly so that we can do our best for him. What about a simple name beginning with B. Ben?"

"I'd go with that," said Dean. "Just hope we don't ever get to C."

"Amen to that." Tom stood, cup in hand. "Okay, I want you all to think about what we've learned from Adam's case. Look again at what we have with Ben; talk amongst yourselves; meditate on your own; do some research – whatever. Then I want you all back here at four o'clock to share ideas and tactics. Go."

A couple of miles away, two elderly ladies stood at the open doorway of a small, neat terraced house. A row of houses at the back and two dividing alleyways, separated Alice Roberts' home from Tom's. Jack resided in both.

"Look after yourself, Edith." Alice smiled at her friend as she helped her on with her coat. "Give me a ring later and let me know how you're settling back in?"

Alice, 78 years old on her next birthday, was filled with anticipation. Edith came to stay following a heart attack a few months ago but now she felt ready to go home. The neighbours that Alice felt were entirely responsible for her friend's difficulties had been evicted and there was a nice quiet Asian family installed in their place.

"Are you sure you don't want me to come with you?" Alice continued as the two women watched the taxi driver launch Edith's bags into his car.

"I have to get used to being on my own at some time, Alice," said Edith, her voice still slightly tremulous. "But I'll miss you and I never forget how kind…"

Oh, no, thought Alice. No more tears. She patted Edith's tweed-clad arm and began to guide her towards the open car door.

"Now, now. No more of that," she said briskly. Then, when Edith was safely settled into the passenger seat, she reminded her of their arrangement to meet at the pensioners' bingo the following Thursday. Normal play to be resumed.

Alice stood on the pavement until the car had turned left out of the street and she was no longer in Edith's sight. She turned and looked at her open front door for a moment, keen to be inside on her own but savouring the short delay. The next minute, she was in her bright hallway, the outside world was behind the door and there was no sound other than that of an old friend welcoming her back. The faint ticking of the dining room clock; the hum of the fridge-freezer that needed re-levelling; a quiet breeze whispering through the open kitchen window. No other voices, no suppressed coughing, no elderly slippered shuffle on the lino. She smiled.

As she started to walk towards to kitchen for her first gloriously solitary cup of tea for many weeks she heard a slight tapping noise. The sound of her window blind settling back into position.

"Hello Jack," she said.

The cat was perched on the shining stainless steel draining board, waiting for her.

"Just you and me again," said Alice as she stroked Jack's smooth black head. He replied with a throaty purr. "You've no idea how good it feels. Let me make some tea and then we can get comfy in the front room."

As she turned to fill the kettle, the cat jumped down from the sink and padded out of the kitchen. Anyone watching would swear the cat understood. Alice didn't hold with swearing.

Alice walked slowly through to her cosy front room, carrying her favourite china cup and saucer; a single ginger biscuit balancing next to her sole surviving wedding set teaspoon. Oh, how wonderful it was to have the house to herself again!

It was almost impossible now to recall the cloying, despairing blankness that filled the rooms after her Jimmy had been killed. She knew of the accident before she was told but it was too late. That was over twenty childless years ago.

She was used to living alone. Well, apart from Jack and her other visitors of course. She was glad to help Edith. But she was even happier to see her go home.

Jack greeted her arrival with a huge yawn that almost threatened to turn his head inside out. She wasn't offended. He waited until she was settled in the easy chair by the window before jumping onto her lap and getting himself comfortable. She stroked his back and began to feel her own back muscles relax.

"Now, then," she said after enjoying the first sip of hot, fresh tea. "How're things with my little friend, eh? And that nice young man of yours?"

Alice first met Tom when he almost knocked her over with a supermarket trolley some years ago. She smiled to herself as she remembered some of the things they'd been through together since then. She touched her head and fingered the slight bump that almost finished her off when she was helping him with a case. Alice didn't mind; it was such a welcome thing at her stage of life. To be taken seriously. To be needed.

She grimaced as Jack flexed his claws into her knee.

"Hey," she said, gently shifting his front paws so that they clawed at the empty air beyond her tweed skirt. She let her mind wander as she stroked the cat's back all the while.

She was expecting something, but the feeling surprised her. There was nothing unusual about the sensation; no dizziness, no noises or colours. No smells. But she recognised it.

Her father had bought tickets for the circus for her sixth birthday. She was so excited she didn't sleep at all the night before they went, terrified that the weather would be bad, or her dad would change his mind or the circus would steal away before the dawn. She remembered the massive grip of his hand as they walked into the Big Top and she felt safe.

But then he came in and the fun stopped. He was dressed in red and yellow. White, horrid painted face. He wasn't funny. He was frightening. Gaping mouth, grinning in blood. Alice's old eyes watered as the same feeling of cold terror ran through her, a lifetime on.

It was growing dusk when Alice opened her eyes. She was alone. She hadn't realised how weary she'd become dealing with Edith; here she was, sleeping like an old woman. She patted her recently permed hair to check for damage before indulging in a yawn to rival Jack's. She took a deep breath. She could do with some fresh air and some more orange squash, so a walk to the corner shop would serve both. Edith was very liberal with the mixers once she felt brave enough to join Alice in an evening vodka.

She reached across to the little note pad and pen she kept on the table by her chair and scribbled down a few thoughts. Satisfied, she got to her feet and took her cup and saucer into the kitchen, humming the tune that her mother always sang to her when Alice couldn't sleep.

Pulling on her coat and gloves, she decided to just take two-pound coins rather than carry her purse. Sometimes it wasn't worth the risk.

Just to make sure, she paused for a moment on her doorstep to check she'd made the right decision. Nodding in satisfaction, she set off down the road.

As she reached the end of her street and was about to turn right towards the shop, she knew they had spotted her. She didn't need to turn round to be aware of them sliding in behind her. As she put her hand on the shop door, she spun round to face them. Two sneering young lads with unfortunate complexions and ghastly clothing stared back at her.

She put her hand onto her pocket and pulled out the coins.

"Not worth waiting outside for me," she said. "I'm getting a bottle of orange squash and neither you, or any of your friends," she jerked her head in the direction they'd come from, sure there were more, "are going to deny me my first drink of the evening." She spoke quietly but firmly. "Go home." She let her gaze sit first on one face, then the other.

It was gratifying to see the clouds of uncertainty pass across their eyes, followed by signs of their brains ticking over as to how they could get out of this without looking stupid.

"Wasn't after nuthin'," muttered the taller one.

"Don't know what you're talking about, yer mad old cow," seconded his fatter friend, aiming for bravado.

"That's alright then," said Alice and pushed open the door.

Chapter 4

The almost hourly dose of caffeine finally got to him. His pulse danced a cha-cha-cha through his veins and he was so wired he felt he could power a small refrigeration plant. Frank, on the other hand, was sitting still and composed as he listened to Tom's summary of the case.

"What lines are the team working on?" Frank asked.

It was nearly five thirty and the evening light coming through the two large windows in Frank's office was beginning to lose its strength. So was Tom.

"Forensics are still testing the car, the holdall and the remains of Ben's clothes. He was found just in vest and underpants. The CCTV footage from the airport tracked the car coming into the car park so we've got some images of the driver. Not surprisingly, he was careful, so we're needing some serious computer-enhancement to get anything to work on. It's typical that the camera was tracking elsewhere when he got out of the car so we're limited there."

"Stolen?"

"'Fraid so. Three months ago in Birmingham. We know the last-but-one owner but she sold it privately two years ago. Tried to be helpful but apparently it was a cash sale to another young woman who tested the car with a man she said was her father. Name of Jones. Then the trail goes cold."

Frank grunted in frustration.

"Who's leading on contact with the community groups?"

"DS Ryan. We're pulling in as many of the community officers as we can to talk to. Mothers' groups; youth centres and church leaders. We're concentrating on the south side." Battling with a yawn that tickled in his throat, Tom rubbed his chin as though contemplating the syntax of his next sentence.

"I'd like to request the secondment of DS Charles Seymour from Scotland Yard. Could you clear it with DCI Grey?"

Frank looked at him for a moment before replying.

"Why Seymour?"

Tom knew he had to be honest.

"He was the most impressive in the meeting on Monday. Clear-headed, concise and objective. He could recall every minute detail of their case. And he was the one who interviewed the voodoo priest."

Frank waited.

"Look, don't take this the wrong way but…" Tom wanted to make sure he got his words right. "All of those things alone would be enough, but well, given what we might be dealing with…"

"Spit it out, Tom."

"Well, it wouldn't harm to have a black officer on the team. I'm not going to say that in front of anyone else, sir, but we shouldn't ignore the fact that sometimes these things can make a difference." Tom stuck out his chin, knowing full well he was in for a bollocking.

"I trust you are not suggesting that DS Seymour is personally closer or more accepting to these kind of rituals and customs because of the colour of his skin?" The Rodent's voice was icy.

"No sir. But I am saying that we need credibility with local community groups and at the moment I've got a team full of white faces. The limitation's with us. That's all I'm saying and DS Seymour told me himself that he reckons he has the advantage in certain situations and is comfortable with it. Like interviewing the priest."

Silence.

"Tom," Frank stood slowly and walked across to the larger two windows of his office and gazed for a moment onto the skyline of Manchester. "I don't need to remind you of the difficulties we had with Yvonne Grey and Dean Wilson over trumped up charges of racism. I don't believe this is your intention but I will not accept this as a reason to ask for DS Seymour's expertise. I will talk to DCI Grey," he turned to face Tom. "But on the basis of your earlier rationale. Your other observations I will ignore."

Tom nodded. Enough said.

Frank began to pull off the dead leaves from a rather sad-looking potted plant. Tom waited.

"We need to get the public involved, Tom. I want us to think carefully about how we break this to the media so that we can get their help but avoiding any racial tension." Frank's voice underlined the last two words. "I've already had one meeting with Mary Andrews in the press office. She's sharing her strategy with me tomorrow morning at nine. I'd like you to join us."

Tom could feel the headache start as he put his key into the ignition. Damn. No way was he going to cry off from seeing Lily even with an army of pneumatic drillers warming up inside his temple. Stopping at the first garage he came to; he bought a large bottle of mineral water and a small packet of paracetamol. Ignoring the dosage advice, he swallowed three tablets and a long swig of water inside the forecourt shop. Out of the corner of his eye, he saw that three black youths were standing around his car. Bugger. Did he lock it?

He walked out of the shop and strode across the tarmac, keys in hand, eyes scanning the area to the sides and in front of him. It was darkening from dusk and his was the only car. The only customer. The only white face.

He relaxed as he closed up on his car, his spare hand in his trouser pocket; fingers comfortably wrapped around his mobile phone.

"Can I help you lads?" he said, voice strong, tone neutral.

"Nice motor," said the largest of the three, his face partly obscured by the peak of a cap beneath the hood of a navy blue jacket. He casually placed his hand on the passenger door. Tom decided against bravado.

"Cheers," he said. "Trouble is, police petrol allowance doesn't cover the cost of old guzzlers like this." He looked back at the ringleader, training his eyes to be impassive.

"Fuckin' bummer," came the reply and in response to some unseen signal, the three drifted away.

Tom got into the driver's seat and closed and locked the door. He checked that the other doors were locked before pulling away from the pump as if he had all the time in the world, puzzled by his reaction to the situation. Maybe they just had an interest in old cars. He couldn't afford to see every black face as a potential criminal. He never had before.

"Of course, you're not prejudiced, Tom!" Lily was perched on one of the stools in his kitchen, watching as he chopped fresh basil and garlic. "Apart from the fact that you're tired and have had enough coffee to make anyone paranoid – well, this case is bound to make you question more than skin colour. It's about culture, different beliefs, sex, male dominance, whatever. Don't start beating yourself up. You need the Ashton objective head back on." She picked up the bottle of white wine and topped up her glass, before waving it questioningly in Tom's direction.

He shook his head. He knew that with his mood as it was, alcohol was only likely to make his headache and his neurosis worse. Seeing that the pan of water was coming to the boil, he gently dropped in six large tomatoes and watched for the minute or so it took to burst and loosen the skins. Still silent, he then rinsed the fruits and began to peel them in preparation for making his special smoked bacon, mushroom and to-mato sauce. Finely chopped black olives and some oregano would finish it off.

"Can you check the bread for me?" he asked, not looking up but focusing on his fingers stripping the fine cover from the red flesh, relieved there was no repeat of the 'steak incident'. He'd made the ciabatta as soon as he got home in order to give it plenty of time to rise. Kneading the dough and rubbing in the olive oil had helped release some of the stiffness in his neck.

Lily hopped down from her stool and peered into the oven behind him.

"Not sure what I'm looking for here," she said. "Want me to take it out and tap it on the bottom or something?"

He gave a small laugh. His ex-wife Sandra was a hopeless cook but Lily was even worse. At least she was trying to learn.

"Well remembered." Tom finished with the tomatoes and turned to wash his hands and watch as Lily held the loaf in one oven-gloved hand and tapped the underside. Her face was so serious that Tom began to laugh again. Properly this time.

"What?!" Lily was all smiling indignation.

"Sorry – you looked as though you were searching for survivors. How is it?"

"Done." She confidently put the bread on the wire cooling rack. "But if it isn't you're not to say anything."

"Agreed. And I've changed my mind. I'll have a small glass before we eat. That won't go with the meal so I'll open some red if you want some more."

In spite of the food, wine and Lily beside him, Tom couldn't sleep. He lay with his eyes closed and his mind open – thoughts and ideas fighting for prominence. In the quiet darkness he examined his conscience. Was he truly objective? Could he really get justice for Ben? How could someone do that to a child?

Lily turned over and snuggled in closer, her head on his shoulder. A soft fluttering noise like a baby's snuffle confirmed that she was deeply asleep. Tom loved that sound.

He had to admit it to himself. He was falling in love with her and the brutal killing of Ben had somehow made her seem even more precious. That bit he could cope with. The most terrifying thing was that he had begun to wonder what it would be like to have his own family. His own son. It was blindingly obvious, he thought as he pulled her in a little tighter and kissed the top of her head. He'd lost his father, his mother was growing senile and his only sibling was miles away in America. And he was in his forties. No wonder he wanted to procreate. He was facing his own mortality. A classic mid-life crisis. Or maybe Lily had come into his life at exactly the right time.

By three o'clock, he decided to give in to his over-active brain and slid out from under Lily's arm and out of bed. He knew a cure for this.

The light in the kitchen punched his eyeballs so hard they began to water. He blinked rapidly to acclimatise before filling and switching on the kettle for tea. The large cupboard above and to the left of the gas hob was his target. He opened the door and looked critically at the selection of herbs, spices and oils. In five minutes, he had every packet, jar and bottle on the work surface. A sachet of liquorice and peppermint tea was infusing at his elbow.

He didn't bother wiping down the shelves. This wasn't a cleaning exercise. It was a stock take.

He was examining the state of a half-grated nutmeg when Jack squeezed through the cat flap. He gave a little yowl in greeting before jumping up onto the work surface and nudging Tom's arm demanding some attention. As he stroked the cat's soft black head, Tom decided the nut was still good enough to use. Jack's inquisitive nose closed in on Tom's other hand but he pulled back his head almost immediately. Clearly not impressed.

Tom watched in amusement as the cat tiptoed through and around the collection, examining each object without disturbing or even touching any of them.

"Very impressive, buddy, but I don't think you're going to find anything you want to eat amongst this lot." He took a swig of tea. It was an odd combination of flavours but it seemed to work at this hour of the day.

Jack obviously didn't. He walked down to the other end of the worktop with his tail swishing in disgust before sitting down to wash the smells from his nose. First one side of his face, then the other. Exactly five strokes each side.

"Just because I'm glad of your company," Tom said as he reached into the fridge to find a little treat. Jack was on the floor beside him in seconds, trying to see what was on offer. Tom opened a plump waxed bag of roast ham from the best deli in Manchester.

"You'd better appreciate this, cat," he said, ripping off half a slice. "Good stuff, this." He was getting soft. It was hardly as if the animal was starving. He knew full well that Alice was always slipping him fresh fish or chicken. He dropped the meat onto the floor.

Shark-like, the cat was onto it and chewing almost as soon as the ham landed. By the volume of purring that accompanied the vigorous chewing noises and the speed with which the cat's head came up looking for more, Tom reckoned he'd more than liked it. He pulled out the remainder of the slice and, tearing it in half again, put the two pieces at Jack's feet.

"This is how it is," Tom said as he turned back to his spices. "I don't know what I'm feeling. What's real. What's in reaction to everything else that's going on – and does it matter?" He threw an old opened packet of paprika in the bin. He carried on chatting to the semi-empty kitchen; Jack by now back on the work-top next to him. He talked about Ben and voiced all the doubts he was feeling. Could he solve this case? How did you make sure it was about justice and not some sort of cultural revenge?

He put the last of the jars in the cupboard and closed the door. And what about his life? He was go-ing to have to be selfish if he wanted a future with Lily, but what would happen to his mother? "There," he said to Jack as he put his cup into the sink. "You've admitted it now."

He climbed back into bed just before 4.30am, his nos-trils filled with a potpourri of promised flavours and essences. Lily stirred. He kissed the nape of her warm, soft neck.

"Hmm?" she murmured, barely conscious. "You okay?"

"Yes," he whispered, not daring to tell her why. "Just need some more vanilla pods and cumin."

Chapter 5

It was ten days since Ben's body had been found. Tom pushed open the door to the CID office, registering that the noise level was way higher than when he'd left the room just half an hour earlier. Dean's voice was clear even above the cacophony.

"No – you are not entitled to any details of how the child's body looked when we found him. And let me remind you, that I have made a note of your name and number. You're wasting police time…" He thumped the receiver down before adding, "fuckin' sicko."

Tom was in front of him in a few strides, eyebrows raised.

"More of the same?"

Dean glared back at him before rubbing his eyes.

"Practically every other one. Not just me, everyone else is getting them. Not just after that kind of stuff either."

Tom looked round, taking in the postures and voices of the other officers. The tension he could feel was a negative force, not the invigorating high energy that comes with getting leads and making connections.

"What else?"

Dean grabbed up a notepad from the desk in front of him and began to recite.

"People wanting to report black neighbours as witch doctors. Others claiming that Ben was their child stolen from them at birth. Plenty wanting to get their rocks off on descriptions of the body; one woman offering her services as a medium and a couple who said they were parking their car at the same time as the Fiesta."

"Who was the medium?"

"Don't worry, it wasn't your Miss Marple."

Tom let the comment go. He'd brought Alice in on a previous case to help track down a missing person and although she'd been invaluable, Tom had yet to live it down. Not surprisingly, he kept very quiet about the other times he sought her company and counsel.

"The couple?"

"Right car park, wrong car."

"We must have something useful, surely! If Mary Andrews is to be believed, the single briefing we gave last Wednesday is all we need to grab people's attention about the identity of a murdered child."

"Seems a bit bloody low key to me," Dean grunted as he reached to answer his ringing phone.

Tom silently agreed but said nothing. He left his colleague dealing with another call and went to the case corner to study the large white board on the wall to the left of the door. The information recorded so far was painfully inadequate. There were plenty of ideas jotted around the edges of the board with question marks but little that was definite. He added another.

"Abducted? Or with people he knew?" At least DS Seymour was arriving today. Tom knew that even just one new perspective could shift the course of an entire investigation. They needed something. He decided to go and have another talk with the PR officer.

"Thank you very much for calling, Miss Jones. We do need you to make a statement – an officer will be round…" Tom heard Ryan's voice break off suddenly before she continued "…I understand. No, no uniform."

He was beside her desk in seconds.

"What've you got?"

"Sounds useful," Ryan looked up and Tom could see the dark rings under her eyes. It was getting to all of them. "Woman who remembers seeing a young woman with a mixed-race little boy at a house two doors away from her. Used to be there all the time apparently. Hasn't seen her or the boy for nearly two weeks now. Didn't think anything of it because they'd both gone but thought she'd let us know. Sounds kosher."

"Halle-bloody-luya. You planning to go?"

Ryan gave him a strange look. "That's another reason why she didn't call at first. She's not in Manchester. She's in Liverpool."

Tom wrote the meagre details from Ryan's call on the board and then went to talk to Frank. Even though they'd alerted all the other constabularies in the UK prior to the press briefing, they needed agreement from the head of the Merseyside Police before getting a local officer to interview Miss Jones on their behalf. Tom was tempted to whiz down the M62 himself and let them know he'd been on their patch after the event but it wasn't worth the hassle. If it was a decent lead, then they'd be getting into a joint investigation and he didn't want to start that on the back foot. On the other hand…

Margery, Frank's secretary, smiled and nodded at Tom to show that he could go straight in. He wasn't offended that she didn't speak to him. He could see the tell-tale bulge of the regular mid-morning cake in her right cheek.

He knocked on the door, opening it and sticking his head around it in one movement.

"We've got a potential lead – need some help, sir."

"Okay, give," Frank responded to Tom's impatience. He listened as Tom leant against the closed door and explained the new development. He listened, but with a pencil tapping on the top of his mahogany desk, when Tom said he was going to go and do the first interview himself. For speed.

"I'll let Liverpool North know of course. We might need to get their people on the streets asking questions but until I can get a feel for what this woman's got…" Tom tailed off as he waited for Frank's brain to work through the internal political ramifications. It didn't take long. Frank picked up the phone and asked Margery to connect him to the Merseyside Area Commander.

"Right Tom, leave this with me. Call me when you've seen her." Frank waved him away as the connection was made.

Five minutes later, Tom was sitting in the passenger seat of DC Talbot's dark green two-year old VW. It was in dire need of a visit to the car wash but that was just fine. Not that Tom's old BMW was much cleaner today but it was a bit out of the ordinary. The last thing a nervous witness needed was anything that would draw even more attention to her visitors. At least they were both in jeans.

"Why are we going over to talk to her rather than someone local, sir?" Talbot said a while later as he manoeuvred into the middle lane of the M62 motorway. "Do you think this is a real lead?"

"Could be. No reason to believe that either Ben or his killers came from Manchester. All we know for certain is that someone decided to leave him at the airport. We need to think as broadly as we can."

Talbot nodded, then added, "I can understand that but couldn't the Liverpool guys have gone to check her out first? Not that I mind getting out of the office…"

"It's a valid point, but sometimes you just have to get as much information for yourself as you can. Second hand is no good. I want to see where she lives, how she describes this missing woman and her child. Ryan's instinct's good. She'll have picked something up from the woman's voice."

They passed the next ten miles or so in silence. Talbot kept his eyes fixed firmly on the road in front of them, occasionally drumming his fingers on the steering wheel. The motorway was busy with lorries battling for supremacy of the middle lane. Tom wondered idly how his traffic colleagues stood the job as they drove past a broken down car on the hard shoulder; police Land Rover parked in front. Then again, they probably didn't get the amount of e-mails he did.

The surrounding countryside, if you could call it that, was flat and uninspiring. The old US air force site at Burton Wood was ripe for development but, according to rumour, there were problems with the land quality so it was still waiting for a new lease of life. Two nearby service stations, one on each side of the motorway, always reminded Tom of those little sweet biscuits called 'Iced Gems', even though he knew there was nothing tempting about the food on offer inside.

Talbot indicated to move across to the overtaking lane, still not speaking.

Tom took the time to consider the man in the driving seat. Joe Talbot started his police career in Derbyshire; joining Manchester CID at the end of the previous year. A stocky man, with clean square fingernails on stubby fingers and a tendency to overdo the aftershave. Today's choice was a bit too heavy on the citrus for Tom's liking. From what he could remember, Talbot was mid-thirties, with three small children and a wife who had clearly passed on her blonde hair judging by the family photo on his desk. Tom was curious to know how he was coping with Ben's case. Hence the lift.

"You and the family settled in to Manchester life now?"

"Getting there. Kids are beginning to make friends which helps."

Even though Tom was divorced, with children, he understood the family state. Six years as an army officer had given him a pretty good idea of some of the tensions that arise when families are uprooted. He figured that while Talbot's kids were doing okay, his wife wasn't.

"Does your wife work? Sharon isn't it?"

The pause was a little overlong to be comfortable. Tom decided to change the subject. Fortunately, they were now at the outskirts of Liverpool.

"We should be looking out for signs to the Mersey Tunnels," he said, looking straight ahead.

Another pause, before his colleague announced rather loudly.

"Sharon's not been well. Post-natal depression from having Libby. Thought the move would help as her sister's close by but it's a slow process."

He indicated to move into the inside lane, ready to take the next exit to the city centre. "Think this is our junction."

Tom knew he had to ask the next question even if it caused offence.

"I'd understand if you wanted to be taken off this case, Joe. You're the only officer with a family and it might be…"

"No! I want to get the bastards as much as you do. And I've always tried not to talk about work at home. I'm staying on this one, sir."

Tom was too aware of the dangers to leave it there.

"You'll need to talk to someone, Joe. This case is a bad one. I just want you to know you can talk to me at any time if it gets too much. Just to offload. I'll not think you're losing it."

He took the resulting silence as complicity and checked the A-to-Z.

"We need to go next right," he said.

Tom stretched his back with relief as he got out of the car. The VW might be German-made but it was nowhere near as comfy as his old BMW. There was a fine drizzle that would do little to relieve the grime on the paintwork although it was guaranteed to make Tom's unruly auburn hair sprout the odd unfortunate corkscrew curl.

"Which house number again?" he asked Talbot as his colleague checked that all the car doors were locked.

"Twenty-seven."

Before they'd taken two steps, a small grubby boy was in front of them with one hand outstretched.

"Mind yer car for a fiver," he demanded.

Tom bit away a grin and crouched down to get closer to the lad's ear.

"Two. But I'll make it a fiver if you give it a good wash."

"Done."

"Good idea," Talbot sounded pleased as they walked away.

"Glad you think so," said Tom. "It's your money."

The black door needed a coat of paint but there was a definite, if slightly patchy, lustre on the brass letterbox and knocker. The number was helpfully painted in white gloss on the wall beside the front door and a small plaque near the roof proclaimed the birth of the terrace in 1902. Tom thought that it was a shame that these good, solid houses were looking their age in a shabby, rather than a dignified way. His own street had probably been the same a decade ago but thanks to the property market in South Manchester his post-divorce bolt-hole was now quite an asset.

The peeling wrought iron gate hung limply ajar and there were more weeds than concrete on the short path. Tom strode along it and rapped on the door with his right hand. Talbot, standing directly behind him, cleared his throat.

"You lead on the questions," Tom reminded him. "I want to watch."

A round-faced woman of indeterminate age opened the door. Her eyes were an unusual greenish-grey colour that stood out against the sallowness of her skin. One eyebrow was raised in query although

Tom was pretty sure she knew full well who they were. She didn't speak.

"DI Tom Ashton," he said quietly. "And DC Talbot. From Manchester. You called."

He was rewarded with a brief nod and the door was opened just wide enough to let them in. Tom was glad of the extra hours in the gym as he managed the gap without having to pull his stomach in, particularly when he heard Talbot noisily inhale as he followed him inside.

"Don't want everyone knowing my business," she said, leading them down the short hallway. "But I was bothered. Such a lovely little lad."

She led them into an L-shaped room at the back of the house. Tom presumed the door in the corner led into the kitchen. The one window overlooked a back yard. The green three-piece suite rather clashed with the flowered wallpaper but it was surprisingly comfortable. Tom felt his spine relax as he leant back into the broad cushion and he gave her his most kindly smile.

"Would you like some tea?"

"No thanks," Tom answered for both of them before Talbot could speak. "We don't want to inconvenience you any more than we have to. DC Talbot?"

"When did you last see the boy and his mother, Miss Jones?"

"Oh, I didn't say she was his mother. I don't know really. I suppose one assumes…" her voice tailed off and Tom felt the creeping disappointment of finding a lousy witness. "And, actually…" she continued, looking sheepish. "It's not Miss Jones. Don't know why I said that. I'm Mrs Stevens."

"Are you sure about that?" Talbot read Tom's mind.

"Yes, look. I'm sorry. The woman on the phone didn't let me correct myself. I only said it at first because I didn't want any trouble and then she persuaded me to see you."

Tom made a mental note to check the conversation with Ryan when he got back.

"Right, Mrs Stevens," Talbot loaded the name with a heavy dose of incredulity before asking again about the woman and the child.

"It was about two weeks ago. I was coming back from town so it was probably a Wednesday but I can't be sure. I got off the bus at the stop at the end of the road and they were waiting to get on. I said hello but she didn't say anything. He did though, the little lad. He said hello back."

"Can you describe them for us please?"

"He was about three or four I'd guess. Half caste or whatever they call it nowadays. Lovely little face and quite sturdy. Well looked after I'd say. She was white. Slim, bit scrawny. Reddish hair."

"How old?" Talbot was scribbling as he spoke. Something was tickling Tom's brain but he couldn't quite pin it down.

"Ooh, now that's a bit harder. Looked rough at times." She dropped her voice into a conspiratorial whisper. "A bit of a drinker between you and me. Maybe late twenties?"

"And where did they live?"

"Next door but one. Number 31."

"Alone?"

Mrs Stevens snorted. "Well, it's not for me to say. She was probably claiming benefits but there was a man around most of the time. And he seemed to have a lot of friends."

Great, thought Tom. A disapproving neighbour might try and create intrigue where there wasn't any just to score a few points. He looked around the room, noting the lack of photos or ornaments. No pets in evidence either.

"Description?"

Tom had to admit that Talbot was not a man to waste his words. Mrs Stevens replied with similar economy.

"Big. Black. Funny hair."

"As in?"

"A strange colour. Sort of orangey-brown."

"Do you live alone, Mrs Stevens?" Tom asked as Talbot noted the meagre details of the man.

"Why?"

"Just curious. How long have you lived here? Who lives next door? When did the woman and boy move in?"

The woman's reply was halted by a sudden and insistent buzzing from Tom's jacket pocket.

"Excuse me," he said, pulling the mobile phone from his pocket and getting up to move back into the hallway. He waited until he was outside the room before taking the call.

"Sir? It's Ryan. A DS Seymour has arrived."

"Great! Put him on – oh, before you do…" Tom asked her about the call she'd taken from Miss Jones aka Mrs Stevens.

"I've got the transcript here," she said and Tom could hear the tapping of her fingers on the keyboard as she accessed the file. She was way ahead of anyone else in the team with her admin. He listened carefully as she recited the verbatim report.

"Thanks. I'll speak to DS Seymour now please."

"You're obviously onto something." Seymour didn't bother with pleasantries.

"Not sure. I'll fill you in when I get back. Shouldn't be longer than an hour."

"If you've no objection – I'd like to look over the files and talk to your people. Who should I start with?"

"DS Ryan. She'll explain where I am and why. Then ask her to take you to see Mary Andrews. She's our PR officer and I told her to expect you."

"Right. Then I'd like to see the boy."

Chapter 6

Mrs Stevens was in full flow when Tom went back into her living room. Talbot didn't look up. He was too intent on writing everything down.

"So I said, that's not really good enough is it? She just nodded. Mrs James next door agreed with me when I told her. I mean, I've been here for fifteen years when all said and done."

Tom hoped that Talbot was capturing something really useful as he came in. This last bit sounded like the tail end of an aggrieved neighbour's whinge. He sat down and waited for Talbot to meet his eye. A few seconds later, he did.

Talbot flicked back each page of his note pad with a flourish and gave a small cough. Tom's spirits sank. In his experience this type of theatrics was for the benefit of a witness who'd given you sod all.

"Mrs Stevens has been very helpful," he said. "She has given me details of most of the other residents on the street. The woman in question is called Karen, but she's not sure of the boy's name. They moved here last summer but have pretty much kept themselves to themselves. The boyfriend was still around until two days ago. She doesn't know his name but thinks that the couple in Number 33 may be able to help us there."

"Why's that?" Tom asked, beginning to think she might be some use after all.

"I saw the man dropping off a visitor to the house. He was driving a big silver car. Karen's boyfriend went off with them later."

"When was that?"

"A few months ago now. I try and get out every day since I took early retirement, otherwise I'd just rot away in this back room."

Tom looked to Talbot for an explanation.

"Mrs Stevens was a teacher," he said. "Stress."

They declined the second offer of tea. Tom called Frank as soon as they were out of earshot and the young boy had claimed his five pounds for caretaking the VW. He watched in some amusement, waiting for Margery to connect him, as Talbot examined every bit of his gleaming car. Tom wondered what was confusing him most – the reminder of just what shade of green it was, or that not only were all the wheels still on, it looked in better nick than when he'd parked it.

"Sir? I think you'd better talk to the Liverpool chief again. We need some house-to-house doing here. We're just on our way back now and I'll get Talbot to send the briefing notes as soon as we do."

"Sounds like a lead – what've you got?"

Tom waited until he was in the passenger seat with the door closed, before replying.

"Young woman with a boy about Ben's age and colour haven't been seen for a couple of weeks. There was a boyfriend. The other neighbours may know something."

"This is good Tom. I'll get onto it and see you when you get back."

Some distance away Karen Abbott curled over on the narrow single bed and buried her face in the damp, musty pillow. The pounding in her head was almost bearable now. Maybe if she could get washed and keep some food down... maybe then Gerard would talk to her. She clenched her eyes tightly and braced herself to roll onto her back.

She concentrated on her breathing while she waited for everything to settle. Her stomach growled with nausea. Blinking furiously, she managed eventually to focus on the swirly cream pattern of the plastered ceiling. How long had she been here? Was this still the first week? God, she didn't know what time or even what day it was. Again. Okay. This time... Karen took a deep breath and exhaled very slowly. First, she gingerly raised herself up on one elbow before pushing herself into a semi-sitting position. Oh, dear God. She felt terrible. Her eyes began to water; a combination of self-pity and shame.

An hour later, Karen sat in the communal kitchen of the refuge clutching a mug of strong, milky tea. Her damp hair dripped down her neck. She was pursing her lips to blow on the drink when her body was gripped by a fit of shivering so vigorous that the tea lurched out of the mug and over the table in front of her. She tried to put the cup down but mistimed the move and instead smashed it against the table edge.

As the hot liquid flooded onto her thighs, she closed her eyes and welcomed the pain.

"Karen? You okay?"

Karen dragged open her eyes at the gentle enquiry. Cherie was small, kind and still covered in the marks of the assault that finally gave her the courage to leave home.

"Not really." Karen's throat hurt but she couldn't remember why. Maybe she'd been sick. She probably had been sick. "Broke the mug," she added vaguely.

"You're soaking! Here…" Cherie laid a blue and white checked tea cloth over Karen's lap. "Give me that," she said as she tugged the mug handle from Karen's grasp.

Karen dabbed half-heartedly at the dampness. How on earth was she going to get him back if she couldn't even look after herself? Another fit of shaking took hold of her and she looked up at Cherie in despair.

"I need help," she said.

Cherie nodded.

"Knew you'd get there," she said. "You need to talk to Jane."

Tom was a few strides ahead of Talbot as they reached the door of the CID office. He opened it to see DS Seymour sitting next to Ryan's desk with an impassive expression on his face. She was reading from some case notes Tom suspected they were details of the responses they'd had from the public. Something in the tone of her voice.

"Good to see you here, Charles," he said with his hand outstretched. "This is DC Talbot – he can fill you in with what we found in Liverpool while I go to see the Chief. I'll let Ray Stephenson know that you want to see Ben. DS Wilson?" He called to Dean over his shoulder.

"Yes, sir?"

"Take DS Seymour over to the pathologist when he's ready."

"Will do."

"Have we got the briefing notes ready?" Frank was standing by the largest of his two office windows.

"Talbot's just giving a quick précis to DS Seymour and then he'll have them typed up. Who's the contact over in Liverpool?"

Frank passed him a piece of paper with an e-mail address and telephone number on it.

"Inspector Geraldine Watkins," he said. "They're ready to go."

"Right. Sir…" Tom wanted to phrase his question carefully, knowing Frank's general eagerness to use the media at every opportunity. "Are you totally convinced that we're doing the right thing by keeping details of the inquiry so low key?"

Frank looked at him.

"Mary Andrews has convinced me that we should use our own people to get information through the community approach. You've seen for yourself some of the responses we got after the TV slot last week. Too many individuals seemed to derive sick pleasure from it. I accept we got a useful lead but in light of the sensitivities of this case I'd rather rely on decent policing than a media push."

Tom wasn't quite so convinced, particularly after his meeting in London. And he wasn't stupid either. He could hear the political sub-text.

"I think we should look again at it if this lead looks like being a dead one. This could be part of a network of activity for all we know."

"I've got an open mind, Tom. Talk to her and see what DS Seymour's reaction was. They met earlier."

Tom sat at his desk, staring into space. Dean was with Seymour, Talbot was typing furiously and both Ryan and Elliott were out getting a breath of fresh air. He decided he'd send Talbot and one of the three other case officers across to Liverpool. Geraldine Watkins had sounded way too excited about being involved with the case. He didn't really want to have to work with another desperately ambitious woman like Yvonne Grey. He mentally chided himself. Sexist. At this rate, he was going to be ticking all the non-PC boxes.

He closed his eyes and took a long, deep breath. His subconscious, primed by the habit, settled at a level that allowed him to be aware of his surroundings but detached from them. He acquired the technique from a fellow officer during army training and just ten minutes was all it took to make him feel refreshed and alert. He sometimes found that answers to thorny questions came unbidden into his conscious mind, although experience taught him that for that, twenty minutes was even better.

Talbot's tapping on the keyboard faded as Tom's internal volume control registered it as an unimportant noise. Tom was vaguely aware of the other sounds in the room; the movement of paper, the humming of computers and printers in stand-by mode; his own, steady breathing.

Liverpool and Manchester. Why the airport? Anonymity? Onward travel? Woman called Karen, her boyfriend and a child. Red hair, skinny. Mother, or guardian? That was it! He flicked his eyes open.

That was what he'd been trying to remember when they were interviewing Mrs Stevens. The word mother had connected with the image of his own, leaping then to the skinny red-haired woman who was lost in her own oblivion at the railway station. That was two calls he needed to make. One to the transport guys at Piccadilly station, and one to Alice.

"Oh yes, I remember her alright. Threw up most of the night and then demanded toast. Must have been pretty once."

DC Green then advised Tom that, in accordance with current policy, he'd given her some information that might help her get herself straight. Tom gathered from the man's tone that he didn't have much time for either the policy or the counselling services it related to.

"I'm sending someone over," Tom said, scanning the room to see who was free. "Need as much detail on her as you've got."

He decided to check his e-mails while waiting for Ryan to get back from seeing DC Green. He wasn't going to mention the idea of the woman at the station being the missing Karen Whoever to Frank just yet but he had a hunch that the details Ryan came back with, combined with his own description, would give them something to add to the Liverpool enquiries. This was more like it.

Ten minutes later he wondered why he'd ever wanted to be a DI. It was getting worse. His mail inbox was so full he couldn't get sight of all the message titles on one screen. Scrolling down, he could feel the weight of administration press down on his head, through his spine and settle in his guts. Goddam it. It was like he'd eaten three Christmas dinners the month after turning vegetarian. As he took a deep breath and stretched his arms above his head to try and get some circulation going, one heading, about a third of the way down the list, caught his eye.

It was from Lily. Ignoring the message just above it on his screen marked with a red exclamation mark and entitled 'Policy and Procedures Update', he clicked on her email.

"Hi there," it read. "Heard about this earlier today. Thought it might be some use? Talk soon. Lily x."

The message finished with an internet link. He opened it. He didn't know what he was expecting, but an economic article about UK investment in research and development compared to Japan and the USA certainly wasn't it. Lily worked in organisational development for the City Council. He was at a loss to see why she'd be interested in that, never mind him.

Convinced she'd sent him the wrong thing, and pissed off that there was no mention of talk when, he sent a quick reply. "Very interesting. Cheers". Then he deleted it.

He did his best to read, answer, delete or file the rest of the messages. He didn't get very far. By the time Ryan breezed back, he'd only managed to shrink the list by six. The rest he was going to have to wade through and actually think about first. It could all wait until the morning.

"Well?"

"Gave an address in Bearley."

"Which is where exactly?"

"Near Stratford-upon-Avon."

"Bloody hell. Anything else?"

"Said she'd just lost her father and her marriage was in trouble. No mention of a child. Gave the surname Abbott. Date of birth would make her just thirty."

"Have we got a number for that address?"

"Not yet. I'll do it now."

Tom strode across to the case white board. He added a line from Ben's name to the name Karen Abbott, finishing with a question mark.

"Sir?" Ryan shouted through to him. "Telephone number listed to a Mr Bernard Abbott."

By the time he'd turned round, Ryan was already dialling. He hovered next to her desk as they waited for someone to answer. The husband?

"Don't think there's anyone there – Hello? Is that Mr Bernard Abbott?"

Ryan nodded at Tom to let him know that she'd got a positive reply.

"Mr Abbott, this is Detective Sergeant Adele Ryan from the Greater Manchester Police. I need to ask you a few questions about a lady called Karen Abbott."

For a moment, Tom's brain went off on a complete tangent when he realised that he'd quite forgotten Ryan's Christian name. How odd. He must ask her sometime if she minded him never calling her by it. Maybe it was because she didn't look like an Adele.

"Your daughter? I see." Ryan glanced up to give Tom one of those looks that told him they'd got something here. "When did you see her last, Mr Abbott?" She scribbled a note on her pad and then was quiet for a while. "Yes, of course, sir. I understand. It is important that we ask you some more questions. We should be able to get someone to you tomorrow if that's convenient? If you're sure. I appreciate that. Yes. No. That would be fine. Thank you."

Tom waited patiently until she had given the man her mobile number and said goodbye. Before she said anything else, Ryan put down the phone and grabbed her jacket off the back of her chair in a triumphant swipe.

"Just a sec," Tom said as he joined her by the smaller white board by the door. Members of the team were instructed to write where they were going each time they left the office during their shifts. Helped to prevent duplication of effort but more importantly made sure his people were as safe as they could be. It was infinitely harder to trace someone in trouble if you didn't know where they'd gone in the first place. He wrote Mr Abbott's address and the time against his name and Ryan's. It was ten minutes past five in the afternoon.

"Sir, what are you doing?" Ryan asked, now standing behind his left shoulder. "We're not going anywhere. He's coming up here tomorrow morning. Should be here by eleven thirty."

Tom stared back at her and gestured to her jacket and bag.

"A date. I've been in since seven and whilst I'm chuffed we've got a lead I'm also glad I haven't got to hot-foot it down to Shakespeare's county. See you tomorrow." She leaned across and, with a damp finger, rubbed out the entry next to her name. Tom regarded her departing back with a mixture of envy and admiration. Anyone with the energy for a date on a Monday night was made of sterner stuff that he was.

He made a note against their names on the white board anyway for the following day. Tuesday March 25th. Interview with Mr B Abbott (father of KA).

Just before ten o'clock the following morning Alice was getting rather warm. She looked at the growing pile of freshly ironed bedding and decided she was going to switch the iron off and have a cup of coffee and five minutes sit down before tackling her blouses. She needed to have a cooler setting for those anyway.

"Both for me and the iron!" she thought to herself as she flicked the switch. It was no good. She was getting old, having to take a breather halfway through the ironing. Last night's disturbed sleep hadn't helped either.

"Oh, who's counting, you silly woman," she admonished herself as she turned to fill the kettle. "The world's hardly coming to an end just because it'll take a bit longer to finish."

Alice was 77 years old. That was what was bothering her, she knew. Both her mother and her grandmother died when they were seventy-eight and there was no way she was ready to follow in that particular family tradition. Her mother remarked on the coincidence just two days before she died, ravaged by arthritis and emphysema. Alice made sure she took her cod liver oil regularly and had never smoked but who knows what would get you in the end?

She looked at the jar of instant coffee in her hand. 'A little of what you fancy' was her maxim and as she spooned the dark brown granules into her cup, she decided today she was going to have it made with all milk. She switched the kettle off and reached for the little pan hanging above the cooker. Before she lit the gas ring, she went into the living room to fetch the cordless phone and put in on the kitchen table in readiness.

Staring at the white liquid, waiting for the first telltale bubbles to grow around the sides of the pan, she thought again about the dream that had woken her just after three o'clock that morning. Maybe it was those boys from outside the off-licence playing on her mind, but that was nearly a week ago, and nothing had happened after all. It might explain the violence she'd been aware of but not the crushing sense of sadness and loss she felt when she'd come to. She wondered whose loss it was.

She reached into the little drawer by the side of the hob, keeping one eye on the milk, and pulled out the pad and pen she kept there for just such occasions. "Write it down," her mother always said to her when she was a child and had seen or heard something she didn't understand. "It'll come clear in the end."

She lifted the pan off the heat just as the milk reached the rim and quickly poured it into her cup. The coffee granules disappeared into the boiling froth and she stirred the mixture with anticipatory vigour. Before she sat down at her new pine kitchen table, she added a small spoonful of Demerara sugar. She needed the extra energy.

The phone rang just as she was about to risk the first super-heated sip.

"Hello Alice?" She smiled as she heard his voice.

"Hello Tom, how are you today?"

"I'm fine. I was wondering if I could pop round on my way home later for a chat? It'd be about half past six."

"I'll be here."

He clicked off before she had time to ask him what he wanted to talk to her about. Maybe she should mention about the lads last week? No, that was something and nothing. She made a note on her pad as she remembered another part of the dream.

She took a tentative sip. Lovely – just strong and sweet enough.

She was looking forward to seeing Tom. It must be nearly a month since they'd bumped into each other outside the newsagents and Alice thought she hadn't seen him looking so well for ages. Must be the new lady in his life. Alice was keen to hear more details. It would also give her the chance to ask him about the little boy. There had been nothing about that in the papers or on the news since last week which she thought was very odd.

Tom smiled as he put down the phone. She'd picked up the phone so quickly it was as if she was expecting him and knowing Alice, she probably was. He'd take round a bottle of wine. She made the mistake of telling him once that she didn't like the stuff, preferring to keep to vodka. It was one of his little quests now, to broaden her horizons. So far, and to his surprise, she'd expressed a liking for full-bodied red wines. White wine, she insisted, gave her heartburn. He'd try her with a Chablis tonight. One last try.

He checked his watch for the umpteenth time. It was still only ten o'clock and he'd applied all the diversionary tactics he could. Giving a deep sigh, he opened up his e-mails and applied himself to some paperwork. After he'd checked these, he'd begin to draft a progress report on Ben's case for The Rodent. With any luck Mr Abbott would be early. Tom sat up suddenly. Why had the man offered to come all the way to Manchester when Ryan hadn't actually told him what it was in connection with?

Chapter 7

Tom took a long gulp of coffee in preparation and then clicked on the Policy and Procedures Update memo. His trepidation was justified when he opened the attached document and saw with despair that not only did it possess hardly any punctuation marks but that it gleefully reported itself to be twenty four pages long. No chance. At least not today. Playing for time, he instructed his computer firstly to print a copy and then pressed the reply button (copying in Frank) to let the sender know he'd seen it and would comment as soon as possible. Soon being a relative term of course.

"Now a good time?"

Tom looked up to see DS Charles Seymour towering over him. Tom leant right back in his chair to give himself the benefit of a bit of visual perspective. His new colleague didn't look too pleased.

"Couldn't be better. Pull up a chair."

"Would prefer somewhere quieter, if you don't mind."

Tom held his gaze for a moment and then let his chair rock back onto the carpet. He stood and picked up his jacket. There was still almost an hour before Mr Abbott was due.

Five minutes later they were walking along the towpath of the Bridgewater Canal. Even though it was only late March the sun was bright and warm. Tom took his jacket off and slung it casually over one shoulder. DS Seymour kept his on, and fully buttoned up.

"So," Tom began. "Why the secrecy?"

Seymour lengthened his already significant stride and Tom thought he might have to break into a trot to keep up. In his army days he always managed to do his basic fitness test with no trouble, but he sensed the Londoner's underlying agitation could take him into the realms of Olympic trials. The thought that there was an aspect to Ben's case that could make the visiting DS uneasy was not a welcome one. Just then, a young couple came into sight around the curve of the canal walking towards them, forcing them into silence until the pair had passed.

"Charles?"

"I'm not sure about either of these things…raising them with the rest of the team would be premature. Blind alleys you don't need."

Tom sidestepped a large dog turd and waited for the revelations.

"I've been looking at all the evidence you've got so far. Bit meagre. But, you're taking a sensible approach to the leads you've got. It was something in the pathology report that bothered…"

An elderly man walking his dog came into view. Tom mentally drew a curse down on him but managed a twisted half-smile in response to the polite nod that came his way. So much for a quiet spot. This was probably the worst place in the world he could have chosen.

"Look," he said. "It's a sunny day and we're going to be bumping into people every five minutes. I've got an interview with the father of a woman I think could be Ben's mother, in less than an hour. I suggest we get the hell back to the station and into that interview room for this. I wanted you to sit in anyway."

"There is something I'd rather talk about away from the office," Seymour said as they retraced their steps back to the large white square building on the banks of the canal that housed the police headquarters. It was known to just about everyone as the Rubik's cube, by virtue of the blue coloured glass windows dotted in regular intervals on every floor. Tom rather liked it, particularly on a sunny day like this when you could almost see what the architect was getting at. On a grey day, the place looked like it was sulking.

"Mary Andrews," Seymour continued. "She didn't seem that interested in what I had to say. Must say that both surprised and worried me, given the experience we've got at the Met."

Tom agreed. "What in particular are you worried about?"

"This softly, softly approach gives the impression that nothing's happening. I know everyone gets paranoid about wheeling out family and friends to do press releases and the whole TV crime appeals stuff that makes it look like we don't know what we're doing but there are ways of keeping the public informed about cases such as this. You've got to build a picture, with fragments of ideas and links and circumstances. She's too parochial. Too northern."

"Meaning?"

"Doesn't want to work with the national press. Wants to keep the public links local. Doesn't make any sense. Ben's death could be part of something bigger, we've no way of knowing but it sure as hell isn't going to be straightforward. There are other cultures at play here. She's either ignorant or out of her depth. What's her background?"

"To be honest, I've no idea. She joined about a year ago. Have to tell you that the DCI used to be mad keen on talking to the media but she's reined him in which I thought was no bad thing. He's gone off half-cocked more than once. Maybe she's swung him too far the other way; he certainly supports her approach."

"Well, I suggest she sits in on your next briefing and gets exposure to how thin your investigation feels at the minute. Particularly when we've decided what to do about this other thing."

Tom picked up the pace. There was only forty minutes before Mr Abbott was due and whatever this 'thing' was, it was big.

Ryan rang his mobile just as they were inside the building. Mr Abbott had arrived early and was waiting in reception. Did Tom want her to take him down to the interview room?

"Well, he's certainly keen to talk to us which makes a change. Get him a cup of tea, will you? I need ten minutes with DS Seymour first. Then you can both join us."

As always, the room smelt. It was usually hard to define exactly what the top note was, given the daily mix of human scents; coffee, bumption and anxiety. Tom didn't need to check the log to know that DC Talbot had been in here very recently. That citrus aftershave had real staying power. DS Seymour grabbed hold of the back of one of the blue plastic chairs but he didn't sit. Neither did Tom.

"I'm all ears," he said.

"There was a scar. On Ben's back. Not recent. Your pathologist had noted it but put no emphasis on it given the overall state of the body. I think it may be significant."

Tom waited as his colleague pulled a note pad from his jacket pocket, opened it at a particular page and held it out for Tom to see. Seymour had drawn an elongated cross.

"And? Does this link in with other cases? Have you seen this before?"

"It's known as Peter's Cross." George took the pad from Tom and turned it upside down so the shorter cross-piece was nearer the bottom of the upright stroke, then took the pad back. "I've made some notes," he said, flicking over the page. "Got this off the internet and I'll want to get some more info on it from elsewhere but basically," he took a breath, "this cross is meant to symbolise humility as Saint Peter refused to be crucified in the manner of Christ, preferring to be hung upside down. But, the symbol of the upturned cross also symbolises an opposition to Christian dogma – and is used as an emblem of Satanism. Those who follow Haitian voodoo or African vodoun have more intricate symbols, this is too simple."

"Where are you going with this?" Tom thought he already knew.

"If I'm right and this scar is meant to signify Peter's Cross then we've got something different than with Adam. We have to question everything." Seymour began to pace around the small room. "There may have been systematic abuse. We can't assume this ritual has the same heritage. There are different elements here."

"Satanists?"

"For one." Seymour held Tom's gaze for a moment and then let his head droop.

For one? Tom's mind tried to sort out the unbidden images of swirling capes, ram's heads, goblets and the creepy guy, perched on the front of a train and laughing at the end of one of the James Bond films. What the hell were they dealing with here? Who were they dealing with?

"I need some protected time with you," he said, beginning his own pacing now that his colleague was still. "On our own. Away from here. There is stuff I haven't even begun to understand. How these rituals started, where they came from, how they link? I know you all gave me quite a lot of stuff when I was in London but frankly – I'm getting more and more aware that I'm in the absolute fucking dark!"

"How close do you want to get?" Seymour's voice was quiet and Tom's heart began to pick up its pace. Clamping his lips tight, he nodded.

A heavy and hopeful pause filled the room, creating a strange vibration that gently buffeted at Tom. He felt his balance begin to slip.

"Then I'd like you to meet someone. Someone who can describe all this much better than I can."

Tom heard the subtext. Someone who was much closer that either of them. Someone involved.

"The priest?" Tom knew the London team had consulted with a Haitian community leader during their investigations, using the description he'd been given although he wondered if 'witch doctor' was probably more apt.

Seymour shook his head.

"I need to make a call," he said. "Start without me."

Tom pushed open the interview room door in an effort to clear out the imprint of their conversation before Mr Abbot and Ryan arrived. He was vigorously wafting the door as she came along the corridor with a tall, handsome man. Tom was struck by the majesty of the man's hair; abundant pewter grey emblazoned with silver streaks. It was perfectly complemented by an expensive-looking blue suit, white shirt, silver tie and a dark overcoat draped over one arm. Tom moved towards them. It was only as he got close enough to put out his hand in greeting that he saw that Mr Abbott was older than he first appeared. And the pain in his eyes was fathomless.

He had seen that expression before. It was the look of an almost unbearable grief.

"Thank you for coming to see us, Mr Abbott," Tom shook his hand and gestured towards the open door. "I'm Detective Inspector Tom Ashton. We'll be joined shortly by another colleague. I trust you've been offered a drink?"

It was a type of confessional, Tom thought some time later. An admission of failure that he needed to share but underpinned with love for the daughter he'd taken as his own thirty years ago. Throughout the interview a photograph of the drunken woman from Piccadilly station lay between them on the table. In it she was smiling broadly and linking the arm of an older woman wearing a broad-rimmed pink hat. Mrs Abbott. Dead from breast cancer two years ago.

"You said that Karen went off the rails when her mother died. How do you mean exactly?"

Mr Abbott sighed, a sigh so deep and long that its vibration whispered in the room well after he started to reply.

"She didn't know she was adopted. We just never seemed to find the right time and well, we were advised not to say anything when we took her."

Tom felt his eyebrows creep into his hairline.

"Advised by who? Surely it was you and your wife's choice?"

"This was thirty years ago, Inspector," Mr Abbott said. "And it was our parish priest who told us that – he'd been so helpful in arranging things – and my wife, well, she never really wanted to admit that Karen wasn't ours. Even to herself at times."

"So why did you tell her?"

"Karen was going to get herself tested. In case she was in danger of getting breast cancer herself. She'd told my wife she'd have surgery rather than leave it to chance, because of Patrick you see. My wife couldn't let her do that. She told her two days before she died."

Tom whistled inwardly. No wonder the woman took to drink. First your mother dies of cancer but not before she tells you you're not actually related.

"Who's Patrick?"

"Karen's boy. My grandson."

"You said Karen had never really asked you for money until autumn last year. Can you remember exactly when that was?"

"It was near my birthday. September 3rd. I thought she'd come to see me for that." He gave a rueful smile. "I thought she'd forgiven me."

Ryan was taking notes but the recorder held every word he said. Every month from then on Karen called him and asked him for money. Increasingly large amounts, for increasingly bizarre reasons. The threat was always the same. She would stop him seeing Patrick.

Now came the worst bit.

"How old is Patrick? When did you see him last?" Tom kept his voice neutral but Mr Abbott wasn't stupid. His dark brows dipped together and he clasped his hands together tightly before he spoke.

"I thought I was here about Karen? I haven't heard from her since February. I thought you had some information for me… that maybe she asked for me." His voice trailed away as he looked deep into Tom's eyes. "What's all this about, Inspector?"

Tom took a silent deep breath and leaned slightly towards Mr Abbott across the table. As he opened his mouth to speak, a brisk knock sounded at the door. For God's sake. He nodded at Ryan, who, anticipating the silent instruction, was already on her feet.

"I apologise for the interruption, Mr Abbott," Tom said, stalling for time while Ryan engaged in a whispered conversation at the open door. "I know this must be very difficult for you."

"Sir?" Ryan's voice was earnest.

Tom apologised again and switched off the tape. "Please excuse me Mr Abbott, this shouldn't take long. DS Seymour, could you make sure Mr Abbott gets a drink and something to eat please?"

Outside the interview room, Tom was faced with Ryan and a red-faced young uniformed police woman who looked at him as if he'd grown a spare nose during the night.

"Well?" Tom demanded.

"There's a lady, sir," the young woman said. "In reception. Said she was your mother and had to see you."

"What?!" Tom was alarmed and annoyed in equal measures. "Why didn't you tell her I was busy?"

When he rang that morning she was just like her old self. One of her good days, she'd said. She was going to do some baking.

Ryan coughed.

"Seems she was happy to sit and wait for a while but when the new desk clerk came on duty and asked her who she was waiting for, she didn't know. She got in a bit of a state."

Tom rubbed his hand across his forehead, his annoyance fading.

"Right," he said. "Thank you. I'll be up in a minute," to the young police constable. He turned to speak to Ryan, who thankfully stayed silent, but then realised the constable was still there.

"Yes?"

"We're a bit pushed today, sir," the flushed cheeks reddened even further. "All the interview rooms were being used… she got very upset when we said we would call you, didn't know why you wanted to see her." She swallowed. "She hit someone. We've had to put the lady in a holding cell."

Tom stared at her in horror before he could get his legs moving. He started to speed along the corridor, Ryan alongside.

"Keep talking to Mr Abbott. Find out as much as you can about who Karen's friends were, when he saw the boy last – any background that might give us some information. We want a photo and something with traces of the child's DNA. Arrange that with the local constabulary." She nodded. "And," he finished, "don't forget you're the lead officer."

Ryan's eyes flickered. "Sir," she said.

Tom took the stairs down to the front entrance two at a time. Who could he call? The GP? No, his mother's next-door neighbour, Mrs Daly. He pulled out his mobile phone from his trouser pocket as he covered the last few yards before the double doors and checked he had her number stored. Yes. He shot through front reception.

"DI Ashton…" the desk clerk uttered his name with such breathlessness as he passed it was as if she'd just found God. Tom ignored her and swiped his identity card to gain access to the cells.

The sergeant on duty was near retirement and totally unflappable. Whatever it was, he'd seen it all before. Tom thought his name was Johnson.

"The lady is in number two, sir." He led the way along the cream painted corridor that always smelled to Tom of toast. Shamefully, his stomach began to rumble.

Sergeant Johnson flipped opened the inspection hatch, nodded at Tom and unlocked the reinforced steel door, stepping back to allow Tom to enter.

His mother was hunched up on the edge of the padded bench, rocking gently backwards and forwards with her head down. He swallowed hard, almost paralysed with the fear of doing the wrong thing.

"Mum?"

Her head came up and she looked at him with tears in her eyes. Tears and – Tom almost sank to his knees – dawning recognition.

"Why am I here, Tom?"

Chapter 8

It would be two o'clock before Mr and Mrs Daly could get there to take her home. Tom knew he'd be able to avoid any assault charge but there was still some explaining to do. Word had clearly travelled, judging by the nudges and stares as he sat waiting with his mother in the canteen. They drank tea and chatted about silly things until, as was now the norm, she took a deep breath and asked him to tell her what she'd done.

"You came to see me for some reason and then got upset when someone asked you why you were waiting." There was no way he was going to tell her the truth. "I was busy so they put you in the cell to be safe as they were expecting a gang of yobs to be brought in." He poured more tea. "Can you remember anything? How you got here? Bus? Taxi?"

A pause and then her face brightened.

"A taxi! I got a taxi. I'd made some flapjacks and wanted you to have some while they were warm. Oh…" She looked around her in panic. "Where's my bag?"

Tom picked it up from the seat next to him and passed it across the table. Apparently, this was what she had swung at the head of a uniformed officer but missed and caught him on the shoulder. She grabbed it from him, and held it tightly to her chest.

"I don't know what I'd do if I lost this," she said.

His mother's neighbours were waiting for them at the front desk.

"Hello, you two," she said brightly. "Thank you so much for coming to pick me up. This really is kind... I just had a bit of a 'senior moment' as Tom calls them..."

There followed a few minutes of chatter as Tom steered the trio through the main entrance. Mrs Daly hung back a little as her husband took Tom's mother's arm and began to lead her towards the car park.

"Tom," she said quietly when the other two were safely out of earshot. "I know you don't often ask for help but what if we'd been out? Or away?" Her kind face was pleated with worry. "You really need to think about getting more care for her. I know your mother won't say and it's not really my place... but maybe you need to think about moving back home?"

She tried to soften her words by patting him on the arm, but Tom knew his expression gave the answer to that question loud and clear.

"Thanks for your help," he tried to smile but his sinking spirits made it difficult. "I'll drop by later."

Tom called for attention.

"Right," he said. "It's eleven days since Ben's body was found. You know that we had the adoptive father of a woman called Karen Abbott in today. There is the

82

chance that Ben could be his grandson Patrick. Hasn't seen the child for nearly six weeks; mother erratic, demanding monies, now she has apparently disappeared. DS Ryan – can you give us the detail please?"

Tom saw how DS Seymour stiffened at the request, barely hiding his annoyance as Ryan walked to join him.

"Okay. Karen Abbott was adopted when she was a few weeks old. She traced her birth mother two years ago after Mrs Abbot died from breast cancer. Both things, according to Mr Abbott, caused her to 'lose her way'. By that he meant drinking heavily, not looking after herself. So much so, that her child Patrick," she wrote the name on the white board, "was temporarily taken into care. She was living in London. He lost track of her for a while after that and she re-appeared last September wanting money."

"Where does her real mother live?" Dean asked.

"A small place called Stillorgan. South of Dublin."

"We need someone to talk to her." Tom nodded as Elliot stuck up a hand. "And what's happening in Liverpool? Talbot?"

Mary Andrews was in a chair towards the back of the group. She said she welcomed the invitation to join the briefing but Tom could see she was uncomfortable. Kept smoothing her skirt across her knees.

"No sign of the boyfriend or the neighbour Mrs Stevens said was pally with him. We've applied for a warrant to search the house Karen and Patrick were living in until a couple of weeks before he was found; a team should be going in tomorrow."

"Why the delay?" This from Mary Andrews of all people.

"It's a rented house," Talbot explained. "Have to talk to the judge to give the case for a search and then to track down the landlord to gain entry. Don't want to cause damage getting in if we can help it. Also," he coughed, "it could be a crime scene so we need to make sure we've got the right people available to examine the place. Want to make sure we are as prepared as we can be. Don't want to go in half-cocked, so to speak."

"You'll be there?" It was more a statement than a question, again from the PR officer, this time directed at Tom.

"Damn right."

Tom next asked Seymour to give his views on what else they should be considering. He was amused rather than annoyed when Seymour also chose to join him rather than speak from his chair. Their southern visitor really was a game player.

Tom watched as Mary Andrews' hands grew still as he outlined the possible significance of the old scar on Ben's back.

"Christ," Dean muttered. "Bloody religion."

"We need to keep an open mind," Seymour said finally, before strolling away to take a seat beside Mary. She blushed and began fiddling with the cuffs of her blouse.

"Now, we've no reason to suspect that any harm has come to Karen Abbott." Tom moved the discussions on. "But then again – open mind – we've no reason to suspect that it hasn't. We've got a half-way decent photo of her from Mr Abbott, but remember when she was in custody last week, she was thinner, and looked ill. Dean, take the lead. You all know the drill."

Heads nodded and everyone moved away to begin calling hospitals and anywhere else a damaged woman might end up. At last Tom sensed the change.

Outrage, impotence and disgust had given way to focus and controlled angry purpose. They'd get justice for Ben. Not just for his sake. But for all the innocents.

By the time Tom finished reading through Ryan's summary notes of the interview with Mr Abbott it was almost six o'clock. They were building a good picture of Karen Abbott but he needed to read the full transcripts from the tapes and maybe listen to them. If DNA did prove Ben to be Patrick Abbott… his brain went into free fall. How did this particular child get caught up in this shit? What had Karen got involved in? None of it made a button of sense.

As he was grabbing his jacket to leave, Seymour took him by the arm and pulled him to one side. Only Elliott was still in the office, and busy talking on the phone, but Seymour still lowered his voice.

"I've arranged a meeting for us both. This Saturday. I can't impress on you enough that we have to attend."

"Where?"

Seymour's voice dropped to a whisper.

"Seven Sisters Road. North London."

Chapter 9

Alice waited. She sat in her quiet front room with just the ticking of the clock for company and concentrated on the glory of being so wonderfully alive. She loved this feeling of heightened expectation; all her senses alert to the information circling her, telling her that there was more to come. She had no idea what it was about or who it involved. But she was patient. And she suspected that, just as in recent times, it was linked in some way to Tom.

A decent man, she reflected as the seconds sang their departure. It was hard to believe they'd known each other for such a relatively short time. She so hoped he would be truly happy one day. A man of his age living on his own wasn't right; when a woman of her age alone was almost the norm.

With a small sigh, she gazed contentedly around her tidy lounge. Her ornaments were gleaming in the cabinet. (Just the right amount, she congratulated herself. Any more would look cheap.) A selection of paperback books and videos softened the lines of the teak shelves next to the TV. Her three precious photograph albums and the box containing the awkward sized ones were safely stored, out of sight, in the heavy old sideboard, sitting snug against the wall opposite the window.

The old piece of furniture was her mother's and the only real reminder of Alice's family home. One drawer still held the faded piece of rose-patterned lining paper her mother had laid within it. The paper had given up its cloying scent years ago. Alice stood at the silent demand of her past and walked across to it, crouched as well as she could and opened the cupboard doors. She stroked the spines of the albums before picking up the old box. The box that once cradled her nearly-new wedding shoes.

Too uncertain of her hips and knees to stay where she was, she got to her feet and went back to her chair. This was a rare and precious moment. After Jimmy died, she'd sat, night after night, stroking his image and then trying to reach beyond the stiff celluloid expression of her mother's eyes for help. The wrinkles in Alice's cheeks stood testament to the many, many tears of those long months. No sight came to help her then.

As time passed, she grew to accept her grief and rejoice in the life she'd had. Even so, she knew it was dangerous to dwell too often on the faces of her long-gone family. Her life was now.

She loved Jimmy from the first moment she saw him and knew he was 'the one'. She smiled as she remembered his early awkwardness and blushing teenage face. Her shoulders relaxed into the back of the chair as she looked at his broad shoulders and impossible grin. This was her favourite photo. A snap taken on a day trip to Rhyl when the sun had shone all day and the train taking them home broke down.

Nobody minded. She knew she was pregnant then but hadn't told him until she thought the danger was past. She sighed and kissed his face. It was just never meant to be.

She closed her eyes; Jimmy's face burning bright behind her lids. A warm glow spread over her as she remembered how deeply they had loved each other. She knew for sure now that it was not her own sense of loss that crushed her spirit every morning when she woke. Someone was trying to reach her.

She was in the kitchen when the knock came. All her memories were safely back in place and she felt secure and full of gratitude for her life. She quickly took her two precious heavy lead crystal wine glasses from the top shelf of the cupboard near the window, figuring Tom would bring something lovely for her to try. Alice really hoped it was fat, red and plummy. And if he wanted to stay to eat they could always have egg and chips.

She was smiling as she opened the door, looking forward to the chat. As her eyes met Tom's she was almost knocked backwards by a foul, unfamiliar stench. Clutching her hand to her mouth, eyes streaming with the acrid fumes, she backed away from him in terror. Heat and flames battered her body. She could still see his face; full of alarm and concern but the world around him was a white haze. Like smoke. Her legs drifted as if the world had suddenly tilted on its axis and she was overwhelmed by despair. Sinking to her knees, she wailed with grief.

Tom shot forwards to try and catch her as she fell. What the hell was the matter with her?

"Oy!"

Tom felt someone drag at his shoulder.

"What are you doing! Leave her alone!"

Tom just managed to stop Alice from cracking her head on the bottom of her white gloss front door and he twisted his head round to see who was behind him. His back muscles wrenched in protest and he gave an involuntary yelp.

"What does it look like?!" he snapped. "She's fainted or something." He was looking into a pair of deep brown eyes, framed by heavy black-rimmed glasses. The owner was a young woman in a t-shirt as tight as a hug, and her mouth was pursed in disapproval.

"I'm calling the police," she said decisively, reaching into the pocket of her jeans, Tom presumed for a mobile phone.

"I'm already here," he said. "Tom Ashton. I can show you my ID if you like but I'd rather get Alice inside." He shifted his position slightly to try and ease the spasms. Alice was awkward and heavy in her unconsciousness. "And you are?"

"Jane Sinclair. I live next door." She nodded her head towards the neighbouring house. "Give me that."

She tugged at the bottle of wine he'd forgotten was still clutched in his right hand, now pressed against Alice's side. She placed it carefully just inside the door and then positioned herself at Alice's feet.

"Make sure you watch her head," she instructed. "I'll take her legs."

Tom did as he was told, heaving Alice's upper body fully into the hallway, conscious that Jane Sinclair's eyes were on him the whole time.

Between them they managed to half carry Alice into the hallway and close the door behind them. Her breathing was rapid and shallow and her face and lips were as pale as moonlight. Tom could see the pulse jump in her neck and he feared she was dying.

"Call an ambulance," he said, trying to get Alice into the recovery position. "And tell them to hurry. Looks like she's having a heart attack."

As Jane turned away, Alice gave a long low moan. Tom stared down at the old, kindly face and willed her to be okay. He needed her. Her eyelids fluttered and she took an enormous deep breath, then opened her eyes and stared. Her expression, when she focused on Tom, wasn't one of pain or distress. It was amusement.

"Hello, Tom," she said. "Sorry to startle you."

"But I'm fine now," Alice protested as the paramedic insisted that she go with them to A&E for a check-up. Less than ten minutes had passed since her collapse but here she was, sitting on her bottom stair as bright as a button.

"I feel a bit washed out," she admitted. "But I was not having a heart attack."

"Sir?" the taller of the two paramedics addressed Tom. "Can't you make her see sense?"

Tom held out his arms in defeat. "I'm friend, not family," he said, fully aware of his reasons for wanting to talk to Alice tonight. He might be fond of her but he didn't need the care of another elderly woman on his shoulders. "I've learned you can't get her to do anything she doesn't want to do."

Jane Sinclair chipped in. "What harm would it do, Alice? At least you'll know for sure and it'll mean I won't be fretting about you."

"No." Alice was firm. "I'm sorry if we wasted your time," this to the paramedics, "but you are needed elsewhere. Honestly, Tom," she tutted. "You should know better."

"What are you talking about?!" He was annoyed in his relief. "I'm not the one with bloody ESP."

"What do you mean?"

Tom had forgotten the neighbour was still there. He rubbed at his forehead and shrugged. "Take no notice. Just been a long day. Look, thanks for your help. I'll make sure she's okay before I go."

He thanked the two ambulance men as Jane Sinclair clucked around Alice, checking she didn't want tea or something a little stronger. It took another five minutes before Tom and Alice were alone. Tom reflected that Alice was fortunate to have such a protective neighbour.

"This had better be good," he said as he poured two large glasses of Chablis, thankfully still cold. "And I don't mean the wine."

A shiver ran down his back when she uttered the almost the same words Dean had used when Ben's body was found.

"It isn't," she said. "It's horrible."

Tom waited for her to tell him in her own time and her own way. Alice didn't always respond well to a direct line of questioning. He waited as she tried her first sip of wine, allowing her to gather her thoughts into some sort of order that he could understand. Her mouth edged upwards slightly at the sides and she looked down at the glass in her hand in surprise.

"Lovely," she said. "All buttery and honey. I like it." She took another gulp, followed by a deep but controlled breath. He raised his glass and swallowed down an equally restorative measure.

"For a week or so now," she began, looking at him straight in the eye, "I've been having strange dreams. Well, not so much dreams, as feelings that stay with me when I wake. Like a cloak around my shoulders. Loss. Grief. An almost unbearable sadness."

This wasn't what he was expecting, and in no way explained what had happened less than half an hour ago. He opened his mouth to speak, then decided to trust her. He took another drink. And waited.

"I wondered if it was for me," she said. "But I've checked. I'm feeling someone else's loss. Of life. Of dreams for the future."

"Did you see anything?" Tom asked. "Any people or places?"

Alice shook her head. "No sounds or smells either until I saw you tonight. That was horrid."

"Can you describe it?"

"Burning flesh and fear," she said immediately. There was no anxiety in her voice or eyes, just absolute certainty.

"Screaming? Crying? Like a child?"

Alice was silent for a long, long, moment.

"Ah," she said quietly. "I see." Again, she fell silent. "I wish there was more, Tom, I'm sorry. I was going to ask you anyway about the little boy. Can you tell me?"

She listened intently as he told her about the case, safe in the knowledge that she could take it, and that it would go no further. Without prompting, he then found himself telling her about Lily and his thoughts of their future, treating her as a confessional; a counsellor. He was aware of Alice getting up and start bustling around the kitchen as he tried to explain his confusion about the growing desire to have his own child, and was glad that she had her back to him as he did.

"How anyone could harm a child…" Her voice was so quiet, he almost didn't catch it. "Such a precious gift." Still facing away from him, she opened the freezer door and pulled out a fat plastic bag of frozen vegetables.

It wasn't a combination he would have tried at home, but a decent French wine combined rather well with egg and chips. He even followed her lead and crammed a slice of buttered white bread with hot, fat chips and a little tomato ketchup. Mouths full, they looked at each other and smiled.

"Thanks, Alice," he said after he'd swallowed the last chunk. "You've helped me get a few things clearer in my head."

"A pleasure," she said. "But you haven't told me what it was you really wanted to see me about yet."

Shame hit him, as it did all too often when he thought of his mother, and he felt the bread and potatoes clump together in his stomach making it uncomfortable to stay sitting down. He pushed his chair away from the kitchen table and stood, leaning against the doorway into the hall. He looked at her and she returned his gaze without demand, but with affection.

It suddenly seemed wrong to ask her about his mother just because she was an old lady too. They couldn't be more different and he didn't want Alice to think badly of him.

"It's nothing," he said eventually. "I'm just struggling with a few things, that's all. Maybe another time?"

"You are allowed," she said.

"Allowed?"

"To be selfish. To want to have your own life."

How did she know this time? Sixth sense or female intuition?

"I feel," he said slowly. "Disloyal. Ungrateful. Guilty. How can I think about wanting a child when I'm starting to resent my own mother? It's not that I don't love her." He realised he was beginning to shout. "But I can't look after her. I just can't."

"There's no law to say you should." Alice was calm. "Is it cancer? Or Alzheimer's?"

Again, Tom felt ashamed. He wished it was anything but dementia. Even if it meant she would have suffered dreadfully but in a way that was easier for people to help.

His forlorn face must have said it all. She stood, went across to him and put her arms around his waist and hugged him. Her tightly curled hair was soft under his chin and the smell of it drew him back instantly to the embrace of his father's mother, granny Peg. He was her favourite and the hug was always followed by a bar of Fry's Turkish Delight and a one-pound note. He put his head against Alice's and, without shame now, began to cry.

It was almost midnight when he left. The short walk home took less than five minutes and as he opened his front door, he felt easier in his heart and mind than he had been for a long time. His mother's illness wasn't just his problem. He could get the help and support she needed. It was going to be a long haul but he had to be practical, unemotional. While he couldn't take on the burden of daily care, he could make sure it was provided, and in a way that she wanted. That meant a tricky conversation. While she still could.

Chapter 10

Mr Kendrick was small and round, like one of those toys Tom had as a child; you could keep nudging it and it would never fall over. Just wobbled around on the spot. Pretty boring really.

Mr Kendrick was the landlord of Number 31 Madryn Street, Liverpool 8 and he was blocking the front door with both physical bulk and anxiety. He wore a grubby stone-coloured jacket with an elastic-ated knitted bit that gripped his middle so tightly Tom wondered what would happen if the fabric gave up the uneven struggle. There was clearly a similar tussle going on in the landlord's mind. He kept saying he wanted to help but wanted reassurance that they would leave the place as they found it. The fingers of his chubby left hand clutched at the bunch of keys dangling from a chain at his hip. His best property. Never had any trouble. Always paid their rent on time. It was getting on for five minutes since Tom arrived, just behind the team from Liverpool.

"Was that in cash, cheque or by direct debit, sir?" Tom asked as he decided that if the key wasn't in the lock in two minutes, he was going to have the man arrested for wasting police time. Or even his Liverpudlian colleagues for not having sorted this out before he arrived come to that.

"Cash. First day of the month. Pushed through my door."

"Okay, enough. We understand your concerns but we need access to this house right now, Mr Kendrick, and we have a warrant. You must stay outside at all times." Another grunt of protest and they were off on the negotiating roundabout again. For fuck's sake.

"Maybe I should handle this?" Inspector Geraldine Watkins stepped forwards. She was average height, with a bland photo-fit face not helped by the regulation hat pressed firmly down onto short brown hair. To be fair, the uniform rarely did anyone any favours, especially if they were on the wrong side of forty. Tom was less than impressed when she arrived with the local CID team but it was her patch after all. Her Scouse accent was almost as broad as the landlord's so maybe she could get through to him.

"There's nothing to see, Madam," came a voice behind him. Tom twirled round on the uneven path to see Mrs Stevens from Number 27 peering around the shoulders of one of the Liverpool officers guarding the space where a gate should be. Useful. He doubted Mr Kendrick would want an audience.

"Morning, Mrs Stevens," he called down the path, loading his voice with just the right note that said the situation was under control. "Thanks again for helping us contact Mr Kendrick. We'll be going inside now so you'd best head home. Bit chilly to be standing around outside."

Maybe it was the bobbing head as she tried to get a better view through the various bodies that did the trick. Less than thirty seconds later Tom was standing in the hallway.

Geraldine Watkins and the two Detective Constables were already inside. Tom shoved the door closed behind him, shutting out the mutterings of the landlord. He did a quick scan of the scene in front of him, gaining that all important first impression. Not bad. Wonder how much rent he got for this?

The cream-coloured walls were papered with that heavy embossed stuff that could be painted over endless times and still bear a pattern. Dark brown and green carpet that wouldn't show the dirt ran along the short hallway and up the stairs ahead. Given the house had the same layout as Number 27, Tom knew the door at the end of the hall would lead to a back room and then the kitchen. He guessed the other door on the right was to a front lounge.

"Before we go in any further," he said as they simultaneously pulled on latex gloves, "a reminder of what we're looking for – signs of a struggle, blood, anything that might indicate this place was the place a young boy was killed. Does it look like people left in a hurry? Any clothes, toys that we can use for DNA testing. Letters, papers, details of names, you know the score. Eyes first, hands second. First sign – we'll get the SOCOs here."

He pointed upstairs. "You two start up there. We'll take downstairs." He was at the back-room door by the time he finished speaking.

It wouldn't be his choice of décor but at least it was clean. Brown curtains hung at the large single sash window and a beige brocade sofa and chair occupied most of the floor space. An unimaginative low teak coffee table, circled with the memories of a dozen mugs, took up the rest. Tom sniffed the air. Bleach. He exchanged a knowing glance with Geraldine Watkins. She nodded.

"Someone's been busy," she said.

They stood, touching nothing but scanning every surface. Tom walked across to the window and looked out onto the small yard. Mr Kendrick had opted for the low maintenance concrete look, softened by a few determined weeds around the sides of the plot. And, unless Tom was mistaken, an ideal place for a bonfire. He called for his colleague to join him.

"Do you see what I see?"

She gave a very impressive whistle.

Tom strode into the kitchen where the smell of bleach was even stronger. No rubbish in the bin, no dishes in the sink, no food in the fridge. A total evacuation. Mr Kendrick would have to find himself some new model tenants, just as soon as they'd finished with the place. There was no key left helpfully in the outside door, or anywhere else obvious. Tom pulled open a drawer to the side of the gas cooker. Empty, apart from a few crumbs in the corners and a small brass screw.

"Best check we've got the key to get out there," she said. "I'll go."

"Sir?" A call came down the stairs.

The bathroom was half-tiled in green, with the rest of the uneven plaster walls above painted a pale blue. Maybe Mr Kendrick thought this colour scheme somehow enhanced the dusky-pink colour of the bathroom suite. Not surprisingly, there were no towels or even a roll of toilet paper on the clear plastic holder. An electric shower unit was fixed above the gleaming bath taps, and a rail was fitted to the ceiling, but no shower curtain hung from it. The presence of chemical cleanser was even stronger in here, this time a cloying pine fragrance overlaid the smell of bleach. Tom sneezed.

Whoever had scoured the place had certainly been thorough, but not quite thorough enough. Tom followed the line of the DC's pointing finger to see a tiny dribble of brown specks retreating down along the side of the wash basin pedestal. He dropped to his haunches and peered at another stain on the varnished cork floor tiles around the base. Blood, for sure. But he needed more than this. Nodding his acknowledgement, he looked up at the younger CID officer.

"Bedrooms?"

"Roddick's in there now, sir."

Tom left the bathroom and crossed the thin blue carpet to the bedroom at the back of the house.

"Bingo." DC Roddick was holding up a small dusty sock. "Stuck behind the radiator," he said. "Together with this." He flicked over a creased sheet of lined paper lying on the window ledge. A child's scrawl. In what looked like red crayon.

Tom picked it up by a corner and let it hang between his fingers. There was a roundish shape, inexpertly filled in with colour. Wobbly letters saying To Mummy and then, from Patric. Seems the child ran out of paper before he could add the 'k'. Again, he nodded, knowing DC Roddick would seal each item in a plastic bag ready for the SOCOs to examine.

"That it?"

"That's it. I've checked the other room. No big items but there must be fingerprints and hairs for the picking."

Bloody hell. They needed more than this.

He ran downstairs as Geraldine Watkins was coming back in through the front door.

"He was determined not to give me the key. Wanted to come through and open it personally. Honestly." She bustled ahead, Tom following close behind.

The outside air was a welcome relief from the pungency of cleaning fluids and Tom took a mighty breath of it.

Sloppy work. Something had been burned here and it must have been quite a large fire given the scorching left behind. It was fourteen days since the car containing Ben's body had been left at the airport so if this fire was connected to that it must have happened at least two weeks ago. Liverpool got almost as much wind and rain as Manchester so this was hardly going to be pristine evidence.

He took a couple of steps and then crouched next to the blackened concrete. He knew from a joint emergency planning course with the other essential services that, in the aftermath of bomb and fire damage, they could find all manner of evidence as to the causes of fire and materials burned. He didn't dare touch it but to his untrained eye, there was a definite thick residue on the slab, and something that could be part of a child's shoe.

"Tom?" He turned round to see Geraldine Watkins peering at a particularly large clump of weeds near the corner of the yard. "Bits of paper stuck in here – could be charred. Maybe blown over here and the weeds shielded them from the weather. And there, too." She nodded to her left.

He made up his mind. He needed drainpipes checked for blood and this residue analysed. If Geraldine Watkins was right, they might get something from the paper remnants. It was going to be a long slog but he knew, just knew that something significant had happened here. And this was where Karen Abbott used to live.

"I'm going to get forensics in here. They're going to have to crawl over the place. You guys need to talk to the neighbours, find out if they know anything. Can't believe our Mrs Stevens didn't mention a bonfire."

"Unless it was done at night. Sadly, fires aren't unusual around here. Cars, rubbish. You know." She gave an apologetic half-smile.

"You can arrange to keep the place secure?" His phone was in his hand and his fingers dialling as he spoke. Almost casually, his gaze rested on the black wheelie bin by the gate. Now that would be a gift. As he explained the situation to Dean to organise the crime scene officers, he flicked open the lid of the bin. Well, well. Someone really was too lazy to do the job properly.

"I rather think we need to have a fuller chat with Mr Kendrick don't you?" he said.

The interview room at Liverpool North headquarters could have been anywhere. Neutral paintwork, plastic chairs around a veneered table. Recording machine fixed to the wall and that distinctive smell of human beings under stress. At least this time there was no parfum de Talbot.

Tom was rather surprised that Mr Kendrick agreed to come in, given that he could have insisted being interviewed anywhere. He wasn't under arrest but the idea that one of his houses was suddenly a crime scene seemed to take the fight out of him. He wanted no trouble, he kept saying. He looked after his tenants, he said. Twice.

He owned four houses, he said as he sipped tea nervously from a plastic cup. He bought the first of them when he'd been made redundant from a company called Plessys in 1985. Did Tom know that Ringo Starr was born at Number 9 in 1940? There was a plaque up and everything.

"Good to know that you keep up with what's going on, Mr Kendrick. However, I'm more interested in who has been living in your house. Number 31. From what we understand from neighbours, there was a young woman we believe to be Karen Abbott and her son Patrick. There was also a man who was seen to be there a lot of the time. We want to know who and where they are. Now, how did you get, check and monitor these tenants?"

Apparently, Liverpool City Council had a private landlord accreditation scheme but there were certainly no regulations around that Mr Kendrick felt it necessary to comply with. This time, he was persuaded to rent the house to a guy called Gerard Baptiste. Met him the once. In a pub called The Eagle Vaults. Tom looked at Geraldine Watkins for clarification.

"Scotland Road," she said. Tom was none the wiser. "I'll get someone down there to ask a few questions," she added.

"Persuaded by who?" Tom turned back to the landlord.

"I'd rather not say."

Tom almost laughed. Where did this guy think he was? An extra in a TV police drama? But he didn't laugh. He set his jaw and leaned across the table; hands held together as if he was going to conduct a prayer meeting.

"I advise you, no I strongly advise you to reconsider, Mr Kendrick. Right now, you are helping us with our enquiries. People withholding information because they think they've got something to hide will find that we look a bit more closely into what exactly they are trying to protect."

He paused and dropped his voice so that Mr Kendrick had to lean forward to hear.

"This is a murder investigation. There are traces of blood in the bathroom of your house. Someone held a bonfire in your garden. A bag with empty bottles of cleaning stuff was left in your bin. Will we find your fingerprints on those I wonder? Did you help to get the place clean?"

It was as if he'd lit a firecracker under him. Kendrick leapt from his chair and began to protest, arms swinging frantically.

"I don't know anything about anything! I was doing a favour. I got my rent and that's all I know." He was almost in tears. "You've got to believe me! I've done nothing wrong!"

So that was it.

"Charged over the odds did you? Just how much rent did you get?"

Geraldine Watkins whistled again when she heard his reply.

"We're in the wrong job," she said.

An hour later, Tom was on the M62 heading back towards Manchester. Geraldine Watkins and her people were going to try to find out more from the regulars at The Eagle Vaults, although she did warn him that they were going to have to pull in a few favours and it could take time. The best thing was that Kendrick, eager to please, suddenly announced that was sure he still had some of the notes from his last rental payment. Tom would have put money on the guy not banking most of his earnings. The prints on the notes would be next to useless, but the envelope was a different matter. He'd left just as Kendrick was being taken back to his house to collect it.

Tom recalled a phrase from his training. The quickening. A point in an investigation when things really began to move and every sense picked up a change in energy. He felt it now.

Chapter 11

"Aren't you ready yet?" Tom yelled up the stairs. Half six she'd said and now it was almost a quarter to. He would rather stick pins in his eyes than go to the theatre but he knew Lily was looking forward to it. Her twin sister Rose had organised the tickets. Apparently, her friend worked for a company that was a corporate sponsor so there'd be free champagne. He'd given in with bad grace partly because it might distract him for a while from what might happen tomorrow; but he needed to get moderately pissed to endure the sodding performance – even for Lily – and now they were running out of time.

"Just trying to look nice for you," Lily shouted back. "And this is the thanks I get. Wine in the fridge if you can't wait."

Pinot Grigio. He poured himself a generous glassful and let his mind dwell as he sipped. Lily was just about the best thing to come out of a difficult previous year. And now, now Lily was a salve; a balm against the horrors of this case and he embraced the thought of her like a toddler with a comfort blanket.

She was the identical twin sister of a university academic that Tom had met during the course of a previous investigation. Rose was just as beautiful, with a brain almost totally devoted to nineteenth century poetry. Sadly, she had come out as a lesbian to Tom just as he was about to make his move – and then she introduced him to Lily. There was a god.

He was smiling into the distance when he heard the tap tap of heels behind him on the laminate floor of her hallway. He turned to tell her jokingly it was about bloody time. But he didn't. He swallowed hard, put his glass down on the breakfast bar and held out his arms.

"Gorgeous," he said, not wanting to take his eyes away from the soft blue dress that clung to her breasts and hips. Simple, classy and absolutely as sexy as hell.

"Take it I'm forgiven?"

"Not yet," he lied, frightened to admit how much he wanted to tell her he loved her. "Haven't got through the play yet."

She tutted as if at a small child and swayed towards him. She put her arms around his neck. Her clear blue eyes caressed and shook his soul, both at once. At times, her gaze was so direct he felt exposed, vulnerable, in danger. Tonight, he didn't care. He leant forward and kissed her mouth, sucking her bottom lip as he pulled away.

"Well, Mr Ashton," she murmured, eyes closed. "I have to say I'm sorry I said we'd go now."

Tom felt his heart rise. Maybe, just maybe, she felt the same.

The taxi driver was tapping his fingers on the steering wheel as Tom opened the back door for Lily.

"Sorry to keep you waiting," she said. Tom wouldn't have bothered. They were going to have to pay over the odds anyway. A Friday night, going into the city centre.

"No problem," the man leaned round and gave an appreciative smile when he saw the full picture that was Lily before giving Tom a cursory glance. "It's your money."

Tom knew the façade of the old Victorian building well, but had managed to avoid going inside it in all the years he'd lived in Manchester. The main entrance to the theatre building was on one side of St Ann's Square; the namesake church on the adjoining side had lost all its windows courtesy of the IRA in 1996 but it was now back to its former glory. Two large wo-men in identical black and white coats blocked the theatre staircase with their ponderous progress. He repressed the urge to yell, "Get a bloody move on!" but only just. He concentrated on Lily's back view as she dipped in front of him, past the women and up towards the glass door.

The inside of the Royal Exchange took him com-pletely by surprise. The cavernous space was domin-ated by what looked like a giant steel spider or lunar landing module, plopped right in the middle of what must have been the trading floor many years ago. Vast cream-painted walls, decorated with massive black and white photographs of people he didn't recognise, reached up to a high multi-domed ceiling. Tom fol-lowed Lily past a brightly coloured staircase sprouting off from one angle of the construction, before seeing that beneath it was a drawn back, blue velvet curtain and behind that, rows and rows of seats.

He tugged at Lily's arm.

"Is that the theatre?" He was incredulous. "How the bloody hell does that work?"

"God, you are a philistine," she called over her shoulder as they manoeuvred past a marble pillar. "It's a theatre in the round."

Well, that's helpful, thought Tom as he followed her gloomily past the crush of people by the bar. He didn't get this poncey stuff. In his view there was something very odd about grown people dressing up and pretending to be someone else. Like the Nolan case, he reflected. The young academic had been a leading light in an amateur dramatics group before he was stabbed to death last year. They'd found who was behind Nolan's murder but not the killer. All pretty unsatisfactory in the end, that case. Although it was through him that he met first Rose and then Lily. He shook his head at the young, shaven-headed man wanting to sell him a programme and hoped there was time for at least one, very large glass of something sedative.

The corporate sponsors' bar was at the far end of the room, underneath the contorted face of a guy with a seriously bad moustache. Tom's spirits lifted slightly when he saw Rose waving at him with one hand, and holding up a glass of champagne in the other. Lily already had hers halfway to her lips.

"Thank God," he said, taking a gulp.

Rose laughed. "Tom, this is my partner, Jodie." She gestured towards a slight, dark-haired woman who was looking at Tom with wry amusement.

"Ah, yes," she said. Her voice was soft and lilting. "The competition."

He raised his eyebrows.

"So long as these two don't start swapping identities, I think you're safe," he retorted.

"Touché! "

Tom decided that he was probably quite a figure of envy with three very attractive women beside him. Things could be worse.

Twenty minutes later he realised that things had very definitely deteriorated. The bar-style seats were comfortable enough but he was squashed between Lily and one of the black and white coated women they'd been behind on the way in. Her left elbow had quickly taken ownership of the joint arm rest, and he could feel her thigh press against his. Not an erotic experience by any stretch of the imagination and, if that wasn't enough, the woman's perfume could fell an elephant.

His attention, wandering since the start, began a serious bid for freedom when some bloke on the stage began to drone on about how no-one appreciated him. Tom could see why. He thought an older woman, flirting like mad with another man, who the first one clearly wasn't keen on, might have been the first one's mother but he wasn't sure. Fighting the urge to yawn, he tried to clench his numbing backside without giving any unintended messages to his large neighbour. Luckily, he managed to rub against Lily at the same time and was rewarded by a squeeze of the hand and the pressure of her shoulder against his.

His eyes scanned the theatre. Odd place, he thought. There was a row of people sitting on what looked like padded benches right by the stage. Well, on the stage, really. Given that the stage was the floor, it was hard to see where it ended and the audience began. It really was a funny old way to make a living, he mused.

Most of the seats were occupied so he guessed the play must be quite well known. He sneaked a glance at the programme lying upside down on his neighbour's lap. The Seagull. He dragged his mind back to the so-called action in front of him in case Lily asked him about it later. Fortunately, he tuned in just as a young woman was presented with what was presumably a dead bird but he lost the plot after a few minutes. Real life was more compelling. And sacrificial murder a damn sight more so.

He was due to meet DS Seymour at Piccadilly railway station at noon the following day. He couldn't remember what time train they were intending to catch but the plan was to be in London no later than 4pm. His stomach tensed at the thought of learning more about the culture, religion, whatever, that led to Ben's horrific death. Sick.

"Are you okay?" Lily whispered.

He looked at her enquiry.

"You grunted," she hissed.

"Sorry," he mouthed and patted her hand, then nodded his head towards the stage as if he was intent on not missing a word.

Thank heaven for intervals. Tom practically inhaled the first half of the glass of champagne and grabbed a handful of peanuts from the dish balanced precariously on the waist-high bar table.

"Well, Tom," said Jodie. "Enjoying it?"

Lily and Rose had tripped off to the Ladies, leaving Tom and Jodie momentarily alone.

"Very nice," he said, deliberately misunderstanding and waving his glass at the table of the refreshments.

Her eyes crinkled at the edges. " I meant the play."

"Ah," he said. "It's – erm – interesting."

"I take it the theatre is not your thing?"

"Never saw the attraction," he confessed. "But Lily…" he stopped as he saw the raised eyebrows and grinned. "Can I get you a refill?"

Inspiration struck him just as Lily returned, no doubt ready to ask him if he was enjoying the performance.

"Before I forget," he said, as Lily took a sip of her drink. "Why did you send me an e-mail about R&D in Japan?"

She stared at him. "You didn't even read it did you?"

"I scanned it." He was indignant. "One of about fifty I got that day and I just thought you'd sent the wrong…"

Lily tutted. "It wasn't very long and if you'd got half-way down there was a reference to a multi-centre clinical trial of a new drug. For Alzheimer's."

He stared at her, his heart jumping at the thought of a chance to delay it, to give them time, give him time.

"Christ!" he breathed. "Could she get it? How do we get her on it?"

"It told you all about it in the memo, Tom," Lily remonstrated, then took pity on him. "Luckily, I've still got it. I'll send it again, then you could print it off and have a word with your mum's GP. You never know."

He grabbed her round her waist and hugged her, kissing the top of her head in gratitude. "You are the most wonderful woman," he murmured in her ear. "Thank you. I'm sorry I'm such a grumpy old sod."

"Yeuch!"

Tom looked round to see Rose and Jodie grinning at them; Jodie then pretending to put two fingers down her throat.

"Soppy pair," Rose said, and passed them each another glass of champagne.

DS Seymour was waiting at the front of Platform 5 as Tom strode through the station concourse the following day. Fifteen days since Ben/Patrick was found. All being well the DNA results would be through on Monday. Knowing the boy's real name was going to be a major boost but then they had to find out who could do this to him. Tom was banking on this trip giving him some insight into that, and the twisted reasons why.

The train was already in and Tom was pleased to see that his new colleague was clutching a large takeaway bag from Café Republic.

"Hope you got yourself one," he said in greeting.

Tom thought Seymour's smile was a little thin.

"I'm learning," he said.

"So, what can you tell me?" Tom asked as they pulled out of Stockport station ten minutes later. Fortunately, as it was lunchtime on Saturday, the first-class carriage was nearly empty and they could talk in relative privacy knowing that the next stop was London Euston, about two hours away. The steward wouldn't be coming though with offers of free drinks for a while. Tom thought he had seemed quite offended to see the large disposable cups on the table as he'd welcomed them aboard.

Seymour sat back in his seat and fixed Tom with a steady gaze.

"I have to know that you will not offer your opinions, even if asked. We are there only to try and understand what might have happened to Ben; not to make judgements."

Tom bristled. Seymour might have the makings of a DI but he wasn't one yet.

"I think you can be sure I will not jeopardise this investigation."

Seymour raised his hand as if to pat an errant puppy.

"I'm well aware that you're the senior officer but on this occasion, I must insist that you allow me to take the lead when we get down to London. Not least because these are my personal contacts."

That Tom could accept. But he was still not going to promise to keep quiet if there was something he wanted to know and it looked like they weren't going to get it. His response was deliberately ambiguous.

"I understand what you're saying. Now I need to know who we're meeting and exactly why you think they can help. And I want the lot."

Alice put on her second-best coat. It looked like it was about to rain and she didn't want to risk being chilly waiting for the bus. Saturday was her day for window-shopping in Manchester – being part of the noise and bustle that was the heartbeat of the city. She rarely bought anything, although she had recently taken to treating herself to a pot of tea and a scone in Kendall's department store on Deansgate. Deciding against gloves, she picked up her black handbag, checking first that she had all she needed, including the envelope for Tom.

She normally caught the Number 188 at the end of her road, but today she needed to take a detour down the alleyway by the other side of her house. As she walked, she remembered all the people who had lived on the terrace. Joe and Mabel Robertshaw used to live next door on the other side, but they'd both been dead now over ten years. Old Molly Williams in Number 42. Tongue like a whiplash and that was before her arthritis set in. Mary Simpson. Said she was a war widow but everyone knew better. Alice heard the voices of long-gone memories, and she picked up her pace. No use in living in the past.

Tom lived two roads behind Alice. As she cut into the second alleyway, she knew she was no longer alone. Smiling, she looked up to the top of the brick wall on her right to see Jack trotting along beside her.

"Hello you," she said. Two minutes later she was opening her bag outside Tom's house.

Alice made a mental note to point out to Tom that his paintwork was looking a little shabby as she pushed the envelope through his letterbox. She'd mention it when he got in touch.

Chapter 12

The sky began to darken as DS Seymour started to speak. Tom thought it was as if the universe, his universe, was listening and grieving. He wished there was a slug of whisky rather than two sachets of brown sugar in his coffee. The train windows began to smear with rain as they sped south.

"Okay. As you know we talked to hundreds of people when we were investigating Adam's death. Some were more useful than others and as you'd expect, more than a few who were downright hostile. Might have been frightened… or simply refused to recognise our authority."

Tom nodded. He understood this only too well. Just like any investigation the world over.

"The person you're going to meet wanted to try and show us the positive side of the voodoo religion, where it came from, how it operates and to dispel the myths and fears attached to it. Only then did they believe we would be able to focus our investigations on the right things."

"And this person lives on Seven Sisters Road?"

"To all intents and purposes."

"Well, what the fuck does that mean?!" Tom couldn't help himself.

"You, see? That's exactly why I need you to keep quiet when we get down there. It doesn't matter where she lives…"

"She?"

Tom stared across the table to be met by a tight-lipped silence. He was about to get really pissed off when he heard a rustle behind him.

"Could I see your tickets, please?"

They were well past Stafford before Tom had the picture. Seymour had given him the full lecture so he could be prepared. The woman was a houngan, a priestess. She accepted the title Mambo, but Seymour advised him to call her Erzulie which best descried her role as a healer. Tom just knew he was going to put his foot in it.

"Right," he said, taking his note book from his jacket pocket. "Let's make sure we've thought of all the questions we want answers to. I get the feeling we're not likely to get a mobile phone number to keep in touch?"

"Not if you insist on that cynical tone of voice."

"You're out of order, Charles," Tom kept his voice low so Seymour had to lean forwards slightly to hear his words. "You've been immersed in this shit for months now. The whole idea of traditional religion makes me uneasy at the best of times so just think what this stuff is doing to my head. I'll deal with it my way. But know this, anyone trying to help me automatically has my respect. Work out the rest."

"And you are out of order, sir." Seymour's handsome face was contorted and his voice loaded with venom. "If you think I haven't had nightmares or imagined the last moments of Adam's life in gory technicolour, well, you're wrong. If you think I listened to some of the crap dished up to us from so-called believers and didn't want to grab them by the throat, well you're wrong. And if you think the brutal death of any child doesn't get to me you are totally, fucking off the scale. I've found a way to handle this to get justice for Adam. I suggest you find your way and quick, if you want to help Ben."

Moments passed when the only sound between them was the constant rumble of the train. Tom suddenly realised that his overriding feeling was one of relief. He gave a slight nod and saw that Seymour's shoulders relaxed, ever so slightly.

"Now I think we understand each other," Tom said and tapped the notepad on the table in front of him. "Right, let's go through the questions and if we've time before London, you can tell me what's really going on with Mary Andrews."

The driver cheerfully announced that they were soon to arrive at Euston Station. Only five minutes late. Not bad. Tom stood, eager to get to North London as quickly as possible. He swayed gently with the motion of the train, for once looking down at Seymour.

"What did you make of Mr Abbott?" Tom more to kill time than anything.

Seymour furrowed his brow.

"Sad man," he said. "Very sad man. Guilty, ashamed. I did think he could shed more light on what his daughter was about but at the end of the interview came to the conclusion that she'd cut him out of her life for years. There are some big blanks." He stood and joined Tom as they made their way to the door, the train slowing as if to give him time to finish the thought.

Tom agreed. "Like who the child's father is. And where she met this Gerard Baptiste, given Abbott thought he was a relatively new boyfriend. Like why she suddenly got in touch with Mr Abbott after more than a year. What happened when she met her real mother?"

"And never mind where she is now. She's good at disappearing, that's for sure. And if she had anything to do with Ben's death."

"What a bloody awful idea."

"Anything's possible, Tom. You know that."

An ear-piercing squeal of metal on metal was accompanied by a lurch of the carriage as they came to a halt. Tom checked his watch. It was just after three thirty in the afternoon.

Karen's hands were shaking and her breathing juddered in her chest. She looked at the phone, lying in wait on the edge of her bed. The little screen was in standby mode and dark but there was a tiny red light on the top that indicated it was ready for action. She couldn't put it off any longer or her courage would fail her completely.

Four days now without a drink. Well, without a real drink. Just a tiny lapse on Thursday when she couldn't cope with the realisation that she'd let them take him away again. Her brain was aching with the lack of sleep and the strangeness of relying on its own chemicals to function. Vivid memory flashes disturbed her waking hours and she didn't know what was real and what wasn't. Apart from Patrick. His beautiful face was at the forefront of her mind and he was the only thing that mattered. She knew that now. Not that woman in Ireland, not Gerard, not her father. Jane had been brilliant.

"You know there are people who can help you, Karen?" she'd said as they sat together in the tatty lounge with mugs of strong tea and own brand chocolate digestive biscuits. Cherie said she'd make sure they wouldn't be disturbed.

Karen was too ashamed to tell the whole story. She just needed to get back on her feet. She could manage on her own then. There was no-one else she could depend on after all.

"The drinking," Karen had admitted. "I've always enjoyed it. Could handle it. Now I know I have a problem. Need to sort it. Everything else will be okay then."

She didn't tell Jane about Gerard, or the lapses. Or about Patrick. Jane was a nice woman but she'd talk to social services and it would go against her, being drunk and getting arrested. It had happened before.

"I found out I was adopted," Karen told her. "When the woman I thought was my mother was dying. They'd lied to me all those years…"

Jane had sat in silence, waiting for her to continue. With sudden horrible clarity, Karen recalled the day she met the woman who'd given her away.

Her father had agreed to look after Patrick and even given her some money for the ticket but she knew he was concerned that she was doing the wrong thing. Not just fearful; angry.

"You're just like her," he'd said.

As she'd waited for the boarding announcement, Karen worked out it was the first plane she'd been on for more than four years. Prior to that she'd been a regular traveller, never dreaming of the day when the short flight from Manchester to Dublin would seem like a major expedition. It wasn't the distance that was the issue, though. It was what she would find when she got there.

"There was a woman who sat next to me on the plane," Karen said. "Big and blonde – full of her new job, selling mobile phones of all things. I was quite jealous of her. So brutally honest about what she wanted out of life and her belief she was going to get it." She took a sip of tea. "I tried to tell her about me. Easier to talk to a stranger, isn't it?"

Jane nodded and gave her an encouraging smile.

Karen's scalp prickled then as she remembered how the conversation had gone.

The woman's name was Erica. She was thirty-one years old, too busy to settle down and desperate to make her mark.

"I'm bang on my career plan," she declared, stirring sugar into her coffee. "Two years in this job and I reckon I'll be ready for a national manager's position."

Karen was intrigued.

"You mean you've planned every step? What if you fancy going off and doing something else?"

"Like what?" Erica looked genuinely puzzled. "I know where I want to be and how to get there."

"And where's that?" Karen knew she was getting personal but she was unlikely to see Erica again.

"A board position," Erica breathed, unfazed by the question. "Mega salary and perks and being able to really make a difference."

Karen wanted to laugh out loud. All this passion and commitment for a company selling mobile phones. It was weird.

"What about you, Karen? What do you do?" Erica took a large bite of her sausage and egg sandwich. Karen's lay untouched on the grey plastic tray in front of her.

What did she do? What a good question.

It was a relief to talk. Erica's expression was of compassionate interest but Karen reckoned she'd be forgotten as soon as they got off the plane.

"I'm taking some time out at the moment," she started. "Am going to meet my natural mother today. Have only spoken to her once before."

Erica murmured something.

"Didn't know I was adopted until mum got breast cancer. She wanted to tell me in case I thought I might get it too. No genetic link, you see."

"Right. How is she?"

"She died. It's taken me a while to get myself together and deal with everything. There's been so much pain…" Karen's eyes closed and she felt the anger begin to rise again, feeding off the nightmare of hurt and betrayal that wouldn't leave her alone.

"I'm sorry. You don't have to talk about it." Karen could hear the note of embarrassment in Erica's voice.

"But I have to. You don't know me and you won't judge any of us. I can't talk to anyone else."

They were interrupted by the stewardess wanting to collect their breakfast trays. A few minutes passed as pleasantries were exchanged and tables stowed away. Before Karen could begin to speak, Erica did.

"Look, I'm sorry. I don't think I can listen to you anymore. I'm not qualified and I really…" Erica wouldn't look at her. "Sorry."

Karen, chastened, turned to look out of the window. She'd just have to learn to keep it all to herself. The plane tilted ready for its approach and she saw a patch of green below the wing; her first sight of the place she was born.

"What happened then?"

Karen realised she must have been sitting in silence for Jane to give the gentle prompt.

"It was raining. I'd never been to Ireland before and it seemed young somehow; bright green fields and few single-storey houses dotted in the fields. Lots of space. I felt sick, nervous."

Particularly when she saw the road sign announce the name of the place. Stillorgan. She was there. At last.

The taxi stopped at a pedestrian crossing. Karen reflected that the woman walking briskly across the road was just as much a stranger to her as her mother. The thought cheered rather than alarmed her. She didn't have to stay any longer than she wanted to. They passed a bowling alley and a cinema and a sign boasting that the shopping centre was the first ever built in Ireland. Karen thought it looked rather attractive if a bit old-fashioned.

The driver turned left. Cheery terraced cottages gave way to larger, neat detached bungalows. Her over-riding impression was that they all looked so terribly stiff.

"This is you, right enough," the driver said as he slowed the car to a halt. Karen looked out of the window to see a single-storey house that was almost too sterile to look at – white paintwork, white net curtains that fell in a stern arch to grant the crystal vases their display. Cold, hard shapes placed prominently on the window ledges to be admired. She hated it all on sight.

"Here you go, love," the taxi driver turned in his seat to face her with a small card in his hand. "Just give that number a call when you need to get back to the airport."

She didn't want to get out. She wanted to ask him to turn round right now. Swallowing hard, she looked out of the window, blinking furiously as her mind replayed the same tired argument, she'd had with herself ever since she'd been told about this woman. Her mother. Annie Colgan. She needed to know what had happened and why she'd been adopted. Hear it straight from her mother's mouth. She wanted to see her, needed to, for Patrick…but she was frightened and angry and didn't want to give the selfish woman…

He cut into her thoughts. "You alright?"

Hysterically, she wanted to tell him all about it. Ask him what she should do but she suddenly registered that the look of concern was masking irritation; she was stopping him getting back to another fare.

"Sorry. Don't really want to do this," she said lamely then bit her lip as his expression turned to anxiety at the possibility of a stranger's emotion. "How much is it?"

As she glanced at the house again getting out of the car, it gave a sign that it knew she was here. One gleaming curtain gave a little twitch, but she could see no accompanying hand or face beside it. Karen's stomach melted and a flush of sweat ran over her shoulders and up her neck. This was it then.

She didn't look back. Striding up the short path before she lost her nerve, she was at the door in a moment. She wanted to pick up a sod of this rich Irish earth and smear it over the gloss. Make it real. Show how dirty life is. Annie Colgan and her pretend, squeaky-clean world.

The anger stilled her nerves and her knock at the door was firm and strong. Karen could swear that the cosmos was holding its breath as she waited, time slowing down as a mark of respect to her situation. The few minutes that passed before she heard the scraping of the turning lock were the most intense of her life. All the world was held in this door and the woman behind it. Her mother.

She couldn't stop her eyes from blinking in double time. It was as if her brain was on a fast shutter speed, generating as many images and memories as possible. The door opened too slowly, no – too quickly – and there she was. Karen swallowed hard as she stared into the eyes of the woman who gave her away. No blinding recognition. No rush of emotion. Just a need to know.

The silence between them became dangerously heavy and Karen suddenly began to fear that the door might close against her.

"Hello," she said, her voice suddenly an apology. "I'm Karen."

The woman drew a tight breath, "I suppose you'd be wanting to come in then."

If the woman's greeting was unwelcoming, the front room did nothing to ease Karen's discomfort. She followed and sat as she was instructed, by the wave of a hand, onto an over-stuffed chair facing the window. A weak sunlight ricocheted off one of the vases and hit her squarely in the right eye. A surge of heat ran through her. Ignorant bitch. She wasn't going to be put at a disadvantage.

She stood and moved to another chair, ignoring the gasp from her reluctant host.

"You may not have wanted me to come," Karen said. "But I'm not going to apologise for it. I think you owe me a proper explanation."

She made herself look at Annie Colgan squarely in the face as she spoke. Karen didn't know if she'd been expecting some sort of generational mirror but it was totally unfamiliar. Pale and thin as though no expression of joy had ever washed over it. Karen began to wonder if her parents had been mistaken when they'd given her Annie Colgan's name.

Karen considered each feature carefully as a clock ticked somewhere in the room. It was an oddly cheerful sound – a gentle reminder that all things pass. Then, at last.

"I've thought of you every day since you were born. I never wanted to give you up. I had no choice."

Karen stared at her.

"That's not what you told me when I rang you. You said it was all for the best. Let me see now…" she paused, pretending to remember. "Ah, yes. That you'd brought shame on the family. They looked after you, made it right. That your faith was more important. The church was your salvation."

"You took me by surprise, Mary – "

" It's Karen."

"Why Karen? I told them I'd already given you a name…" She stared into space before adding, "Mary, after my grandmammy."

I don't want this, Karen thought fiercely. I don't want to be given the shadows of another family. I just want to know why.

"All you've given me in thirty years is less than five minutes' conversation. You said you made a mistake. I was a mistake." It had to be now. "Why did you let them take me away?"

"I'll make some tea." Annie began to get out of her chair.

"No. No tea. Just an explanation."

Karen gulped, her throat dry. Jane patted her arm.

"Are you okay? Do you want another drink?"

"Please. Just water."

"Won't be a sec."

As Jane came back into the lounge, she said, "Do you want to talk about how you felt when you first spoke to Annie?"

Karen shook her head. Her mind was still locked in the memory of that afternoon and she wanted to get the whole story told.

Tears began to stream down Annie Colgan's face as she told her story. Karen listened in silence as the pinched old woman described how she came into being. Sad and sordid. It was the grateful teenage fumbling of a plain girl with a passing fairground worker called Mickey. Not surprisingly, her family were furious. Annie Colgan talked on, calm now as she made her confession.

Karen began to feel resentful of the contrition. This wasn't about her at all. It was about Annie Colgan reaching some sort of peace. She needed to get some space to think. She interrupted the flow.

"I've changed my mind," she said. "About the tea."

Annie stopped suddenly, her mouth drooping open. Karen felt embarrassed rather than sympathetic. The woman looked stupid.

"Oh. Yes."

Karen sat alone in the bright room, so devoid of the things that make a place homely and welcoming and wondered how soon she could leave. What kind of a family does that to their own? With anger rising the answer came back loud and clear. Her own.

She made up her mind. She didn't need to hear any more. Her grandmother forced her own daughter into the care of nuns who didn't know the meaning of the word, just because she was pregnant. She, Karen (never Mary) was treated like a bad thing that had to be got rid of. Knowing this was never going to help make sense of anything in her own life. The only mother she'd ever needed was dead. At least she'd loved and wanted her. And she still had her father. And her son.

She was getting to her feet as Annie Colgan came back into the room, carrying a massive tray that was too generous for its surroundings. As Karen stood awkwardly, caught in the act of moving towards the door, she registered the unmistakeable whiff of whiskey, and a glimmer of understanding.

"I can manage," Annie said, genuinely or deliberately misunderstanding Karen's intentions.

There was one thing she needed to know before she left.

"You said your father was a hard man. Did he drink?"

Annie carefully placed the tray on the largest of a next of tables near the mantelpiece.

"He had the taste for it – as many men did," she said eventually. "They were hard times back then."

"And that makes it okay?! You said he took the belt to you more than once before they sent you away! Was he a serious drinker? An alcoholic?"

"You hush your mouth! He was a good man."

"Yeah, right! And you? Have you got the taste for it, or was that slug you took in the kitchen purely medicinal?"

Annie's pinched face flushed. Karen didn't wait for any reply. She knew now. Her grandfather and mother between them had bequeathed her a truly sorry genetic gift. She felt as though she had swallowed a glass full of ice.

She picked up her bag.

"Did he ever say he was sorry?" She said as she reached the front door, sure that Annie was close behind her.

"It was the way of the time. He was a proud man. I'd let him down. Please don't go."

Karen had no intention of getting drawn in. It was not her responsibility to heal this woman. She had to look after herself.

"Goodbye," she said, staring at the white paintwork and suddenly wanting to hurt. "And, by the way. You have a grandson."

She opened the door and didn't look back. Let the woman reach for her god – either the one in heaven or the one at the bottom of a bottle.

Jane hadn't made her feel awkward or anything. Didn't ask any questions. Just talked to her about support for those with alcohol and drug problems and gave her some leaflets. Karen said she'd call. As she sat, back in her room, she wondered if maybe she'd talk to Jane some more.

Her hand closed around the phone and she took a deep breath. He was going to be angry, but she needed him. This number was only for emergencies, he said. She closed her eyes as the ringing phone called across the ether. Please answer. She heard a click and the ring tone changed. Please.

"So, you're still alive then?" he said.

Chapter 13

"You look disappointed, Detective Inspector," the woman said, a wry smile playing on her lips.

He was. He expected bright, swirling clothes and a hat. With feathers. And beads. Instead, he was looking at a beautiful black woman dressed casually in jeans, scarf and a sweatshirt. She wasn't even wearing any jewellery. But then she didn't need any.

He held up his hands. "Not disappointed," he lied. "You're just not quite… I mean…"

She laughed. A fat, glorious, throaty chortle.

"Sit," she commanded. "We have little time. My friends will be back soon. They may not understand. You understand?" As she finished speaking, a phone in the corner of the room began to ring. Erzulie made no move to answer it, but calmly waited for the noise to stop.

He sat, or rather perched on the edge of a black leather sofa. Seymour sat on a wooden chair to his left, positioned so that he was facing Erzulie, and could make eye contact with Tom.

They were in a small room above a book-binding workshop. The décor more than made up for Erzulie's lack of adornment. The walls were painted a deep red, the carpet richly patterned in swirls of red, gold and black and there were three small lamps covered with gold tasselled cloths that wafted gently from the heat of the light passing through them. In the corner of the room, farthest away from the door, was a shrine. Candles flickered around a statue of the Virgin Mary in her trademark blue and cream dress. She had beads. Strings of them were placed around her neck and more were draped across the table on which she stood.

"Ask your questions. A child has been killed. This is against all our beliefs. I will help." Her accent was hard to place but the words were perfect.

"We think we understand the significance of most of what was done to this child," Tom said, ignoring the sharp intake of breath from Seymour. Damn it, it was his investigation and she'd spoken to him first. "There was scoring, by a sharp knife, around the nipples and navel. And he was left with a small bag of stones that had traces of lavender oil on them."

Her eyes didn't waver from his face as he spoke. They were the type of eyes that poets would struggle to describe – wide and dark, fringed with long, long lashes that cast shadows on her cheeks in the sub-dued light. Tom began to feel rather hot.

"The nipples and navel are symbols of vitality," she said. "Cutting them may indicate the sacrifice was offered for someone who had lost or was losing their own. The stones…" She paused. For what seemed like hours. Tom began to grind his teeth. "A person would be given that favour as a talisman against an enemy. I don't know what was meant."

"Could you take a guess?"

Seymour clearly couldn't bear it.

"He means no disrespect, Mambo," he said quickly.

She silenced him with a wave of her hand and fixed Tom again with her steady gaze.

"Maybe this time the enemy was death itself."

He wanted to stay. He was fascinated by the idea that people could follow both traditional Christianity and the voodoo faith – and why some took the ideas and principles to extremes. He wanted to learn, to understand. A middle-class upbringing in Manchester, followed by a stint at a University in the Midlands and then army officer training in leafy Berkshire hadn't exposed him to much that could help him here.

"You mean that people live their entire lives by what they see are the instructions from the spirits?" He tried to keep the incredulity out of his voice.

"There are zealots in every walk of life," Erzulie said calmly. "And death follows faith wherever you look."

No! his mind shouted. Ben's killing was a brutal sacrifice driven by the selfish desires of some ignorant adult. Nothing else. No bigger picture. He rubbed at his forehead.

Tom was about to say that faith rarely led to the ritual slaughter of the young, then thought of the ethnic cleaning in Bosnia and Africa. He knew that children were subject to rape and murder. How did you divide race, culture and faith? And, closer to home – what about the early days of the troubles in Northern Ireland? Is attacking a teenager so different from a four-year old? You couldn't tell Tom that shaving the head of a girl, smearing it with tar and sticking feathers wasn't some bloody sick ritual. And taking someone's kneecaps out was hardly the stuff of righteous compassion. And it hadn't stopped there. Murder was murder however you wrapped it up. His head began to hurt trying to figure out how he should think – greater minds than his hadn't got to the bottom of this stuff.

The only sound in the room was the faint creaking of the radiator behind the sofa as it relaxed with the warmth of the water rising within it. Seymour was so far from Tom's peripheral vision that he might well have stayed in Manchester. Then Tom realised what she was doing for him. He looked across at Erzulie and saw that she knew he understood. She was opening his mind.

"Well, are you any the wiser?"

Tom made sure the switch in the cab showed that the driver couldn't hear them.

At least the fragile truce was holding. Seymour had only given him a half-hearted ear-bashing as they left the flat and waited for a vacant taxi to get back to Euston. Tom had pulled rank and vetoed the idea of taking the tube. The meeting had taken less than half an hour and there was a good chance that he could salvage a whole evening with Lily now that it looked like he was going to be able to catch the five fifteen. Seymour was staying down for the weekend and would make his way home from the station.

"Not yet," admitted Seymour. "She was firm about the strong symbolism linked to running water – for purification – but that doesn't seem to fit here. But what she said about loss of vitality would indicate someone was ill, maybe not wanting to accept traditional medicine or that wasn't working. Cancer, that type of thing."

Tom thought back to the image of Karen Abbott.

"Or alcoholism?" he ventured. "Christ, no. That's too bizarre, not for herself... look, I can't get over the fact that Karen Abbott doesn't seem to fit! Could she really be a willing party to all this? From leafy bloody Stratford-on-Avon?"

The unspoken question hung between them like a soap bubble, glinting in the light, ready to pop. Seymour's face showed he knew why Tom hadn't asked it, but acknowledged it all the same.

"Voodoo is a religion, Tom. Like Catholicism. Open to all. I rather thought you got that."

Tom didn't reply for a while.

"I did get the message," he said. "And then some." He grabbed hold of the strap above the cab door as the driver took a tight left turn at speed.

"You got any children, Charles?"

"One of each. You?"

"Not yet." Tom caught the slight, knowing smile and looked away to watch the scene passing by.

"As soon as we've got the DNA results back we need to get Mr Abbott in again or go down to talk to him. Though what the fuck we'll do if Ben isn't his grandson..."

"Well, he isn't, strictly speaking is he? Hope the West Midlands plods have taken the right samples. Be great if they've taken some of his hair to be tested rather than anything from the boy."

"Oh, that's just great! Weren't you there when Ryan briefed them?"

"Just assumed it was under control. I seem to remember she made it clear I was a bit surplus to requirements."

Tom pulled out his phone. He reckoned he was going to piss her off but he needed to make sure. His own fault for not checking at the time.

"Ryan? I need to check something with you…"

He was outside his front door just before nine o'clock and pissed off.

Lily, figuring he was going to be away for the whole evening was out for a 'girlie' night with some bloody woman who needed cheering up. He tried to persuade her, just as the train left Stockport and to the obvious amusement of a fat guy sitting across the aisle, to get a taxi to his house when the friend had gone home but he was told that wouldn't be kind and what if she needed to stay?

Dean was seeing Fiona. They'd weathered a few storms and were now settled into relatively comfy coupledom. Now here he was, on a Saturday night in Manchester, forty-two years old and on his own. There'd come a stage after his divorce when he positively basked in his own company but now, he rather disliked weekends alone.

Something crinkled under his shoes as he let himself into the dark hallway. Flicking on the light he saw a small white envelope. Glad of any distraction, he picked it up and ripped it open, closing the front door with a nudge of his right foot at the same time. He took out a folded sheet of white paper, half-covered with small, neat writing; the type only old people could do. There was a newspaper cutting nestled inside it.

Dear Tom,

I don't know why this is important, but I keep thinking about it. Maybe you just need to keep it

*in your files for now. We can talk again. I'm at
home this evening if you want to call, but please
make it before the film at 8.30pm.*

   Yours, Alice.
   PS. I'll feed Jack.

He opened the piece of newspaper. It was a short
article about forced adoptions in Ireland in the 1950s
and 1960s, written with reference to a film that had
just been released on DVD. For a mad moment he
thought about trying to rent a copy, or see if it was on
the movie channel. Sod it.

He decided to give his head a rest. He was expected
at his mother's for lunch tomorrow, so tonight it was
going to be whatever sport he could find on Sky, a
bowl of pasta with smoked salmon and crème fraîche
(dried dill would have to do) and a bottle of Cabernet
Sauvignon. Good for the heart, apparently. He'd talk
to Alice another time.

Chapter 14

Sunday started rather well. Tom's slight, but manageable hangover was more than eased by his mother's roast chicken. It was so perfect he couldn't believe there was anything wrong with her. He told her about the possibility of a new treatment that they could talk to her GP about. She agreed that Tom could call the surgery on Monday to make an appointment.

He left her in high spirits and drove round to see Lily, hoping to spend the rest of the afternoon in bed. He was feeling positively randy when he pulled up outside her house and leapt out of the car like a teenager on his first promise.

The first signs were not good, but Tom was still optimistic. Lily's eyes were red-rimmed and her nose was shiny and when she opened her mouth to speak, all Tom got was a hoarse croak.

"Not so well?" he ventured, hoping she would do the female thing and rally. They kept saying they could take illness better than men.

She shook her head, and a little drip fell from the end of her nose before she could get a tissue to her face.

"Sorry, Tom," she sniffed. "I was alright last night, then this morning…" She gave a rasping cough and he knew all was lost.

"Run you a hot bath? Massage your back?" He knew he sounded desperate.

She smiled and gave an almighty sniff.

"You don't want to catch this Tom, trust me. Just need some sleep."

He gave a manful sigh then offered to get her any medicines she needed.

"Am okay," she said. "Betty got some stuff for me this morning before she left."

Well, whistles and hooters for Betty, thought Tom. He'd never met the woman but he decided he didn't like her given she'd stolen his Saturday night. Promising to call soon, Tom mooched back to his car, his shoulders slumped in defeat. The weak afternoon light was struggling to stay in charge and for the second time in less than twenty-four hours, he was at a loss. More than that, he was crushingly disappointed.

He sat in his car, engine off and ran through the possibilities. Clean the car? No point. Sort out his paperwork? Absolutely no chance. Gym? Not in the mood, although he'd probably feel better if he did. He pulled down the sun visor and peered at himself in the small mirror, trying to talk himself into it. His dark blue eyes looked back with a weary gaze. Who was he kidding?

He looked back longingly at Lily's closed front door. Funny how quickly he'd got used to her in his life. In reality, there hadn't been many times in recent years that he was without female company.

Realising that the bleak years after Greg's death and his divorce were firmly in the past gave him the courage he needed. He knew exactly where to go.

The massive wrought iron gates stood open and the fading light was softened further by a steady drizzle. Tom drove through slowly and parked just inside the entrance. Grabbing a waterproof jacket from the boot, he locked the car and stood for a moment to get his bearings. He'd only been here once before and that was on the day of the funeral.

He set off down the wide, tarmac path through the graves. Massive stone angels guarding long forgotten loved-ones, watched silently as he passed. His breath misted in the cool air and he shivered. A Celtic cross, unsettled by the years, leaned away from the grave, it headed like a domino about to fall. Ben's back. The scar. That was wickedness, not faith.

Tom stopped to read the inscription beneath the carving.

Thomas Alex Waring
1896 – 1938.
A loving husband and father, now resting with God.

Almost my age when he died, Tom thought. At least we've both had a life. The injustice of what had been stolen from Ben burned in his guts. No-one would ever know what he could have been or achieved. Frank was right. Some murders were worse than others, that was just how it was. Tom knew that if he didn't find who had murdered Ben and get them punished, it would hang over him for the rest of his life.

He took one wrong turn that led him past a row of newly dug graves, little mounds of fresh earth each marked only with a simple wooden cross. One was covered with decaying bouquets of flowers, drab and limp in the dim light. That was not for him, even though he'd be past caring. Tom had already made it clear to his brother Alex that he wanted to be cremated and scattered in the Lake District when his time came. Bloody hell, he thought and pulled his collar tighter around his neck. Fifteen minutes ago, he was feeling quite positive about the future and here he was, working up his funeral.

He retraced his steps. Finding the correct path, he picked up his pace, anxious to find the place before the light faded all together. He saw no-one.

Surely it was here? Tom peered at the headstones, convinced he was in the right spot but unable to find the name he was looking for. The marble and granite monuments were more discrete in this part of the cemetery. He couldn't remember what it looked like. Then, like a beacon, he saw it. Just the name was enough to punch him in the chest.

Thomas John Ashton.
Died 7th July 1998.
Sorely missed.

Sorely missed? Was that really all they could think of to say? It was so much more. In the months after his father's death, when his mother's grief was almost too unbearable to be around, Tom dealt with his own loss by ignoring it. He worked hard. He looked after the arrangements for the funeral, sorted out the transfer of bills into her name only and finished off the little jobs his father was always meaning to get to.

Kept promising that he would visit the grave regularly but could never bear to do it. In the early days it was too final an acceptance, and then it was like returning a phone call that became embarrassing in its delay.

He thought of his father often. A tall man before the cancer buckled his bones. Enjoyed his malt whisky, football and The Archers. Tom never got round to telling him that he preferred cricket. Typical of an engineer, Ashton senior kept his garage and shed perfectly ordered, with jars of nails and screws fixed to the wooden cross beams in the ceiling, held firmly in place by a large brass screw through each jar lid. Tom wanted to talk to him more than anything in the world.

There was a soggy leaf on the top of the headstone and Tom leaned across to flick it away. His breathing sounded unnaturally loud; the trees, stones and rain flattening the steady rumble of traffic from the nearby Parkway to a murmur.

He stood in the grey damp air, letting his mind seek out the memory of his father's voice. He'd only ever sworn once that Tom could remember (the time he cut his thumb almost to the bone) and even then, he only managed a heartfelt "Oh, bugger". He could make or fix anything, never criticising Tom or Alex when they made a pig's ear of trying to do the same. Maybe it was just middle-age creeping up on him but Tom couldn't remember any time as a child when he didn't feel loved or secure. He got a few wallops mind you, and was sent to his room more than once when his hormones overtook him. But when his father told him that he was the proudest man alive at Tom's passing out parade at Sandhurst Military College, Tom knew he owed him big time. Both of them. Life was a lottery. And getting decent parents was the biggest prize of all.

The rain was coming down heavier now and evening was well on it way.

"Thanks Dad," he said.

Maybe they were right, he thought as he squelched his way back to his car. There comes a point when acceptance is catharsis, or whatever you called it. He felt now he had come through it all – dealing with Greg had been the start.

He drove away, happy to be alone with his memories. Greg was his best friend. They met on their first day at Sandhurst. His wicked sense of humour and willingness to take a few chances made him great company. They'd joined the Army Air Corp together, Greg as a pilot and Tom as a navigator. Great times. Tom smiled as he eased the car into fifth gear. Sandra was his sister. Tom thought his life was complete when she stood at his side as his wife and Greg as his best man.

The investigation concluded that the accident was pilot error. They were flying low, tracing the snow-covered Norwegian coast…light on fuel and less than a kilometre from base. The water was ice cold and everyone said it was a miracle that Tom survived, barely injured. Greg died instantly and Sandra never really forgave Tom for coming home alone. The agony of that knowledge, combined with his own remorseless feeling of blame, squashed their marriage to a barely civil nodding acquaintance. Leaving the army and joining the police force was a new start for Tom but not for them. In the years since the divorce, they'd rarely spoken. He rang her to tell her about his father. She didn't come to the funeral.

Greg was buried near the family home in Yorkshire, surrounded by trees and on the top of a hill. It took Tom a sorry twelve years before he could bear to go back there too.

Tom shook his head at himself. Maybe he'd put himself through the mill at times but there'd been a fair amount of shit to deal with too.

"Now," he said, his voice sounding unnaturally loud. "You've only really got three things to focus on. One," he indicated his intention to turn left at the traffic lights by a Victorian church now enjoying a new lease of life as a student pub. "Finding out who killed Ben; two, enjoy being with Lily and three, looking after the old girl. No particular order."

Confident of his ability to multitask, he sped down the road towards Rusholme to buy some fresh spices for the curry he was going to make when he got home.

Tom was eager to get into work the following day. The alarm beeped him awake at six o'clock and he was out of bed and in the shower within a minute. His head was clear, his stomach still content from a quite masterful king prawn rogan josh and he felt he could take on the world. A late-night husky call from Lily had helped to send him into a smiling, dreamless sleep.

The kitchen was still fragrant with the smell of curry. Tom's stomach rumbled. He decided to stop for coffee and an almond croissant on the way into work. Back to the muesli tomorrow.

"We're going to get something today, Jack, I'm sure of it," he said as he squished out the contents of a sachet of cat food onto a saucer. "All the prawns have gone mate, sorry," he added, as Jack gave him a look of stoic despair. Tom patted him on the head with a promise of some ham from the deli and grabbed up his keys and mobile phone.

He was about to leave the house when he saw the envelope from Alice lying on the hall window ledge. He picked up the newspaper cutting up from beneath it and pushed it into his pocket.

Chapter 15

Monday morning at seven o'clock meant the roads were clear and he was in the office in less than twenty minutes, even with a stop to pick up some breakfast.

Dean was the next to arrive, for some reason wearing a bright yellow polo shirt. Chances were, it was a present from Fiona and she was still around when he was getting ready for work. Poor sod.

"Good weekend?" he said.

Tom opened his mouth to speak, then wondered how he could summarise everything that had happened since he left the office on Friday. He'd ricocheted from high-brow theatre, to political and cultural awareness in London and then via his father's grave to self-acceptance. Hmm.

"Busy," he said.

Dean nodded. "Likewise. Met Fiona's parents yesterday."

"Ah."

They shared a grin that said it all.

"Lily okay?"

Tom knew he wasn't asking about her health. "Couldn't be better," he said. "How about we all get together for a drink soon. Maybe later this week?"

Dean's response was interrupted by Elliott's usual noisy entrance. "Fuckin' traffic. Bloody short women in bloody stupid 4x4s they can't control. Don't worry about silly little things like parking – just abandon the sodding tanks in the middle of the road because they can't manoeuvre the thing."

"Classic sign of penis envy," Dean observed as Elliott stomped across to his desk near the window.

"Who? The women with their big cars; or Elliott 'cos he's still driving that Mondeo?"

"Yeah, yeah. Very funny." Elliott hit at his computer keyboard with gusto. "Briefing at 8.30 as usual?"

"Would that be the regular eight thirty Monday morning briefing you're talking about?" Dean loaded his voice with enough sarcasm to rile the Dalai Lama.

Elliott gave Dean the finger. Tom laughed.

It wasn't quite the regular Monday morning briefing. Frank didn't usually attend and Mary Andrews' appearance was unexpected. Charles Seymour rang to say he was on the first train from London but wouldn't arrive until just after 9 o'clock. In a way, Tom was glad. He didn't intend to share his meeting with Erzulie with the whole team today. He wanted more time to think about it all first.

"Let's keep this snappy," he said. "It's now seventeen days since Ben's body was found and nineteen days since the car was left at the airport. Ben may, in fact, be Patrick Abbott. We've done a search of a house in Liverpool." He leaned over to the white board and tapped at the address that had been added the previous week. "There's strong evidence of a major clean-up there but we still found traces of blood, a child's sock, a drawing by Patrick. There's also the chance an envelope given to the landlord with a bloody outrageous amount of rent in it may give us some fingerprints. Right," he perched on the corner of a desk. "Let's hear the rest. Ryan?"

"We should have the DNA info back from the West Midlands guys by the end of the week," she said. "They didn't have much to play with, given that it's a while since Karen and Patrick visited and all the bedding et cetera has been washed but they did get a toothbrush and a few hairs from under the beds."

"Talbot? What did Karen's natural mother have to say for herself?"

"Watch this space, I'm afraid." Talbot was clearly unhappy at not having anything worthwhile to report. "Called her house umpteen times last week. No joy. Finally got the local Garda to go round to the house. Neighbour said Annie Colgan was on a retreat and not back until today. I'm going to try her as soon as we've finished."

"Try now."

"Will do." Talbot moved away from the others and picked up the phone.

"What's the latest on Karen Abbott?"

"No sign," Dean said. "We've done the usual but she must be very good at hiding herself. No contact with her father. I reckon she's either dead or up to her eyes in this bloody mess and done a bunk."

Mary Andrews put up a slim arm. Tom nodded at her.

"Could she be being held against her will?"

"She could," Tom conceded, ignoring Dean's grunt of annoyance at his omission. "As DS Seymour has told us more than once we need to keep an open mind. Elliott – check the neighbour statements again from the Liverpool team. See if there's anything we've missed."

"I'll have another go with the winos," Dean regrouped. "She's got some sort of drink problem so maybe she's been noticed."

Frank Dawson said nothing.

Tom was about to dismiss everyone to get to get on with it when the door was wrenched open and Seymour strode in. Talbot edged in front of him, clearly fit to bust.

"What a cow!" he said, waving his notepad. "Listen to this," he said, not that there was any danger of people doing anything else.

"Annie Colgan, biological mother of Karen Abbott, has just spent nearly a week at a convent praying but still managed to call her daughter wicked and beyond redemption. That she wanted nothing to do with and never had. That Karen, or Mary as she called her, was unwanted and she told her so when she turned up at her house two years ago. She doesn't know where she is and has no interest in hearing anything more about her."

"No wonder she went off the rails," muttered Ryan.

"Did Mrs Colgan tell you what they talked about at that visit?" this from Frank.

"That was it," Talbot admitted. "The woman was practically spitting."

"That much agitation means there's more," Seymour said quietly.

Tom nodded. His thoughts exactly.

"You're out too much as it is, Tom." Frank fussed around his potted plants as they spoke in his office an hour or so after the briefing. "You know that being a DI means spending more time behind the desk. You need to let your team learn their craft. It's up to you, of course. It's your investigation. But I think you should consider sending Ryan."

Tom clenched his teeth. Even though a tiny, really weeny voice in the back of his mind was saying that the Rodent had a point, he just didn't want to let this go. What if Ryan wasn't quite ready? What if this was the only chance they got with Karen's mother and they didn't make the best of it? Now you're being arrogant, said the little voice. Sod off, he said silently back.

"I know what you're saying…" he started.

"Spare me the bullshit, Tom." Frank glared at him. "I know how much this case is getting to you and you want to try and do it all yourself, but you have to learn to trust your people sometime. And there's the question of resources. You're too costly to be spending days away from the office."

"Days away from the office?!" Tom began to pace. "Hardly days. And I'm doing what I'm paid to do! Get answers. I can get to Ireland and back in a few hours…"

"Liverpool first, then Ireland? You'll be down to Stratford next." Frank sat down behind his desk and rubbed his face.

"Look, Tom," he said. "We have a duty to make sure the systems and processes in this place run as smoothly as we can. We're an accountable body and I need to know I can rely on you to support me in that. I get leaned on more often than you know…"

Tom realised just how tired the man must be, trying to come to terms with what happened to his family at the same time as trying to operate here. That said, Frank wasn't going to be pleased when he saw the expenses claim for the trip to London.

Inspiration hit.

"Why don't you come across with me, sir? This is a very sensitive case and given the fact that we'll have to involve the Garda… and we could use the travelling time to discuss a few things. Personal development, departmental policy – that sort of stuff."

Frank's eyebrows shifted upwards and a twitch started at the corner of his mouth. As he prepared to deliver a suitable reply there was a knock on the door.

"Yes," he called, then quietly to Tom. "We're not finished yet."

Dean stuck his head around the door.

"Sorry to interrupt but we think we've found Karen."

Tom didn't wait to hear what else Frank had to say.

"I'll brief you when I get back, sir," he said, eyeballing his boss and daring him to stop him leaving. Frank nodded.

We'll pick up the other matter then, too.

"What do you mean, you think you've found her?" Tom said to Dean as they strode towards the car park.

"Purely by chance to be honest. We did a trawl of hospitals last week as you know." Dean pulled open the door. "Got nothing. Seems someone matching her description was admitted to the MRI last night. Got a call this morning from one of the nurses I'd spoken to. Fortunately, she remembered to keep an eye out."

Dean's ability to impress himself on the female of the species was legendary. Probably due to the fact that he was six foot three and with shoulders broad enough to tease out the primeval need for protection from all but the most ardent feminist. And, as Lily pointed out when Tom first introduced them, he was also quite a hunk. Tom couldn't see it himself.

They took Dean's car.

"Guess she's not said much then?" Tom said as they turned the corner onto the main road out of the city.

Dean looked across at him.

"Seems she's in no state to do much of anything."

Alice wasn't overly worried but she was getting rather perplexed. She'd expected to have heard from Tom by now, even if it was just a quick call. She knew he was under strain but it was unlike him to be so remote. She realised how important he had become to her – she must tell him so, when he was in the right frame of mind to hear it. She'd hate him to think of her as another burden.

The only thing to do, in her opinion, when you felt that something was stopping you from 'getting on' was to do something about it.

She didn't normally go into Manchester on a Monday, but the washing was all done and hanging nicely out to dry. The forecast was good, chilly but no rain so it should be alright until she came back. Anyway, she was only going to be gone for a few hours.

She checked her bag to make sure her bus-pass and purse were in it before pulling on her tweed coat; fastening the large brown buttons while looking at her reflection in the oval gilt mirror in the hall. Bright blue eyes in a calm, lined face considered her in return. Alice nodded at herself, sure of what she needed to do. Finally, she patted her neat, white hair with satisfaction, thinking of poor Agnes Whitchurch whose baby pink scalp shone through the few wisps she had left. Thankfully, strong hair ran in Alice's family.

"Does this one go to St Peter's Square?" Alice asked the young scruffy girl next to her at the bus stop as the single-decker came into view. A student most likely. All denim and big shoes. Quite a sweet face though, underneath all that muck. The bus stopped a few hundred yards away at the traffic lights.

"Yeah."

Alice normally caught the Number 85 to Market Street and the shops, so today was a bit of an adventure. She was in the mood to chat.

"I'm going to the library," she said cheerfully as she rummaged in her bag for her bus pass.

"Right."

"It is on St Peter's Square, isn't it? The central library?"

"Mm." The girl began to twiddle with the earpieces of her stereo and then took a mobile phone out of her pocket. Her fingers and thumbs began to fly over the little buttons. Alice thought it was all for show.

"I usually go to my local one," Alice carried on regardless. "But they don't really have a very good information section. I'm doing some research you see... for a friend."

The girl didn't reply. She rocked slightly on her heels and then took a deliberate step away. The bus began to move towards them again.

Alice was feeling mischievous. The girl probably thought she was looking up a family tree or something but even with her ears plugged she was confident the young girl would register the next bit.

"It was all about sex really," she said, letting her gaze fall onto the middle distance. "And families convinced their pretty daughters would get into trouble. Shocking how they were treated. And not that long ago, either. Yes," she gave a theatrical sigh, "sexual repression has a lot to answer for."

Alice had the girl's attention now. It was probably the dreadful realisation that old people might know quite a bit about it.

Alice decided to soften the blow, and smiled at her.

"You're lucky in lots of ways, my dear," she said. "Opportunities; freedoms. I hope you're making the most of them. Ah, here we are!" Alice stretched out her arm to make sure the bus was going to stop.

Alice presented her permit to the driver with a flourish and made her way to the first available seat on the bus. The young girl gave her a strange, but not unfriendly look, as she passed her and continued down the aisle. You never know, thought Alice. It might make her see the world, and older people, just a little bit differently.

The traffic was relatively light. The morning rush had yet to give way to a lunchtime surge and Alice happily spent the next fifteen minutes watching strangers going about their daily business. A vast woman with numerous chins wobbling with the effort of breathing and walking at the same time, rested for a moment just as the bus drew alongside her. Alice could see the straining throat and the little pink mouth gulping at the air. She must be so uncomfortable, Alice thought. Still, at least we've got rid of those ridiculous roll-ons and stockings although, glancing back at the woman, it looked as though she wasn't wearing any tights either. Poor soul. They probably cut in too.

A group of young men swaggered along the street with their hands in their pockets, all the movement of their bodies focused around shoulders and hips. Alice knew she was as guilty of making generalisations as anyone – aimless; yobs; wasters. But what talent lay hidden there? What skills were trapped; drying out and dying in those young fingers, arms and brains?

Jimmy's face swam into her mind. Her father was less than pleased when she took up with him. "A common labourer, Alice. You can do better." She remembered answering back for the first time in her life. "No, you are wrong father. He is truly an uncommon man." Never a good reader, Jimmy was still possessed by more common sense and intelligence than any man she'd ever met. Well, maybe apart from Tom of course but then he was well educated. That said, he could be incredibly dense at times.

"Bye."

Alice gave a little start when she heard the girl's voice and looked up to see her waiting at the door of the bus ready to get off. They smiled at each other and Alice felt as though the day had given her a rare and precious gift. She watched as the young woman walked confidently off towards a large white building, the steps of which were packed with other young people. She rarely travelled this way into Manchester city centre but she knew this was the University. If her memory served her, the Manchester Museum would be coming up in a little while. It had seemed dreadfully dark and dusty to her ten-year-old eyes but days out were such a treat it didn't matter. Alice almost didn't recognise it – the old red building had a sparkling chrome and glass entrance. Very posh. Maybe she would take herself in one Saturday for a look around instead of her usual stroll around the shops.

She reckoned there were only one or two stops now before hers. Oxford Road had widened and there were three lines of traffic heading into town. The Palace Theatre gaily proclaimed that it was showing 'Cats'. She craned her neck to gauge when she should press the red button to alert the driver that she wanted to get off, and as she did so, caught sight of Tom's face in a maroon coloured car going past in the other direction. How very frustrating not to know where he was going.

"I'm not convinced we're going to get much," Dean whispered as they strode along the grey and cream corridor towards the high dependency unit. Although there was no-one else around, Tom understood the hushed tones. It was a mixture of solemn respect for those fighting for their lives and fear of the knowledge that one day it could be you.

"Presume you didn't tell them why we wanted to talk to her?"

"Only that she was a key witness in a serious case," Dean replied. "The ward staff know we're on our way."

"Where was she found again?"

"A women's refuge in Longsight. Normally people wouldn't interfere, but apparently, she was making some really weird noises so they broke into her room when she wouldn't shut up."

"What kind of noises?"

Dean waited for a porter pushing an empty trolley to pass them before answering.

"According to the nurse who rang me this morning, her colleague called it a cross between a wail, a moan and a curse."

Tom raised an eyebrow at the choice of words and shook his head. Whatever had made Karen Abbott create that noise sounded like seriously bad news.

Chapter 16

She was in a single room off the main ward. Tom expected to see a mass of tubes and wires attached to her but she lay, almost too flat to be real, with just a drip feeding some clear liquid into her arm. Even without any medical knowledge, Tom could see that she was desperately ill. Faded somehow. Her lips were clamped shut and her face was not soft and relaxed. It looked as though she was frozen. She was definitely the woman he'd seen at the station but the strength and energy that had given everyone such a floorshow was nowhere in sight.

"Hello, Karen – can you hear me?"

He watched her face carefully but there was absolutely no flicker. Tom looked across at the male nurse standing by the window that overlooked the rest of the ward. There was no view of the outside world in here, just six beds with sick, fragile people and the machines keeping them alive.

"She's sedated." His tone was apologetic. Tom gave Dean a glare and was rewarded by a helpless shrug.

"She was struggling and moaning when she was admitted and her responses were all over the place. We've managed to stabilise her and we're just keeping her hydrated until we know what she's taken. The toxicology should be back later today."

"What did she come in with?" Tom asked. "Bag? Clothes?"

"Just these." The nurse opened a locker by the side of the bed and indicated a bundle of clothes.

"I presume you weren't here last night?" A shake of the head.

"I'd like to see the handover notes then," Tom said. The nurse nodded and left the room. Tom reached across and removed a clip file attached to the end of the bed. Lots of lines, figures and little dots joined by arcs drawn in blue biro. He peered at it. He knew that they'd be keeping an eye on breathing, temperature and blood pressure but that was about it. What bit related to what on the chart he had no idea. He put the file back.

"Looks in a bad way," Dean whispered as he pulled out a pair of latex gloves from his pocket and put them on. A minute or so later he was standing by the locker with Karen's clothes in a pale grey, plastic evidence bag.

"Reckon she was trying to top herself?" he said.

Tom considered the slight figure, watching as the covers undulated slowly and slightly with her breathing. Wondered if the notes would show signs of injections or bruises.

"Maybe," said Tom. "Or someone's trying to make it look that way."

The nurse returned clutching a light blue paper folder.

"You can't take it off the ward – I'm sorry," he said, pre-empting Tom's next question. "I'll try to answer any questions you have but I need to attend to another patient first."

Tom nodded and held out his hand to receive the file. Just as he moved to sit on the typical NHS plastic easy chair in the corner of the room, Karen gave a long, low moan. The nurse was halfway through the door, but twisted on his heels and reached her bedside in seconds. Tom watched as he took a painfully thin wrist between his fingers and thumb, at the same time leaning across to examine her face. What was he looking for? Distress? Or emerging consciousness?

Dean was still by the locker.

"Is she coming round?" he asked.

The nurse opened one of Karen's eyes. "I don't think so," he said. "I need to just get someone."

It was a cold place; a sterile room in an unloved house. The old woman looked at her with distaste, her eyes a hard, ice-grey. She opened her mouth to speak but only a fine mist drifted from her lips and suddenly, there were others; noisy, raucous people. And music, drums beating – the white-haired one began to twirl in time to the rhythm and the room began to undulate and pulse, like a heart. A red, red heart. A child singing and the man's voice saying over and over, "It's for the best, it's for the best." Karen tried to answer, to get someone's attention, but the party was too big and too loud. She tried harder, but her words were whispers and sighs, lost in the madness.

Tom flicked open the pages of Karen's file. They'd been asked to wait in the visitor's room on the other side of the corridor and he was impatient to see if there were any signs of injury on her when she was admitted.

The writing on the notes was small and neat to look at but really difficult to read. It was only when Tom twigged that the odd 'v' shape was actually an 'r' that he could decipher it.

No signs of needle marks. He made a note to ask them to look again. Just to be sure. No injection site meant that any drugs in her system had probably been swallowed. Not necessarily knowingly or willingly – but possibly both of those things. Come on Karen, he thought as he read on. Just wake up and do us all a favour.

Dehydrated, fast pulse, high temperature. Some slight bruising, and two small lesions on the groin. Mouth ulceration and evidence of urinary and faecal incontinence. Nice.

"Anything?" Dean was perched on the end of the chair opposite.

"No idea," Tom said before explaining about the lack of obvious signs of physical abuse.

"Who brought her in?" Dean said.

"I thought they'd already told you that?"

"Only that it was someone from the refuge." Dean rubbed his face. "Shit. I'll go and ask at the desk."

Alice was rather disappointed as she stood in the entrance of the library. There really wasn't much to see apart from curved stairs heading upwards at either side of the hallway and more that apparently led down to a theatre. She walked past a shabby screen and into a small room with a sign that read 'Reference Library'. She'd expected massive wooden doors opening into a huge circular room that had been filled with books and people for decades. This place just seemed home to old men reading the newspaper.

She retraced her steps and took the stairway to her right. And there it was. The place she imagined. Long oak wooden tables fanned out from the centre of the room like the spokes of a wheel. Beautiful old chairs, and shelves and shelves of books. She breathed in deeply, savouring the particular aroma of warmth, dust, leather and paper. All that knowledge, all those words.

She gazed upwards to the domed ceiling, framed by a circular stone-carved declaration. 'Wisdom is the principal thing, therefore get wisdom,' she read. 'And with all thy getting get understanding'. Well, she wasn't too sure of the grammar but she liked what it was saying.

Inspired, she wandered across to the central desk and picked up an information leaflet. The building was opened by King George in 1934. Heavens, the place was younger than she was! Alice smiled to herself at the idea. She wasn't wearing too badly at all. She read on, learning that the library housed a number of books printed before 1501. Amazing. Incunabula they were called. What a wonderful word, she thought. She determined to drop that piece of information into the conversation at the bingo on Wednesday.

Making a mental note to come back again to browse properly, she examined the sign detailing the contents of different floors and departments and felt quite daunted. She decided the best thing would be to ask for help otherwise she could be here all day.

The young man behind the information desk had a long ponytail and a weak chin. He looked at Alice with an expression of weary patience, no doubt expecting her to ask for directions to the Ladies or the Mills and Boon section. A badge, pinned to the left side of his dull blue sweater held the name Brian.

"Hello, Brian," Alice beamed at him. "I need some help."

He became quite animated when she told him the nature of her query. Taking her to the end of the desk, he found her a chair and then began to search through the library files on the computer. Alice listened carefully as he explained what he was doing.

"A lot of background to the Magdalene Laundries is held in the social sciences section because of the impact on communities and the basis of religion…" He hummed slightly as he stared at the screen. Alice couldn't see what was written on it but she wasn't concerned. Brian was on the trail. "These papers are probably going to be a bit academic…"

"Of course," he said, turning to her with a smile that minimised the dragging effect of his lower face. Alice smiled back. "There was a film," he said. "Called The Magdalene Sisters. There are quite a few reviews of it on the web." He tapped on the keyboard again. "Lots of links to other documentaries and interviews – that sort of thing."

"Can I look?" Alice stood and tried to peer over his shoulder.

"Best if I log you onto a terminal and you can surf yourself."

Alice blinked.

"Pardon?"

Brian smiled again.

"Follow me," he said.

163

Thirty minutes later, Alice was engrossed. After a few hiccups when she'd pressed the mouse when she shouldn't and lost the piece she was looking at, this surfing was proving surprisingly easy. And such fun! She was definitely going to come in and use the library more often. More to tell the girls on Wednesday, too. Alice felt confident enough to take her hand off the mouse and shrug out of her coat. She kept her eyes on the screen the whole time, just in case.

Settled back in her seat, she looked around to make sure no-one was watching and then clicked onto a link about a film called Sex in a Cold Climate. Brian had assured her that she wouldn't find herself looking any rude sites by mistake but this sounded a bit near the knuckle.

She began to read.

A creeping sense of disbelief rose in her chest. This was truly shocking. Young women to be so badly treated by the church… and with the complicity of their families… She blinked to make sure she'd read the dates right. The last place didn't close until 1996.

Glad she'd had the forethought to get her notepad and pen from her handbag (now wedged firmly under the desk by her feet) Alice began to write down the names of the places described in the film. As she finished writing the words 'Good Shepherd, Limerick', she realised that her feet felt strange. Cold and damp, as if she'd been standing in a puddle in cheap, badly soled shoes. Alice sat back and watched the words on the screen, increasingly aware of a dragging ache across her shoulders. Now she knew she was right.

An hour later, exhausted but with numerous pages of notes in her neat handwriting, she got up to tell Brian she was finished. She couldn't remember what he had told her to do when she was ready to leave, so she just left the screen showing the face of a pretty dark-haired actress who played one of the lead roles in The Magdalene Sisters. Alice really hoped Tom had taken the hint when he read the cutting.

"Find all you want?"

"Thank you, yes. And for all your help. I'm afraid I've just left it. I couldn't remember what you told me to do…"

"No problem," Brian gave her long look. "Are you okay?"

Alice tried to smile. "Just a bit tired, that's all." The description didn't come close to the bone weariness she was feeling. She didn't think she would be able to face the walk to the bus just yet.

"Is there somewhere I can get a cup of tea?" she said.

The café was downstairs. Although the light was dim, it was restful and the tea was piping hot and very, very welcome. Alice could feel her muscles relax and she bit with relish into the chocolate muffin. The flat slices of fruit cake also on sale just didn't seem to offer enough energy. The café served as the bar for the Library Theatre and she let her eyes wander over the posters displayed on the walls as she ate.

By the time she'd finished her cake and was onto a second cup of tea (from the same pot, so a little stronger), she was ready to make her way home. She reflected on what she had learned. Tens of thousands of young girls, branded 'wayward', had been locked away in those dreadful workhouses, robbed of their childhood and often their children. Made to work all hours; worse than being in prison. Not only that, they were subject to all sorts of abuses from nuns and priests alike. If she hadn't spent the last hour or so reading about it, and the interviews of victims, Alice wouldn't have believed it possible. How families could let this happen, out of respect for a church that supported it... well. She shook her head and wondered how this linked in to Tom. It couldn't be about the boy. He, and his mother, were clearly too young.

"I think it may be best if you call back later," the nurse said. Tom was of the same mind. Dean had a name and the address of the refuge where Karen had been staying. They could be more use there.

"How is she?"

"Her organs are struggling and there are signs of infection. These crises often occur when there's a cocktail of drugs in the system so we're working to minimise the damage to her heart and kidneys."

Tom was alarmed.

"She might die?"

"We hope not, but she's very ill." He moved back towards the door of the visitors' room. "If anything happens, we'll call you."

Chapter 17

Tom and Dean walked quickly away from the hospital entrance to the car park.

"No offence, mate, but I'm going to call Ryan to come and pick me up. Probably best if you get back to the ranch." Dean's bulk alone might make some of the women at the refuge nervous but he was also known for his blunt approach to life that could, on occasion, be misconstrued.

Tom spoke as lightly as he could but prepared himself for a blast of outraged disapproval. Frank would probably have a go as well about him staying out of the office but, sod it.

"Damn it, Tom! This was my lead!"

Tom's phone rang just as Dean was about to really get into his stride.

"Ashton."

"Elliott, sir. We've got the DNA results back from Liverpool and Stratford. Ben is Patrick Abbott."

"Now we're getting somewhere!" Tom clenched his fist and nodded in response to Dean's mouthed query. "Anything more from Liverpool?"

"Talbot's onto DI Watkins now, do you want to hang on to talk to him?"

"No. Tell him I want a full briefing when I get back. Put Ryan on will you?"

Tom's mind raced as he waited for Ryan to come on the line. Given that the information from Liverpool might give them a lead to the boyfriend and possibly the killer or killers... fair enough, the women at the refuge may give them some background on Karen but now that they knew the dead boy was her son... he was going to have to talk to Mr Abbott...

"Ryan – I need you to go with Dean to the women's refuge where Karen was staying. Grab your stuff and pick him up outside the MRI."

Dean was standing by a large sign about the car park tariff with his arms folded.

"Something more interesting come up?"

Tom ignored the jibe. Friend he might be but he was still Dean's senior officer.

"Find out what you can about when she arrived, anything about her background, the boyfriend. Get Ryan to ask if she talked or met with anyone recently. Find if she's got a phone." Tom took in the glowering brows and clenched jaw.

"Oh, come on Dean! Sensitivity is hardly your strong point; you don't need me to tell you that! Just let Ryan front the visit and you listen carefully and nudge when needed. Now we know that our boy is definitely Karen's son we need all the info we can get – and from wherever we can get it."

"You don't need to tell me how to do my job," Dean's voice was low and dangerous. "And I especially don't appreciate the inference that I can't do it properly because I'm not a woman."

Bloody hell, thought Tom. The accusation of sexual assault, thanks to Yvonne Grey, was known to be false but the wound was clearly still weeping.

He took a step forward. With Dean backed up against the sign, Tom was now firmly encroaching on his colleague's personal space.

"I'm on your side, mate and I'm telling you to let it go," he said firmly. "You're a good officer and detective. We've all got our strengths and weaknesses. Ryan's superb at drawing confidences. You know that. If we need anyone to be terrified into submission – you're the man." Dean didn't smile.

Tom sighed.

"Look, it's not meant as a criticism. Just realistic. Some of the women at the refuge might panic at being questioned by a big bloke. Especially if they've been at the receiving end of somebody's fists. It's not personal. Use your bloody brain."

He stepped back. Dean didn't say a word, just dropped his car keys into Tom's outstretched hand, before walking back towards the main entrance of the hospital to wait for Ryan.

I didn't want you. I never wanted you. I don't want to see you again. The white-haired woman spat the words and then she began to swell and darken; clouds of sweet smelling smoke filling the room. Karen struggled against the assault of the words and ran away down the long corridor towards a bright light where she knew Patrick was waiting; the red floor pulsing and beeping under her feet.

Talbot was deep in conversation with Charles Seymour when Tom got back to headquarters. It was just before noon.

Tom nodded a general greeting to the pair before propping himself against the wall near Talbot's desk.

"What else have we got?"

"One of the neighbours confirmed the boyfriend's name as Gerard but she pronounced it the French way." Talbot gave Tom the benefit of his impression.

"Did we get a description of the guy?"

"Well, they're all in agreement with our Mrs Stevens. General consensus is big and black with brownish-ginger hair. But we've also got 'polite' and 'quiet' to add to that."

"Bloody hell. Did we get anything from the landlord's envelope?"

"Decent enough prints apparently but nothing coming up on NAFIS."

Tom sighed. That would have been too good to be true.

"Well at least we can cross check them against the prints we got from the car. And what about the pub? They must be able to give us a lead…"

"DI Watkins said they're working on it." Talbot suddenly grinned. "We did just have another thought?"

Tom looked at Seymour and Talbot and back again.

"Well, let's hear it then!"

DS Seymour coughed. "We did get one thing clarified by the pub. That this Baptiste spoke with a funny accent. So, we reckon it's not just his name that's French. Maybe he is too. Or French colonial."

"This is NCIS territory then."

Seymour nodded.

"They're our route to Interpol so it's worth a try. He may or may not have a criminal record but he's right in the frame. Easy enough to get the prints lifted, checked in their database. We built up quite a good relationship with them over Adam. They're shit hot."

"Do we know when we'll have anything?"

Seymour grinned.

"Tomorrow," he said.

"Nice one, you two – write it up, Talbot!" Tom pointed across to the case corner. "Now all we have to do is hope and pray that Karen Abbott doesn't give up the ghost before we can ask her about Mr Gerard Baptiste."

Leaving his two colleagues beaming in self-congratulation, Tom decided to grab some lunch and make some calls at the same time.

"On my mobile!" he yelled to whoever was listening and trotted out along the corridor, downstairs and outside into the fresh late March air. He increased his pace as he left the building behind him and strode with purpose along the canal towpath. They'd found Karen, they knew Ben was her child, they were homing in on Gerard Baptiste. Too much still up in the air but he could feel they were getting closer. Bugger. He hadn't told The Rodent.

He called his boss' number. Margery answered.

"He's at lunch with the City Council today. Tom," she said. "Is it urgent?"

Tom assured her that it would wait until later, but would she please pass on the message that there had been some developments in Ben's case. She would.

He rounded the first bend and picked up his stride even further. He'd be at the edge of Deansgate and the café in ten minutes if he kept this up. As his mind began to consider his sandwich options, a shaft of sunlight pushed through the clouds and brightened up the Manchester skyline in front of him. This was shaping up to be a good day.

The café was busy but not so bad that he couldn't get a quiet spot to himself at the back away from the large picture windows that overlooked the main road. He loved the industrial look of the area; Victorian red brick engineering brightened by chrome and neon. New bars and restaurants, together with the Comedy Store, had really brought the place to life.

He carefully placed his lunch and large cup of black coffee on the table before settling himself down. He picked up his sandwich and gave it the benefit of his full attention. Moist focaccia, sprinkled with rosemary and black pepper, stuffed to bursting with roasted vegetables, feta cheese and rocket. Bloody marvellous.

The clientele was a mixed bag. A good number of young, be-suited professionals (male and female) but with a liberal sprinkling of middle-aged men trying to look trendy. Tom examined himself in the reflection from the mirror on the wall next to him and realised with a shock he was one of them. Maybe it was time to take Lily up on her offer to help him get some new clothes.

He took a bite of his sandwich and gave an involuntary hum of pleasure as the tangy flavours exploded into his mouth. Tom silently saluted an older woman sitting at the next table who'd made the same lunch choice as him. She seemed rather out of place with her wild mop of corkscrew grey hair and clutch of plastic carrier bags at her feet and he wondered who she was and why she was here. He revised his assessment of her when he noticed how avidly she was reading The Guardian, and saw that one of the bags held sheets of white paper. Probably an academic, he decided, taking another bite.

A sharp beeping from his jacket pocket broke his reverie. The woman glared at him in annoyance at the interruption and any early ideas that she was a lonely old soul well and truly disappeared.

Tom flicked open his phone and checked the screen. A reminder to call the GP between 1pm and 2pm. He hadn't forgotten. It was five minutes to one.

He took a gulp of coffee and considered the possibilities. Lily had warned him not to get too excited but he couldn't help but feel this just might be a 'Get out of Jail' card. Even if it just halted things for a couple of years… maybe by then they'd have found a cure… or Alex might come back in the meantime and he wouldn't have to manage this on his own. More coffee. Actually, he admitted to himself, he really rather hoped he wouldn't be on his own anyway.

He picked up his phone from the table and, ignoring Medusa's tut, rang Lily.

"Hi there," he whispered as she answered. "Just thinking about you so I thought I'd give you a quick call, see how you're feeling. Okay for tonight?"

Glad to hear her quick positive response, he suggested a time and place to meet.

"Might know something about the trial," he said. "Receptionist told me to ring back before two o'clock to speak to the doctor. Keep your fingers crossed."

"They're unlikely to commit to anything today, Tom. Try not to get your hopes up too high, eh? Your mum might not fit the criteria."

Tom felt narked. He knew she was being sensible and cautious but he didn't want to hear it. He wanted her to tell him it was all going to work out just fine, not snatch the future away from him. He took a swig of coffee to stop him saying something petty. He was behaving like a teenager.

"Tom?"

"Yes, I know," he said. "Sorry. Just want…" he bit his lip. "Look, I'd better go and get the call done. See you later."

As he put the phone away, he realised he was under the full beam of his neighbour's glare. He stared back.

"I couldn't help overhearing," she said. "Maybe we can be of some help?" She leaned down and rummaged in one of the bags. Oh-oh, he thought. He quickly wrapped up the remainder of the sandwich in his napkin, drained his cup and began to edge his chair backwards to give him room to get up and away.

She thrust a green and white leaflet at him. There was a black logo on the front, and Tom could see it was a set of scales, but it looked like there was a man on one scale and a rat or something on the other. By this time, he was on his feet.

"We're a patient group who support the use of animals in the research for new medicines," she said. "If you're talking to a GP about taking part in a trial then we could use your voice. And we may be able to answer some of your questions."

He took the paper from her to avoid getting into any kind of discussion about medical ethics. Frankly he didn't care either which way so long as there was some possibility of help for his mother. Thanking the woman, he shoved the leaflet in his pocket and left the cafe.

Although it was lunchtime, there were few people around but the noise of the traffic was too intrusive to talk outside. He knew where he could find a quiet corner. He flashed his ID card at the box office at the Comedy Store.

"Just need to make a few calls – don't mind if I park myself in the corner, do you?" He picked up a copy of the current programme of events as he asked. He might need a laugh if Lily was proved right.

Well, it wasn't a 'yes', on the other hand it wasn't a 'no' either. Lily was partly right in that the GP wouldn't commit either way but at least she promised to look into it and call him back. It was something. Now he had to call Mr Abbott. Good news first (we've found Karen) or bad news first (your grandson is dead)? Not much to celebrate in the good news either given Karen's state of health. And the death of a child is not something you tell someone over the phone if you could help it. In reality, all he had were different grades of bloody awful news to pass on.

Tom sat quietly for a moment before making up his mind. Mr Abbott would want to see Karen and then Tom could tell him about Patrick face to face. He wasn't going to give the poor man that information before he faced the drive up from the Midlands.

He called the Stratford number. Damn. No answer. He'd have to leave a message. Okay, aim for non-committal but he was probably going to freak the guy out anyway.

"Hello Mr Abbott, this is DI Tom Ashton. Could you give me a call back as soon as possible please? It's now twenty past one on Monday 30th. I'll be on this number for the rest of the day. Many thanks."

He was almost back at the police headquarters when Karen's father called back.

"Inspector Ashton?" The man's voice was crackling with anxiety. "You have news for me?"

Tom checked quickly behind him that there was no-one to overhear.

"Karen is in hospital, Mr Abbott. I'm afraid she's not very well but the doctors are doing all they can to help her."

"I'm on my way. Which hospital?"

Tom gave him the details. "Is there someone who can come with you?"

"Why? Is there something you haven't told me?"

Tom berated himself. The man might be getting on a bit and worried sick but he wasn't stupid by any means.

"I was thinking of having someone to share the driving, that sort of thing. Parking at the hospital is a bit tricky."

If Mr Abbott thought the remark as lame as Tom did, he had the good grace not to say so.

"I'm quite capable, Inspector," he said. "But I would appreciate details of a cheap B&B close by. Perhaps you could help? I'm sure the hospital will let you know when I arrive." With that, the line went dead.

Tom stared at his phone for a moment. If Karen Abbott survived, she and her father were going to need more help than he could provide to come to terms with what had happened to Patrick. He picked up his pace, striding along the towpath towards the car park at the back of police HQ. He needed to get in touch with DI Watkins in Liverpool but first, he was going to find Mary Andrews.

Chapter 18

"She's with the DCI," said Margery when Tom asked her if she'd seen the PR officer.

"How come?"

"The boss thought it might help to have Mary there because of the new website. Make sure it's on message with the city council I think."

Tom sighed. There was his career plan foreshortened. The higher echelons were too bloody political. Mind you, he ruminated, maybe you develop the sense when you get older just like a fondness for gardening. He'd better start flexing his antennae then; he was already officially middle-aged.

"If you see her before me, can you let her know I'd like to grab five minutes? Or better still," he said, leaning over to pinch a boiled sweet from the dish on Margery's desk. "Give me a buzz when they get back and I can see them both together."

"Will do – and you owe me at least a packet of mint humbugs. That's the sixth one you've had already."

"Not keeping count, surely? Can't you claim them out of petty cash?"

If Frank Dawson's phone hadn't started to ring just at that point, Tom reckoned he would have been given some insight as to why he was unlikely to ever be Chief Constable. He was grinning as he strode out of Margery's office, knowing she hadn't seen him pinch a second one.

"You look pleased with yourself." DS Seymour was coming out of the gents as Tom strode past.

"Just in touch with my inner child," Tom said, slowing his pace so they were in step, then stopped altogether in front of the social events notice board. "Karen Abbott's father is on the way up. Poor sod."

"Does he know about Patrick?"

Tom shook his head. "Thought it best left until we're face-to-face. Nothing to gain by telling him sooner."

The two men stood in silence for a moment.

"We'll get the bastard, Tom." Seymour's voice was deep and hard.

"I bloody well hope so," Tom said with feeling. "And I reckon there's going to be a whole queue of people wanting to see him swing."

Seymour set off along the corridor towards the stairs.

"Just going out for a while, then I'll just give NCIS a call. You never know."

"I'm going to chase DI Watkins. Can't believe they haven't got us a decent description of this guy from the neighbours and the regulars in the pub. She can lean on the landlord again, too."

Tom had a thought and wondered why it hadn't come to him before.

"Charles?"

"Yeh?"

"What colour would your hair go if you tried to bleach it?"

The office was quiet. Only Elliott was in, and he was leaning over Tom's desk, sticking a post-it note to his computer screen.

"Ah," he said as he caught sight of them. "Hospital called. They've got the toxicology done. Seems Karen Abbott is in the grip of a drug-induced coma. They're faxing through the report now."

Tom twisted on his heels and walked quickly across to the fax machine. The flashing green light told him there was a message on its way.

"Did they say anything else?" he said, killing time as the instrument did its usual warming up routine.

"Only that it was a pretty lethal combination. She's lucky to be alive given there was booze on top of it."

He read:

Evidence of flunitrazepam ('Rohypnol'), plus active metabolite together with traces of alprazolam – an anti-depressant. Relatively low levels of latter observed in blood and urine suggests ingestion likely to have occurred within the last 24-36hrs. It is noted that the levels are still more than would be expected from the normal maximum therapeutic dose (1.5mg per day). Hair samples taken and sent to regional toxicology lab for analysis. Results will show any evidence of previous abuse. Liver function compromised indicating long-term alcohol and/or substance abuse.

Tom wasn't surprised. Still didn't explain if she was involved with her son's death but it did show she was well and truly screwed up. There was a postscript.

Skin lesions and mouth ulceration. T4 cell count lower than normal range – blood sample sent to GUM clinic for analysis.

What the hell was that about? The single sheet was headed with the details of the pathology department at the MRI, but there was a name scrawled at the bottom.

"Was it a Philip Jones who rang?" he called in Elliott's direction as he walked back to his desk.

"Yep. Gave his number in case. What's the problem?"

Tom read out Philip Jones' report, at the same time reaching for the phone.

"They'll be looking for HIV," Seymour observed.

"Shit," Elliott said. "She's got herself in a right bloody mess, hasn't she?"

Tom paused for a moment, hand over the receiver. Mr Abbott didn't need to know that bit. Not just yet. He'd better call the ward first, to let them know he was on his way.

Philip Jones' voice boomed down the line. Tom reckoned he was probably of operatic proportions and with a tendency to waistcoats. He shifted the receiver an inch or so away from his ear.

Mr Jones responded with great enthusiasm to Tom's request for more information on the drugs in Karen's body.

"She'd have been well out of it," he thundered cheerfully. "Goodness knows how she's survived – must have quite a tolerance built up, at least to the flunitrazepam. Presume you know that's called the 'date rape' drug? Mind you, that doesn't tend to happen with the alprazolam I understand. Tolerance, I mean." He explained that he had consulted with a pharmacy colleague before sending through the fax to make sure he was fully informed.

"Apart from being 'well out of it'," Tom said, "what would be the immediate effects of this cocktail?"

"I can send you through a full data sheet if it would be helpful, but essentially – sleepiness, confusion, slow heartbeat, difficulty breathing. She'd appear drunk. Some people get hallucinations, convulsions, memory loss. Nasty."

"Why the HIV test?"

"Ah, well spotted. Routine now for drug users. In any event, she's got mouth and leg ulcers starting. Bit of a clue."

"When will we know?"

"Takes a bit longer. By the end of the week. I'll take care of it myself."

It was nearly three o'clock when Dean and Ryan finally returned.

"You two took your time," Tom said, glad he could make a dig. He wouldn't have dared if Dean hadn't been grinning.

"Had a bite of lunch at the same time if you don't mind," he said. "My colleague here gets very tired leading interviews you know. That's women all over."

"This great lump gets tired just dragging his knuckles along the floor," Ryan said mildly as she wriggled out of her coat.

"Good job Seymour's out," said Tom. "He'd think you two were having a thing." Inwardly he applauded both of them. Lunch had clearly also been a bit of a heart-to-heart and whatever Ryan had said, it had worked.

"So," he continued, "what did you get?"

"We spoke to a lady called Jane Sinclair," said Ryan as she flopped into a chair. "Young, very capable, no nonsense. Been at the refuge for the last two years. Not cagey but very careful at first. Client confidentiality and all that. In the end we told her the whole shebang. She was obviously shaken. Seems Karen told no-one she had a child."

The name rang a distant bell, but Tom couldn't place it.

"Karen first appeared at the refuge a few weeks ago." Dean was sitting on the edge of a desk. "They have a policy not to ask too many questions at first, just a first name and if the woman wants them to provide any help over and above a safe haven and shelter. People can stay for a few days before they need to get some funding sorted out. They'll contact the police if it's asked for and they'll put women in touch with all sorts of support agencies for rape, domestic violence or whatever. They knew Karen had a drink problem but waited until she was ready to talk about it. Apparently, she was friendly with another client there, called Cherie. She didn't want to speak to us. Jane was going to see if she could get anywhere with her for us but she wasn't hopeful. Cherie and the police don't have a happy history."

"Did she talk about the boyfriend? Her mother?"

Ryan tilted her head to one side. "No and yes," she said. "She told Jane about going to see her natural mother in Ireland. Not a great visit by all accounts but then we knew that. Her mother and grandfather had a weakness for the bottle too."

Tom picked up a pencil and began to twirl it through his fingers. Passing it over and under the index, middle and third fingers at increasing speed. He knew it annoyed Dean enormously because he hadn't figured out the technique but it helped Tom to think. He'd seen a sergeant in the army do it when they were stationed together in Norway. The guy was one of the calmest Tom had ever met.

"This feels like nothing new," he said, finally. "Just helping to colour in the picture we've already got. Did you get into her room?"

Ryan shook her head. "No warrant. Jane was keen to make sure none of the other women there saw us go through Karen's stuff. The staff don't even do it as a rule but given the circumstances, she went in and looked around for us. A few clothes and toiletries, that was it."

More twirling, this time with the left hand for added difficulty.

"Her bag," he announced. "All women have a bag, drunk or not. Wasn't with her when she got admitted into hospital. No purse, no keys, phone, no nothing. Somebody's got it. Was it Jane who rang the ambulance?"

"No, she wasn't on duty, but Cherie was there."

"Well, if our mystery friend isn't happy talking with us, I reckon it's because she's got something to hide.

And that something just maybe Karen Abbott's hand-bag."

Suddenly, an image came into Tom's head.

"This Jane Sinclair. Is she slim, brown eyes with dark-rimmed glasses?"

"Yeah," Ryan was surprised. "Do you know her?"

"Just clicked where I'd heard the name," he said. "Lives next door to Alice Roberts. Could be useful." He didn't bother to explain further. "Give this Jane Sinclair a call. See if she can delicately ask around in the refuge if anyone has seen Karen's bag."

Dean and Ryan exchanged a look.

"Over to you, buddy," said Dean.

The Rodent looked very pleased with himself.

"Ah, Tom," he beamed. "Come on in."

Mary Andrews was sitting at the oval conference table near the window.

"Hello, Tom," she said, closing the notebook in front of her.

"Good lunch?" said Tom, then caught the glint shining in his boss's eye. "I mean, useful?"

"Very. We need to do all we can to encourage the public's confidence in us and one way is by making sure they see the joined-up approach to local government working on their behalf. Most importantly, to see that the police force is part of that."

Tom nodded, sagely. He couldn't argue with that.

"I reckon the public confidence would go up a notch it we told them what was happening with Ben's case. Not to reveal his real name yet but to ask for help tracking down this guy Baptiste given Karen Abbott might not last the day."

Frank Dawson pulled out the substantial leather chair from behind his desk and sat down, his hands clasped together as if in prayer.

"Details please, Tom."

Mary Andrews sat quietly as Tom brought his boss fully up to date.

"What else has Liverpool had to offer?" Frank asked.

"I'm waiting for a call back from Geraldine Watkins. She was back at the pub where the landlord and Baptiste met."

The Rodent tutted. "She's as bad as you. Trying to be in with the action instead of concentrating on being at base and contactable."

"Not mutually exclusive, sir," Tom observed. "But she's hardly likely to want to have a cosy chat with me when she's in that place. I'm rather hoping she's waiting until they've got something more useful to report."

"Hope?!" Mary Andrews' voice made both men jump. "That sounds a bit relaxed given what this man has done. We should be trying everything we can to find him, surely?"

Tom's eyebrows shot up to his hairline, beating Frank's similar expression by less than a second. Tom's mouth worked first as well.

"You've changed your tune," he said. "What happened to the softly, softly approach?"

"DS Seymour has spent some time with me," she said. "And I've talked with the communications teams in a number of other forces. While we have to be very careful not to be sensationalist or racist – from what you say there is enough evidence now to put out a message that we are trying to trace this person in connection with a child's death. No accusations but asking the public for help. Particularly as it looks like we're not going to get much from the mother."

At last, thought Tom. She's talking 'we' rather than 'you'.

"Right," Frank was on his feet. "Round the table you two. Let's get the press briefing sorted."

"We'll need DS Seymour," Mary was firm. "He and Tom should do it."

She could see him so clearly. Brown eyes crinkling at the corners. Giggling every time, she got close enough to catch him before he wriggled free and ran off. She was tired, so tired. Please Patrick, she called. Wait for me.

Chapter 19

Tom knew the evening was probably lost. The hospital called just after 5pm to say that Karen Abbott's father had arrived. Tom drove straight down to see him, leaving the final details of the press briefing to the others. It was set for first thing in the morning.

The two men sat in uncomfortable silence at her bedside. God, she looked dreadful. He wanted to suggest they went to have a cup of tea somewhere so he could tell him about Patrick but the poor man was clinging onto his daughter's limp hand as if he could transfer his own life force to her. Tom glanced around to see if there was a clock nearby – he didn't want to be so obvious as to look at his watch. It was nearly six o'clock.

"Will you excuse me for a moment, Mr Abbott?" he whispered, and rose without waiting for a reply. He was pretty sure the man didn't care whether he was there or not.

He trotted to the exit and joined the mass of people either smoking or using their mobile phones. Tom positioned himself so he was away from the smoke. As soon as he turned on his phone, it began to beep furiously to tell him he had missed calls and messages.

Lily, Lily, Alice, Ryan and Mrs Daley. Shit.

He called the latter first.

"Mrs Daley?"

It could have been worse. Apparently, his mother had put a pan of water to boil and forgotten about it.

"I saw her throwing the pan out onto the back lawn and popped round to see her. She was more annoyed than anything, although she couldn't remember what she was heating the water for."

There was no real damage, the neighbour added. Just a horrid smell lingering in the house. She thought Tom ought to know.

He rang Lily to explain why he wouldn't make their date. As ever, she picked up on the flatness in his voice.

"Is there something else bothering you?" she asked. He wanted to kiss her.

"Just the old girl," he said. "Bit of a kitchen accident but nothing to worry about. I'll call round later and check she's okay."

There was a pause.

"I'd like to meet her, Tom," Lily said. "Why don't we invite her for lunch on Sunday? You cooking, of course!"

He wanted to kiss her again. He knew absolutely that he was a very lucky man and he was ready to share all of this and more.

Panic gripped her. The light was changing – not fading, but moving towards her and then away from her. She couldn't see Patrick anymore; she shouted for him in despair… The white-haired woman's face swam in front of her, cackling with vicious delight and Karen pulled all the phlegm she could from the back of her throat, wanting to poison her with hatred. She was being sucked, dragged – her arms felt pinned and she was drowning. She opened her mouth to scream but there was ice on her tongue. A frenzy of tears began to choke her and the darkness closed in.

Tom needed to take a few minutes alone – he couldn't face the hopeless look in Mr Abbott's eyes again just yet. The man's entire family was almost lost to him and Tom was beginning to really understand how that must feel. Absolute and utter crap.

He walked away from the hospital doors and headed towards the main road, trying to concentrate on what he might cook on Sunday. His legs appreciated the stretch and he increased his pace, aiming for the small supermarket near the church. He needed chocolate.

Ryan called while he was making his choice. He grabbed a king-size bar with fruit and nuts and hurried across to the till. Amazingly there was no queue.

"Just hang on a sec," he said, finding some coins in his pocket. A minute later he was outside the shop. "Find anything?"

"You were right," she said. "This Cherie had taken Karen's bag. For safe-keeping apparently."

"Yeah, right. Have you got it?" He started to walk.

"On my way back with it now. Jane Sinclair suggested I met her away from the refuge to hand it over. No recriminations."

"And?" Tom rounded the corner into the side road. "Did we get the mobile?"

"We did. And there's a purse, keys and a diary."

189

Hallelujah.

"Don't suppose there's a helpful photo of her with her boyfriend?" He hurried across the road towards to the hospital entrance, weaving between the almost stationary traffic.

"No. But there's two of Patrick on his own and one with her. Look very happy. Makes it hard to believe she'd have anything to do with his death, doesn't it? Keeping them with her all the time?"

"People are capable of anything Ryan, you know that." But she had a point.

They arranged to meet after the briefing the following day by which time the phone and bank records ought to have given them something else to work on. He wasn't counting on it though. This case was all bloody smoke and mirrors. Just when you thought you had a clear lead, a haze descended and the person or fact in your sights began to disappear.

He switched off his mobile phone and took a deep breath, quickly followed by a large chunk of chocolate. Chewing and crunching, he made his way back to what remained of the Abbott family. It was only as he came out of the lift on the third floor that he remembered about Alice. She must think he was ignoring her.

Tom was intercepted by the same male nurse as he turned into the high dependency unit. The expression on his face was hard to read and Tom was gripped by a sudden dread. He'd been gone for less than half an hour.

"Is she dead?"

"What? No – she's had another fit. Her father is in a bit of a state; we've had to put him in the relative's room while we sort her out."

"Will she be brain damaged? If she comes round?"

The nurse gave a slight shrug. "It's hard to judge. Her heart may have stopped for a few minutes and that can mean the brain is starved of oxygen. But these cases are almost impossible to predict. She's stable now so we just have to wait and see. She'll be carefully monitored."

Tom shook his head. What a nightmare. He made up his mind. There was never going to be an easy time to tell Mr Abbott about his grandson, and if she did die…well, how the hell was he going to do it then? And then pump the man for any extra bits of information he had? Shit.

"I'll go and sit with him," he said.

The room was gently lit. Pastel-painted walls were dotted with uncomplicated prints of soft countryside scenes; kind images for tired, fixed eyes to rest upon. Mr Abbott was alone.

He was slumped in a faux leather easy chair and the despair emanating from him was thick and heavy. Tom went and stood next to him and put a hand on his shoulder. The older man gave a sudden, raw sob and Tom wished he knew what the hell to say.

"I was only away for five minutes," Mr Abbott whispered. Tom pulled over another chair and sat beside him.

"Just had to nip to the toilet… she was so calm." His voice wobbled and the words rolled over themselves to be heard. "I felt I could leave her… just for a few minutes…" He took another wavering breath. "When

I came back, she was moaning, then raving, spitting out venom." He began to cry properly now. "The noise was so terrible and I couldn't comfort her. There was nothing I could do. I couldn't even get that right. Useless." His head and shoulders drooped.

Tom patted his arm and wished that Ryan was here. She was instinctively better at this sort of thing. He took a crumb of comfort from the idea that bad news didn't hit so hard when someone was already in the pit of despair. It was as if the existing pain absorbed the impact of the new.

"Mr Abbott?" he spoke gently but firmly. "There is something I have to tell you and some questions I need to ask you. I know this is a terrible time, but I really need your help."

The grey head lifted. His eyes shone with unshed tears, but there was a glimpse of determination.

"I thought so," he said. "If it helps my daughter and Patrick, then I will do anything I can. He's missing, isn't he? Not in care again like she said?"

Christ. Tom breathed slowly and shook his head, momentarily thrown. In care? When had she said that?

"Patrick is dead," he said. "A body was found. We weren't sure of his identity until we ran some DNA checks with Karen. I'm so sorry."

Mr Abbott thrust out his chin.

"Tell me," he said. The words were pushed out through tightly clenched teeth. "And tell me straight. No flannel."

Tom talked, uninterrupted, for twenty minutes. He told him about finding the body, visiting the house in Liverpool and about Gerard Baptiste. He described his first sighting of Karen at the railway station and how he had linked her to Patrick. The news that she had been staying for odd days at a refuge and where the investigation was heading. He tried to leave out the details of the mutilation but Mr Abbott was adamant.

"I could have looked at the body to identify him. Why did you need DNA? Was he burned?"

As Tom tried to explain, the older man stood and began to pace around the room.

"Dear God," he said, his fists clenched against his sides. "Dear God." He stopped dead by the door, his back towards Tom. For a moment, he was static, caught in his own thoughts. Then, he twisted round on his heels and stared at him.

"Do you think she had anything to do with this?" His face was dark and his voice angry. "I'll not believe that! She loved that child! I'll not believe that!"

Tom waited until he was sure the man would hear his response.

"We need to talk to Karen," he said. "Nobody knows except her. But in case that is not possible, I need to find out as much as I can about her and the people she was with."

He heard it just fine.

"You think she's going to die, don't you? Have they said anything to you?"

"All I know is that it's hard to predict what will happen. But I want to do all I can to get justice for Patrick. That's it," said Tom.

"What do you want me to do?"

Tom drove away from the hospital deep in thought. He knew he should have asked Mary Andrews' opinion before asking Mr Abbott to join the press briefing but it just might make a difference. Karen seemed to be stable again and the nurse had advised him to go and get some rest but the old man insisted on staying close by her bed. Tom promised to let the B&B know and arranged to pick him up just after 8 o'clock in the morning. After the briefing, Karen's health permitting, Tom wanted to ask him some more questions.

For starters, who was Patrick's real father? Where had Karen been between the death of her mother and last September? When and where did she meet Gerard Baptiste? What were the circumstances of the child being taken into care in London (he'd set Elliott on that) and when had she told her father it had happened again?

He indicated to turn right by a new student bar. Bright green lighting guaranteed to make anyone look like they'd just left the primordial swamp – which students did anyway most of the time. The place was relatively quiet, but he did catch a glimpse of a couple deep in each other's throats in the corner. Now that brought back memories. He drove on, remembering his own early fumbling. Alex was always more successful with women. But now there was Lily.

He rang his mother so as not to startle her by turning up unannounced. Her voice was bright and cheery and he inwardly cursed this disease that meant you never knew where you bloody well were. For the lack of something constructive to do, he stopped at a small corner shop that smelt of spices and disinfectant and bought two bunches of daffodils that were still in bud. She liked yellow.

Chapter 20

The sound of a soft wheeze swept across her ears. Then other sounds, slight and distant, crowded in. Beeps; a voice; a low, insistent hum; a heartbeat. Awareness tapped on her eyelids, demanding to be let in.

Karen's tongue found its way across her lips and she drew in a short, shuddering breath. She could smell illness and her mouth tasted foul. She tried to reach back to oblivion but suddenly there was cool liquid dribbling down her throat. She swallowed.

"Karen? Love?" Her father's voice echoed in her head. Not him. She didn't want to see him. Not now. Tears of self-pity and shame grew and pushed against her lashes but she kept her eyes shut.

"It's alright," he said. "I'm here."

A wave of nausea shot through her and she began to retch. Cold sweat poured over her entire body and her leg muscles started to twitch. More voices and then she was on her side, her head hanging down. Someone was holding her forehead and her mouth was open. Fluid poured out, burning her throat and nose. Her entire body heaved and twisted, but she still didn't open her eyes.

"Okay, Karen, it'll pass. Easy now." Another voice. Capable and truthful.

She thought she heard someone say "blood" but she wasn't sure and she didn't care. She felt like she was turning inside out. Another wave and she began to cry. It hurt. Everything hurt.

She felt someone take her arm. Please, make it all go away, she thought. Make it all go away.

A while later she lay on her back, drained, aching and desperate for escape. Her newly wakened mind and the nurses would not allow it.

"You've been unconscious for nearly two days," one said. "We're not going to let you go to sleep again just yet. This drip will help to make you feel better. Your dad's been worried sick – I'll let you have a bit of a catch-up."

She didn't want to talk about anything to her father. She needed to talk to Jane. Thoughts and images danced around in her skull and fear crept up her spine. Had she blown it?

"It'll be alright," he said. Stupid man. What did he know? She looked at him through half-opened eyes, hoping he would register the message of dismissal. Funny. When did he get that old?

"What day is it?"

"Tuesday."

She closed her eyes again and tried to remember what had happened. Tuesday? Which Tuesday? Her fingers found the top of the sheets and she plucked at them as her mind jumped.

"I need to talk to Jane," she said. "Patrick…"

She felt the air around her father stiffen and press on her chest. Her eyes flicked open and she saw his face, even whiter now with sunken cheeks. His eyes burned at her with a fire that she didn't understand. It looked like fear. Her heart grabbed her soul.

"What?! What do you know? Patrick? Is it Patrick? Tell me!" Her whole body was shaking. What was this? Her father? Why was he here? What did he know?

She was suddenly aware that he was patting her arm and saying, "Hush, hush now," like she was a child again.

"Tell me." She concentrated all her strength on the words so they came out dark and sharp. "Or so help me, you won't see either of us again."

He didn't speak or look at her. Short rasping breaths whistled through his thin lips and she willed her hands into fists. Her right arm fell in a pathetic arc as she tried to hit him – it fell with a soft thud onto the bed.

"Try and get some rest, Karen," he said eventually. "It's still the middle of the night. We can talk in the morning and I can get your friend Jane here…"

This time she did make contact. Her fingernails found little resistance in the papery skin of his hand, and she pressed as hard as she could onto the bones. If threats wouldn't do it, she knew what would.

"Please, Dad."

This time she tried to fight the blackness of sedation but its fat embrace held her tight. Her father's voice tiptoed alongside her.

"I'm so sorry, love. So sorry."

Tom managed to get a parking space right outside the hospital. Hopefully Mr Abbott would be ready and waiting so they could be away before eight o'clock. He locked the car and took a deep breath of the damp morning air. He'd have heard if anything had happened during the night so he was feeling quite upbeat. His mother was so delighted at the invitation to meet Lily that the pan episode had been brushed aside as a nonsense and Mary Andrews was frighteningly on-side with Tom's idea to have Mr Abbott at the briefing.

The corridors hummed with activity. A short, shapeless woman was working hard to keep a circular floor polisher under control as various staff and visitors danced to avoid it. Talk about a thankless task but then the place was never going to be quiet enough to do it properly. He strode past the woman and was greeted with a strong whiff of old sweat. Nice. Seeing the number of people already waiting by the lift, he decided to take the stairs. Five minutes later, and only slightly out of breath, he was outside the high dependency unit.

He pressed the security bell and waited to be admitted.

"Morning," he said as the door opened. He'd not seen this woman before. "DI Tom Ashton. Here to pick up Mr Abbott."

"Wait here please," she said. "I'll go and tell him you're here."

He supposed he shouldn't be surprised that he was left outside but he still felt a bit peeved. He wanted to see how Karen was doing for himself.

The corridor was deserted but not quiet. All sorts of background noises floated by to keep him company. He jangled the change in his pockets, suddenly conscious of a funky rhythm he was making with the general distant hum of machines. He began to walk away from the unit in time with the beat. After a few steps, he heard the click of the door and turned back.

He only realised he was smiling when he felt his face muscles droop at the sight of the man coming out. Christ. He looked utterly diminished.

"Mr Abbott?"

Karen's father raised his chin. Weariness was etched all over him but he responded with a courteous nod.

"She came round," he said, in a tone so thin and flat Tom had to strain to hear. "I told her about Patrick. She had to be sedated. Shall we?" He started to walk towards to lift.

Tom knew he was going to have to play this one carefully. He waited until they were outside the building before he spoke, guiding Mr Abbott across the road towards his car.

"That must have been very hard. I'm not going to give you any platitudes here, there's nothing I can offer that will make this any easier. Did she say anything, anything at all that might help us?"

He was rewarded with a deathly silence. They both got into the car and fastened their seat belts but Tom made no move to switch on the engine. He turned to face Mr Abbott, and waited.

"She had nothing to do with Patrick's death. She's distraught."

Tom said nothing. The growing traffic to the hospital rumbled past the car window. More tragedies unfolding. At least Karen was still alive. The machinery of care that focused on you hardly stopped for the length of a heartbeat when death came. Space had to be made for the next person, as it had for you. Just like when his father died.

"I know my daughter."

Tom caught the stubborn tone and bit back the temptation to say, "I doubt it."

"What happened?" He turned the key in the ignition, indicated and moved quickly away from the kerb, getting a hoot from behind for his impertinence. "Exactly?" For God's sake, give me something, he thought as he took a left turn to join the bypass. It was beginning to rain.

His passenger gave a long, mournful sigh.

"I couldn't sleep. I just sat by her bed, watching her face and trying to match the features to those of the tiny creature we picked up when she was a couple of weeks old. Remembering when she lost her front teeth, and when she gave herself a black eye trying to do a wheelie on her bike. Pink it was." Another sigh. "All of a sudden, I could see that her eyelids were flickering and her mouth began to twitch. The light isn't too bright in there so I wasn't sure at first but then I could tell. I gave her some water." A pause. "She was so sick. It was horrible. She didn't want to talk to me at first. Wanting somebody called Jane. Then said I wouldn't see her or Patrick again if I didn't tell her what was going on."

"Jane? Jane Sinclair?"

"She just said Jane. Why? Who is she?"

Tom explained. "I'll get someone round to see her," he said. "Go on."

"It was horrible. She was digging her nails into my hand the whole time. But she was fully awake. The look in her eyes was terrible. Fierce. Like a tigress. That's why I know she had nothing to do with Patrick's death."

Tom didn't react, but concentrated on the road ahead.

"I just said that a child's body had been found and that it was Patrick. That's all. Nothing about how he…" he took a moment to steady himself. They were almost at HQ.

"She tried to get out of bed. She was screaming and calling me a liar. That I was trying to steal him from her. She didn't believe me. That she knew when he was taken into care, we were behind it… and who was I anyway? Just some sad old man…"

Jesus. Poor sod.

"They gave her something to calm her down. I don't know what I'm going to do…"

Tom knew what he was going to do. Use this with the press.

It was all green. Like moss, soft and dense. She tried to push her way through but her body wouldn't respond. She couldn't move. There was something on the other side of the curtain but she couldn't reach it. A flicker of light switched on and off in front of her. Like a neon sign, swinging to her left, then to her right. Her feet lifted as she tried to see what it said. She had to see what it said.

Alice took a long sip from her glass. She may have overdone the vodka a little but she was feeling unsettled. Still no word. Maybe Tom didn't trust her any more. She looked at the clock on the wall by the kitchen sink and saw that she was a bit early with the drink tonight. Ah, well. Who was going to worry about that? It was really time to put the potatoes on to boil but she wasn't sure she fancied that pork chop after all. Maybe she'd just have a poached egg on toast later.

The music coming from the TV announced the start of the news. She made her way through to the lounge to watch. Jack was already there, curled up on her chair. She gave him a nudge which he totally ignored. Smiling, she put down her glass on the little table under the window and picked him up. He was soft and floppy like a rag doll, relaxed in a way that only a cat can achieve.

The coal effect gas fire popped and hissed as it threw out its heat. She wondered if it was time to have it serviced – it didn't used to be so noisy. She settled back into the chair, one hand resting lightly on Jack's back. She couldn't feel his usual purring vibration so he really was fast asleep. She stroked the sleek black fur and let her shoulders ease.

She wasn't sure that tie suited the newsreader. He always put her in mind of a turtle and the big purple knot at his throat was neither the right colour or size for such a scrawny neck. She liked his voice though; deeper and smoother than you'd expect. She reached for her glass as he began to read the national headlines, realising with a shock a few seconds later that she was looking at Tom. He was sitting at a long table, with a black man on one side of him and a distinguished but ill-looking older man on the other. There were microphones in front of them but she couldn't hear their voices. The newsman was speaking.

"…and police in Manchester are appealing for help to find those responsible for the brutal murder of a four-year-old boy. More later in the programme. But firstly, the Prime Minister…"

Alice moved quickly, putting down her glass and reaching for the notepad and pen she kept in the

magazine holder by the side of the chair. This was significant. Maybe Tom felt he didn't need her help but
he was going to get it. She listened with growing impatience to the main story about the war in Iraq. It
was the ordinary people she felt sorry for. They always paid the price. Mind you, give the Yanks their
due, they were the first into the fray this time.

It was nearly six thirty before Tom came back onto
the screen. She was sure it would be covered on the
following local news too, but she concentrated hard
to get every bit of information she could.

The older man was the grandfather and the black
man was from the police in London. She made a note
of their names and little points about their appearance that would help her in the future. Tom was coming over very well, she thought. Calm but authoritat-
ive. He looked straight at her, and those dark blue
eyes showed a glint of steel. He's asking for help, she
thought. But he's also sending out a warning.

Her heart was in her mouth when Tom invited the
old man to speak. What a dreadful position to be in.
She did hope Tom hadn't leaned on him too heavily.

"I would ask anyone involved to look to their conscience," Mr Abbott said. "This was an innocent child.
A much-loved son and grandson. My daughter is under sedation. It has ripped our family apart. You know
what you've done and you will be judged. You should
try and atone in part now for your sins."

Goodness, thought Alice. She wasn't sure that was
going to do the trick. A bit too churchy for her tastes.
Tom, on the other hand, looked quite comfortable
with it.

The piece ended with the other policeman, Seymour, explaining that there were similarities between
this case and that of Adam, the boy found in the

Thames. Alice was sure that would make some parents look with more love and fear at their children. The news bulletin ended with a recap of the day's news. Alice felt depression slide across and sit on her shoulders. What a harsh and horrible world it can be, she thought.

"This won't do," she said crossly, and shook her head. Aware of her mood, Jack was awake and off her knee a few seconds before she stood. The depression began to fall away down her back. "Desperate times call for desperate measures."

She hadn't had the cards out for years. Carefully, she took the inlaid wooden box from the drawer of her mother's sideboard. She needed the full light in the kitchen to do this properly. But first, she needed to have something to eat. Consulting the Tarot was never a good thing on an empty stomach.

Chapter 21

Karen opened her eyes. She was alone and her mind was clearer than it had been for months. Gerard had lied to her. He knew where Celeste was, where she had taken Patrick. Her father and mother had lied to her for the whole of her life. He was still lying to her. It was time she took control. She pressed the call bell.

"Well, hello there," the nurse said cheerily. "Welcome back. Ready for a drink?"

Karen nodded, accepted the help into a sitting position, and plotted.

She gave what she hoped was a winsome smile.

"Could I make a phone call?" she said.

"Indeed, you can." The nurse leaned across and pulled something white down from above Karen's head. "These are new. TV and phones by your bed. You need to buy a card."

Karen stared at the screen with dismay. Did she have any money?

"I don't think I have any… my bag?"

The nurse gave her a kind glance. "You didn't come in with anything other than the clothes you stood up in. I'm sure your dad will buy a card for you when he comes back."

Karen's heart sank. Then she saw a way out.

"But it's him I need to speak to!" She let her voice climb. "Please! Can't you get one for me and he'll pay you back? Please?!"

"I'm sorry." Cheery nurse suddenly became strict nurse. "We're not allowed. Now, don't distress yourself. I'll be back shortly."

Karen's head flopped back onto the pillow. This was an emergency. She dragged the covers back from her legs and tried to swing herself out of the bed. She'd forgotten the drip attached to her arm and it tugged and hurt. She was trying to disconnect it when the door opened behind her.

"Now, Karen! Your dad's been on the phone. He'll be in for visiting."

Tears of frustration poured down her face. He'd mess things up. The nurse took hold of her legs and swivelled her back into bed.

"You've just time to try a bite to eat before then. Yes?"

Karen's mind did a flip.

"What time is it?"

"Just after half six. You've missed the dinner round but I can try and get you some toast? And tea?"

Okay. Six thirty in the evening. What evening? No matter. Get some cash from the old man tonight. Yes.

"Yes please," she said.

"Good girl. At this rate, you'll be moved out of here tomorrow."

"You've been avoiding me." Alice glared at Tom. His wiry auburn hair was sticking up and the blue dressing gown he was wearing was rather too short in her opinion. Good strong legs though.

"Alice! It's seven o'clock in the morning! Why didn't you just give me a call?"

"I have. And left you notes." She took a step towards him. "I need to talk to you. Shall I make some tea while you put some clothes on?"

Tom went back up the stairs wondering if he was having one of those dreams. He was still in a state of wide-eyed bemusement when he gave his hair a final rub with the towel – maybe he'd been hypnotised. He wouldn't put it past her.

She was standing in the kitchen with a steaming mug in her hand. Alice always had a bit of bother getting up onto the bar stools, so she'd clearly decided not to risk it. Jack was sitting on the work surface next to her. Both of them staring at him this early was bit bloody much.

"I have been rather busy," he said, moving past her to get to the cupboard. "Tell me what's on your mind while I have this." He poured a generous portion of his own mix muesli into a bowl. He showered it with milk and began to eat. Not a great choice he thought as his ears filled with his determined crunching. He wasn't going to hear a word at this rate.

"I saw you on the TV last night," she said. "What do you know about the father's family?"

"We don't know who the father is yet," he said, trying to extricate a bit of hazelnut from a back tooth.

Alice looked at him very strangely.

"What?" Tom chewed on a clump of rolled oats and dried fruit.

"He was sitting next to you," she said.

"Sorry. Adopted father of Patrick's mother you mean." He swallowed. "Why?"

"It's this Irish connection," she said. "There's something there that we're missing. What has he said about Karen, before and after the boy was born?"

Tom couldn't see where this was going and told her so.

"Karen was adopted. She didn't know until Patrick was two years old. Why would Mr Abbott's family have anything to with anything?"

"I rather think he and Karen are related. Either him or his wife."

"They adopted her! The whole thing was facilitated by the church. Natural mother lives in Ireland. The Abbotts lived their whole married life in the Midlands. I'm sorry Alice, I'm going to have to go to work." He dropped the empty bowl in the sink and began to walk towards the door.

"It was in the cards," she said. "You just ask him. I think Karen's mother is either his or his dead wife's sister."

"And what difference would that make?"

"I don't know. But I think there's a lot more he's not telling you."

He took her arm to give her the message it was time to leave.

"And ask him about the Good Shepherd in Limerick," she said, as they left the house and stood together on the pavement. "And… Tom?" Now she sounded anxious. "Someone or something is stirring. There's trouble coming."

He was still shaking his head as he opened up his emails. He wasn't sure why he was feeling impatient with Alice this time, maybe it was just too much mysticism on top of everything. He needed to focus on good, solid detection. He looked again at the list of memos. Only ten this morning. Mind you, it was only a half past eight so there was still time. He was deep in thought trying to word an appropriate response to the last one when his desk phone rang.

"Detective Inspector Ashton?"

"It is. Who's calling please?" He deleted the last sentence of his memo. Too sarcastic.

"This is Ward Sister Gregson at the MRI. I'm sorry, but Karen Abbott has disappeared."

It seems she was there at nine the previous night because she'd asked for something to help her sleep. No longer on regular monitoring, she'd not been missed until after the tea round at six thirty that morning. She wasn't in her bed when the auxiliary went in to offer her a drink but thinking she may be in the bathroom, hadn't said anything until she was clearing the cups. They'd done an immediate check of the hospital but couldn't find her. She could have been missing for nearly seven hours.

Tom was incredulous. How could someone just walk out of a ward that had security locks on the doors? Wasn't there someone on duty the whole time?

Sister Gregson was clearly mortified, but explained that the security was to stop people getting in, not out. And while, yes, they were somewhat short staffed, the level of care supervision last night was at an acceptable level. Tom absorbed the jargon and recognised the words of someone who would shortly be under an internal inquiry. He advised her to expect a visit.

"Of course," she said.

Karen's father was distraught. The hospital had called him too, so by the time Tom got to speak to him, the man was almost incoherent.

"You've got to find her! She's ill, she doesn't know what she's doing… they should have looked after her… I've frightened her… all my fault… should have waited to tell her… she needs help…"

It took Tom a few minutes before he could get a sensible answer from him. Yes, he had been in to see his daughter last night. Yes, she had asked for money. To use the phone. To keep in touch, she'd said. No, he didn't know if she had called anyone.

"I went and bought a card for her, for those new-fangled things they've got by the beds now. She was very tired. I didn't stay for the whole of visiting. I told her I'd be in today. She seemed to be glad I was there – I thought we were getting somewhere…" His voice tailed off.

It didn't take too long to track down the call Karen Abbott had made. The women's refuge. At seven thirty-five last night.

Tom rang the number and asked to speak to Jane Sinclair. Initially stiff, she warmed considerably when he reminded her that he was Alice's neighbour.

"Is she okay?"

"Fine." More than, thought Tom thinking of his surreal breakfast meeting. "This is not about Alice." He explained the situation. "Is Karen with you?"

"I haven't seen her. Let me go and ask my colleagues and call you back."

"Find out who she spoke to please – I'm presuming it wasn't you."

"I would have told you." A bit of frostiness crept in. "We're here to support and protect our clients but within the bounds of common sense. I realise Karen's in danger. We'll do all we can to help you but we have to consider her wishes at all times."

He gave her his direct and mobile telephone number.

She knows something, he thought as the phone disconnected. Was she playing for time? He grabbed his coat and scribbled on the white board. Gone to Longsight. He was halfway out the door when he bumped into Dean.

"Blimey – where are you off to? Had enough already?"

Tom told him.

"I'll go to the hospital," said Dean. "See if she had any more visitors after the father left."

"Ask for Sister Gregson. Keep in touch."

Tom called Ryan as he got down to his car. She was sitting in traffic on the Princess Parkway so it was easy enough to get her to cut through to Oxford Road and meet up with Dean at the hospital. Then he rang Mary Andrews.

"Get ready to send out an alert on Karen Abbott," he said, giving her the basics. "Just as soon as I give you the nod."

His phone rang as he was pulling up outside the women's refuge. Jane Sinclair came straight to the point.

"She spoke to Cherie. Cherie's not here just now."

"Any ideas where we can find her? A mobile number?" He got out the car and strode up to the front door, reaching to knock as Jane began to reply. She'd tried apparently but with no luck.

She didn't seem surprised to see him, but she was annoyed.

"They're not here," she said. "I told you I'd call."

They stood across the open doorway, each with a phone clamped next to their ear until, by osmosis, they realised the stupidity of the situation and switched them off in sync.

"It's not about trust," Tom said. "She's ill and she could be in danger. She could hold the key to what happened to her son. We have to find her as soon as possible."

He saw the expression on her face and realised her antagonism was fuelled more by frustration than anything.

"If I could tell you anything, DI Ashton, believe me I would. This is not a prison. The women here can come and go as they please; most of the time they prefer to keep us informed, but if they don't…" she sighed. "I've told the others to try and get hold of Cherie. As soon as I hear anything, I'll be in touch. Night or day."

He held her gaze until the silence was on the verge of becoming uncomfortable.

"Anything, Jane," he said firmly. "You may think it's nothing but we need any fragment… a name, place… shared dreams. I'm going to be sending someone down here…"

"For heaven's sake! Come in."

Startled, he did as he was told. She turned to face him in the hallway and spoke quickly and quietly.

"Some of our other clients are in danger too. For all we know, this house may be being watched by people who could do them harm. Or neighbours who only grudgingly accept the refuge on their doorstep – too much police activity can lead to unfortunate incidents." Her face was flushed. "Do you understand? We are on your side here, but please, can we keep it low key?"

He nodded, then had a brainwave.

"Would your clients find it easier to talk to someone? Not the police or from social services…"

Jane folded her arms and stared at him.

"What? Like a journalist? I saw you on the TV last night. Very powerful stuff using Karen's father like that."

"Don't be naive," Tom snapped. "Give me some credit."

Jane shrugged but didn't reply. Tom sighed. He was handling this like a junior DC.

"No, not a journalist," he said. "Alice."

This time the stare was more puzzled than antagonistic.

"Alice Roberts? What on earth has this got to do with her?"

"Look – can we take ten minutes for a coffee somewhere?" Tom could hear the noise of someone moving around at the back of the house and he didn't want to crank up the tension again.

"Please?"

She insisted on paying for her own drink. Tom watched as she poured milk and then added two sachets of sugar to her coffee; her hands strong and capable. Short nails, devoid of polish, and a single gold band on her wedding finger. He wondered what Mr Sinclair was like, decided to ask Alice then in the next moment, concluded it was totally irrelevant.

The café was sandwiched between Doreen's Coiffure and an electrical repair shop. Dusty vacuum cleaners stood in the window like abandoned pets pining for the return of their owners.

Tom had little or no expectations of the menu, but he'd been pleasantly surprised to see a coffee percolator behind the counter. Granted, it wasn't what he was used to these days but could have been a thick mug and a spoon of instant. At least it was still early and the stuff was fresh. He blew on the surface of his cup and took a tentative sip.

"Alice," he began, "is a very unusual woman."

It transpired that Jane and David (well, he had a name now at least) had lived next door to Alice for ten years. Jane knew she was widowed but they never really talked about much, both households appreciated the coup of quiet, non-intrusive but pleasant neighbours.

"She knows she can always knock," said Jane. "But generally, we just say hello from time to time over the wall. David does shifts and of course, I don't talk about my job. Confidentiality." She took a drink, then put her cup down and put her hands under her chin.

"That said," she continued. "Alice has something about her that would make you want to confide in her. Not motherly as such…"

Tom watched as she considered his request.

"How would I describe her?"

"Just tell the truth. That she is helping us to find Karen. She's helped the police before; you know her; and that they are safe to tell her anything, without prejudice."

Jane thought for a moment, then nodded.

"Okay. But let me talk to Alice first? I'll go home at lunchtime. Explain who our clients are and a little of their situations. I'm sure you're going to speak to her anyway so will you let her know? It'll be about half twelve."

Tom checked his watch. It was just after nine thirty. He hoped Alice would be at home.

"Can't you get round there now?" he said. "Karen's been missing for nearly eight hours already."

Alice was restless and it meant that her week had gone completely awry. She had woken early and, unable to get back to sleep, got on with her usual Wednesday chore of cleaning the bathroom and kitchen. She was finished by nine o'clock. Normally, her porcelain figurines wouldn't be dusted until a Thursday.

She put on the smaller of her two cotton aprons (the one with the single deep pocket), tying the bow tightly at her back. She stood in her lounge and considered the gleaming display in the teak cabinet, suddenly aware of how pointless a task it was. Barely a speck of dust would have landed on the things since last week. And even if it did – so what?

Alice knew full well what her mother would say.

"It's the slippery slope once you let things go. A woman needs routine. A home needs routine."

Alice sighed and patted her hair; shampooed and set as always on Monday evening. The world wouldn't end if she didn't bother today, maybe she was sickening for something. She sighed again. It wasn't that. She knew why she was feeling like this. The truth was she was edgy; waiting. Even Jack was elsewhere so she had no distractions at all.

She glared at 'Susan', the elegant lady with a blue and white crinoline and always the last to be done. Alice decided that just as soon as she finished wiping

Susan's petticoats, she would have a cup of coffee. Made with all hot milk.

Alice eased open the sliding glass door of the cabinet. As her hand reached in to lift 'Madeline', with basket of flowers and a pink dress, from her place on the top shelf, the phone began to ring.

"Oh, thank God!" she breathed and turned on her heel, blessing whoever was responsible for the interruption. "This is it."

"Hello?"

"Alice – it's Tom."

Chapter 22

Karen knew she could trust Cherie. Cherie was used to keeping secrets. She did not know the whole story anyway.

They would be looking for her but she still had time. The first thing she had done was clear out her account, money from the man who called himself her father. There was more than she remembered but not nearly enough. It was time for that woman to pay.

The phone booths, all ranked along the wall near the ticket office, were vacant. No-one was looking at her. If anyone stared, they would see a neat, thin woman with tired features hidden under careful make-up. Her hair was gathered in a pony tail at the nape of her neck.

"Directory enquiries?"

"Could you check a number for me please? For an Annie Colgan, Stillorgan, near Dublin." Karen read out the number she found on a scrap of paper in her purse. It must be hers. Important numbers she kept stored in her mobile phone but that woman – she did not belong in there. It must have been some sort of sixth sense, keeping this piece of notepad for all this time.

"That number is ex-directory," came the reply. "Can I help you with another query?"

That was a bit of a surprise but no matter.

"The STD code," Karen said. "Is that right for Stillorgan?"

Assured that it was, she hung up and began to tap in the numbers, visualising the pathetic woman forever alone in her sterile house.

The ring tone bounced in her ear like a metronome and she worked hard to ignore the growing cramping sensation in her stomach. She had tried to eat some toast earlier but only managed a few bites. There would be time for food later. Her hand holding the receiver began to shake in disbelief at the possibility that Annie Colgan was out or moved or worse. Was dead. No. She could not be. She owed her.

At last, there was a click and a thin, quavering voice stretched across the Irish Sea.

"Yes?"

Even at this time of day, Karen reckoned the woman was drunk. She pushed a pound coin into the slot.

"It's Karen, or Mary, if you like," she spoke quickly. Don't hang up – I need money and you owe me." The line was silent but Karen was taking no chances. "I could make things difficult for you after what you did. Giving me away because the church said so. But this is not for me. It's for my son. Your grandson."

Karen had it all planned. She had set up transfers from her father often enough. She carried on, ignoring the emptiness of the connection.

"This is what you will do…"

"You are trouble. Nothing but trouble. Why would I help you? You were a mistake, a stupid mistake. You walked out on me…"

Karen laughed. Well, that was rich! But now she knew it would work. A surge of adrenaline pumped round her body. Annie Colgan was hooked, otherwise the phone would have been slammed down by now. She gave her instructions slowly and clearly.

"I'll call again in an hour," she said. "Make sure you are in and it's done." She waited until the line went dead and then pressed the receiver down. Picking it up again, she checked the number on her mobile phone and dialled again.

Alice felt no concern at all that her ladies would be unpolished for another week. Or even two. This was far more important. She was sure Jane had not noticed.

She listened carefully as Jane explained the situation. Alice was well aware of the trust being placed in her, even without Jane's firm request that nothing must be said to anyone other than Tom. She grew increasingly certain that there was little point in talking to those poor women in the refuge. Karen Abbott, in her view, was bound to get in touch with her mother because that was where it all stemmed from. It made sense. It was in the cards.

"This friend of Karen's," she said, making sure she understood and assuming the Tarot was not a good concept to raise just yet.

"Cherie," Jane said.

"Cherie – what can you tell me about her?"

It made for a depressing conversation. Apparently, she left school at fifteen, bright but without direction.

Four years and two abortions on, she had a crack habit and more bruises than a first-time skier from an insecure man not liking the idea of her getting clean. Cherie wanted to work in a nail bar.

"Kind heart," Jane added. "And loyal."

"Did she know Karen had a child?"

Jane shook her head.

"None of us did. We knew she was struggling with an alcohol problem and there was some serious pain in her life but that was it. She was with us for some time to get herself straight. To be safe."

"When would be the best time to try and talk with the women?" It was just after 10am.

"I thought I would take you back now if that is alright with you? Most of them tend to get up quite late and are often out in the afternoon. I have noticed there is an informal get-together in the kitchen at about eleven."

Alice nodded. She just wanted to ask something else before she went to get her things.

"Did she talk much to you? Karen, I mean."

"After a couple of days. Mostly about the trip she had made across to Ireland to meet her natural mother. Not a happy occasion by all accounts."

"In what way?"

"Let me tell you about it in the car," Jane said. "I'd rather we got back to the refuge if you don't mind?"

Alice was out of her chair and towards the living room door at a speed that belied her seventy-seven years.

"I will just get my coat on," she said.

Had it always been this crowded? Karen pushed her way between bodies and bags; briefcases and umbrellas. So many people, hardly registering her existence as they followed their own invisible trail. She needed to sit down and get something to eat. Very badly. Now was the time to think; to plan. To make sure that everything was perfect.

Out of desperation, she dashed in front of a large man, talking intently on his mobile phone to someone called John.

"For God's sake," she heard as she swerved past to the doorway of a café that boasted French Coffee, Patisserie and All-Day Breakfasts.

The place was larger than she expected and classier than the signage predicted. There were brass rails around the tables, crisp white cloths and a rack of tabloid newspapers just beside the till. A TV, mutely showing the business news, was positioned high up in the corner by the door. She slowed her stride and took a deep breath, gratefully accepting the smile of a small, dark-haired woman in a long linen apron.

"Good morning, Madam!" The deft fingers of her right hand whipped a menu card from the counter, while the left hand gestured Karen further inside. "A table for one?"

She showed her to an alcove table with maroon velvet, padded seats. Karen sat facing the door, acutely aware of the sights, sounds and smells of this world. The colours danced in front of her eyes and a blackness began to creep into the corner of her vision. She took another deep breath and a grateful sip of the chilled water the waitress had placed on the table with her menu.

Karen tried to concentrate on the text but the words swam into each other. She put down the laminated sheet and raised her hand. A sudden childhood

221

memory of eggy bread on Saturday mornings had given her the choice.

"Fresh orange juice, black coffee and two slices of French toast with bacon please."

The waitress scribbled the order on a leather-bound pad.

"I am rather hungry," Karen said.

A glass of juice was in front of her in moments, followed soon after by a plate of egg-coated fried bread, dusted with icing sugar. Four strips of crisp bacon were nestled to one side. This place was clearly used to people in a hurry. The little table just had enough room for the coffee and a jug of what Karen hoped was maple syrup.

She ate quickly, hardly tasting the flavours of the first few mouthfuls. It was only after a gulp of sweetened coffee that the darkness at the edges of her sight receded and her mind sighed with relief. She sat back and observed her fellow diners. Three men and three women. Each in their own world; fuelling their bodies for the day ahead.

She poured syrup over the bread, letting it soak through before cutting off a piece. Together with some smoked bacon, it was a glorious combination. She let her mind wander, knowing what she wanted to do and becoming sure of what had to be done. She knew where to go. They would help her. She'd been there before when she'd first met Gerard. As soon as she'd finished her breakfast and written the letter, she would call Annie back. Then she would find a news-agent.

If Alice had her way, she would give the walls of the kitchen a coat of pale lemon paint and scrub those beige tiles with a nailbrush. She supposed it was clean enough but the lingering smell of old cigarette smoke really would get her down.

Not that she would dream of saying anything. She knew her presence here was a source of some alarm for the women gathered around the old wooden table. They and the atmosphere were fragile.

"Tea or coffee?" Jane asked, moving across to the kettle. "Then I'll leave you…"

"I'll do it." This from a large woman called Marie with short blonde hair and stubby fingers, heavy with gold rings and yellow from tobacco.

Alice waited until Jane had softly clicked the door behind her. She looked slowly at each of the women, letting her gaze rest on each of them in turn.

"I'm only here to help," she said, quoting the ancient maxim, "nothing else."

Marie, she felt, would find peace with another woman. Angela, thin and tight as a wire, had an aura of fear around her. Alice couldn't see her future but she knew what to say to her before she left. Sharon, angry and lost, would go back to her home and find a frightened and changed man. Cherie – Alice let her eyes linger for a few moments longer – Alice felt sure she would find her place, not in a nail bar but with abandoned and difficult children.

No-one else said a word, waiting for Alice to speak again.

"I've no qualifications," she said. "Or any reason to be here other than I've lived a long life with the gift, or burden, of second sight."

Marie gave out a guffaw.

"Oh please!" she said.

Alice carried on, unabashed.

"I Know, I know", she said, her hands up as Marie pushed her chair away from the table. "But let me tell you this." Alice leaned forward and described her visions and images of Karen's son. It was going to shock but she knew these women would connect straight into Karen's state of mind.

"It seems she didn't know he was dead," she said. "In fact, she still may not believe it. Thought he'd been taken into care because of her drinking. You'll have heard about it on the TV?" She let the thought hang in the stale air.

"The little boy found at the airport?" Cherie's voice was tiny. "Karen's father was on the TV with the police, wasn't he?"

Alice nodded and waited.

"Poor cow." This from Angela with sympathetic noises from the others. Now was the time.

"She's ill," said Alice. "Out of her mind with grief. She shouldn't be out of hospital. Everyone is worried about her. What she might do. She needs care. Can you help… at all?" She paused for a moment.

"Did she give any idea of where she might go; mention anybody?" Alice made sure she kept her expression neutral, taking care not to look directly at Cherie. She needn't have worried.

"Go on Cherie," urged Sharon. "You two got on and she called you. Jane said."

Cherie's face was white and stricken. She swallowed twice in succession and then nodded.

"I promised her – but I didn't know all this, I swear." She looked pleadingly at Alice. "She said she needed to get some answers; to make everything right. She said she had to talk to a woman called Celeste. Her boyfriend knew her. Someone in community services she said. In London."

Chapter 23

"I just must tell someone this," Alice said. "But can I stay and chat with you a little longer?"

She'd brought her Tarot cards with her. They could always say no but sometimes the fact that someone cared enough to take the time to discuss the issues of their life was healing in itself.

Angela shrugged.

"Nothing else to do," she said.

Tom disconnected his phone and leapt to his feet at the same time. The CID office was almost full – the team working (he hoped) on their monthly reports.

"Right," he said. "We've got a possible lead for Karen Abbott. Seems she could be either heading for London, or even," he checked himself, "she could be there already. Ryan, get onto the transport police at Piccadilly with her description. They've had dealings with her once already so ask for Sergeant Green. Dean, can you do likewise with the guys at Euston – pull Seymour in if you need him. Where the hell is he anyway?" His pulse was racing. "I'm going to talk to her father, see if any names come to mind from when she lived there. Elliott – give her natural mother a call, will you? Just in case."

Within seconds, the room was filled with voices. Tom called through to his boss.

"Just thought you'd want to know," he said. "We think Patrick's mother is on her way to London. Could already be there. We're on to it…"

"Source?"

"One of the other women at the refuge, called Cherie. She and Karen were friendly."

"Can she be trusted?"

Tom thought back to the conversation with Alice.

"Yes sir," he said.

"Use Seymour," Frank said. "We don't want DCI Grey having any reason to complain."

"Sir."

Where was he?

"Anyone seen DS Seymour?" he shouted across the activity. Elliot, clearly holding for Annie Colgan to answer her phone, mouthed 'comms office' at him.

Tom was out of the office and along the corridor to the press room in a time that would have had his army regimental sergeant glowing with pride.

It took a few seconds to register what he was seeing when he opened the door. Charles Seymour's dark head leaning close, too close, to the sleek blonde hair of Mary Andrews. Stupid sod. Stupid, married, on loan, gold-plated idiot. Tom went into the room and turned his back on the couple as he shut the door firmly behind him. He let a few seconds pass before he faced them.

He knew his face was like stone.

"Tom?" Seymour began to walk towards him. "Before you jump to…"

Tom cut him off with a glare.

"Not now. I'm going to pretend I saw nothing. Just make sure this doesn't happen again. I need your help. Both of you. We've got a lead on Karen Abbott."

Karen finished writing, put her pen down and took a long drink of water. She folded the paper and put it in the envelope Cherie had brought into the hospital for her. She addressed it and left it on the table, putting a decent tip on top. She was relying on the good nature of the waitress to put a stamp on it and post it for her. She checked her watch.

The street outside was still busy but Karen now felt part of the bustle rather than a fearful onlooker to it. She walked briskly towards the tube station, realising that she'd left all her change in the café. Sod it, she'd reverse the charges. Annie would accept it. She didn't want to use her phone in case they were tracing her calls. Gerard warned her about that. Anyway, this time tomorrow, it wouldn't matter.

Mary Andrews was standing by his desk. Her cheeks were flushed but she didn't avoid Tom's gaze. He could see the flash of defiance in her grey eyes and hoped that she knew what the hell she was letting herself in for. Charles Seymour would let her down and go back to his wife when this case was over. In fact, he may not come back to Manchester at all. He was out of the office and on the train to London as soon as Tom had told him the latest.

"Any luck?" he said.

"Yes. The BBC's confirmed they can get a slot on Karen in the lunchtime news here and in London. Probably the local rather than the national programs but they've got the photo of her with Mrs Abbott, a description of the clothes Cherie took into hospital and a statement. Calls to go through to a CID hotline and an e-mail address. I also gave them my mobile number if people wanted to text any information."

Tom was impressed and told her so. The flush rose again but this time with modest pleasure rather than embarrassment. At least this might give them something. Seymour's news that Gerard Baptiste did not show up on the NCIS database was disappointing to say the least. It could mean he was operating under a false name; was a clever guy or even someone who was clean. More likely, just undetected.

Tom checked his watch. It was just eleven thirty.

Elliott suddenly slammed his hand down on the desk in frustration.

"Goddam!" He stood and turned away from the desk to face Tom and Mary. "That flaming woman is like the scarlet pimpernel this morning. First time I tried she was on the phone, then there was no answer for about an hour and now the line's engaged again! Shall try the phone operator, see if there's a problem? Or just get onto the Garda?"

"The Garda," Tom said firmly. "Then the operator. Can't believe she's got that many friends. Could be Karen." Alice's words rang in his ears. She was insistent that Karen would get in touch with Annie and he was inclined to believe her. Even if her evidence base was a bit suspect. Tarot cards. The Rodent would have a fit.

The whole team pressed into the communications office. One of the first things Mary Andrews did on her arrival in the job was to order a large, flat-screen TV

228

which took up most of one corner. It rankled with some people who thought it was a waste of money but today, at least, it was coming into its own. Tom watched the faces of his colleagues as they waited for the local news bulletin. All the early strain was gone. He could see anticipation, professional detachment and alert curiosity. Only Talbot was still sporting dark rings under his eyes, which he said was more to do with the continued struggles of his wife than with the case. Tom had no complaints with his diligence, maintaining links with DI Watkins and her team in Liverpool, following up any possible lead. He did look knackered though.

"Police are anxious to trace…" Tom's attention shifted to the TV.

The image of Karen Abbott and her adoptive mother filled the screen. The female newsreader's voice relayed the detail sent through by Mary Andrews; how Karen Abbott had discharged herself from hospital, that she was ill and needed help. She added how the missing woman's appearance had changed since the photograph was taken.

"Police have reason to believe that she may be heading to London. If you have any information, please contact…"

The room filled with a collective sigh as the news item finished.

"Well, let's hope that brings us something," Tom said. "The same piece went out in London so I want as many of you as possible around this afternoon. Mary's done a great job getting this sorted so thanks to her."

"Yeah, spot on," said Dean as he headed to the door. "Anyone fancy getting some decent coffees before we lock ourselves in for the duration?"

"Great idea, Deano," said Ryan. "And for volunteering. Mine's a two-shot cappuccino, ta."

Various voices yelled out ever more complicated orders with Talbot getting a two-fingered salute for his request for a skinny decaf latte with a shot of vanilla.

Laughing, Tom waited until they'd left the room before turning to face the PR officer.

"I meant it," he said. "This could give us a real break." He paused, knowing he was stepping out of line. "Just be careful?"

The characteristic flush rose in her face but she nodded.

"Thanks Tom," she said. "But there's no need. Charles and I are just friends. No need for you to be concerned." Now, she bustled behind her desk and took up a file. "Best get on. Report to finish for the Council."

Karen smirked with satisfaction. She span on her heels away from the phone, her mind racing. She knew Annie would do as she was told. Her final atonement? Pathetic, really. At least now everything in the letter was fine.

"Can I see him?"

Karen nearly lost control when she'd asked that.

"Maybe," she'd replied. "We'll see."

A few minutes later she was at the Underground station. She took a moment to study the tube map. Her memory was a bit blurry. There was a lot of stuff that happened when she lived here that she couldn't quite get into order now. Her old flat was in Tottenham but the place she needed to get to was further north. How could she forget the name? It would always be linked in her mind with wicked women and abandonment because of what she found out during that time. She used her finger to trace the coloured lines of the network – and then she found it. Seven Sisters. Victoria Line.

Tom was standing by the window near the case corner when his phone rang. Even though the tone told him it was an internal call and unlikely to be any reaction to the news broadcast, his stomach clenched. He raced across to his desk.

"Tom Ashton", he said.

"There's a Mr Abbott here to see you."

"I'm downstairs if anything comes up," he called as he headed for the door. The least he could do was to give the man some time while they waited.

"Is there any word?" Mr Abbott was sitting stiffly up-right across the table from Tom. He was clean shaven and his shirt and tie described him as a man of propriety but even so he somehow looked shabby. His very spirit had lost its lustre. "I saw the news. You should have told me."

"Nothing yet, Mr Abbott," said Tom. "I'll let you know if anything significant comes up – you'll have to forgive me if I don't let you know everything we're doing. You have to trust us." He struggled for a moment, aware of the fragile state of the other man. "You really should go home." This was the second time he'd suggested this in as many days but he was no more confident his advice would be taken. "There's nothing you can do here and we'll be in touch as soon as we hear anything. And you could look through any old letters she sent you from London. Even a postmark could be helpful. She may even try and contact you there."

The older man gave a bitter laugh. "You think so? I know you would rather I was out of the way but I need to be here. Close to the investigation. Believe me, Detective Inspector, there's nothing for me at home."

Tom spoke gently.

"It could be months, Mr Abbott," he said. "There are plenty of places for people to lose themselves if they want to. Please think about it."

There was a long pause and Tom could see the shadows of hope and hopelessness chase each other across Mr Abbott's face. Eventually he spoke.

"I'm booked in the B&B until Sunday. If there is no news by then, I'll think about it."

"You told us a little about when Karen lived in London but is there any detail you might have forgotten to tell us? Who she knew, that sort of thing?

He was answered with a deep sigh.

"It was a difficult time, Detective Inspector," came the weary voice. "My wife was dying. Karen was determined to be independent, bring up Patrick on her own, living away from home. She said she had a job, friends… We hadn't been happy when she got pregnant, things were strained between us. She came back to us for a while but it was difficult. There was no talking to her… She began to steal from us, my wife… I asked her to leave. We hardly saw her. When her mother told her she was adopted, she was upset, angry, confused. I didn't want her to contact Annie. Worried it could make things worse for her."

"I know I've asked you this before but given the circumstances… did you maintain any sort of contact with Annie Colgan after you took Karen?"

"No." Mr Abbott sounded puzzled rather than annoyed and Tom began to wonder if Alice had got it wrong.

"What about the priest who arranged it all?"

"I don't know – he may have done but he's been dead years now."

"How did you and Karen know where Annie was living then?"

Mr Abbott shrugged his shoulders slightly.

"There were some letters," he said. "Early on. We didn't reply. Turned out, she hadn't moved from the family house; people of that generation often don't. It was easy to check."

"Did you keep the letters?"

"Karen took them."

"Did Karen keep in touch with her? After they met?"

"I don't believe so."

Tom picked up a pen and let it dance between his fingers while he thought.

"I know you and your wife brought Karen up as a Catholic." He said. "Does she still practice, do you know?"

"No."

Definite this time. Tom couldn't decide what he was hearing. Bitterness? Or anger?

"No? Since when?"

"Young people today, Detective Inspector, are exposed to too many external influences. They question things. University, travel – they broaden the mind but that can lead to all sorts of ideas and discontent."

"Like what?"

"Just… just challenging everything! The true, Roman path. Saying there are similarities between Jesus and Mohammed; that there is room in a person's life for more than one faith. She knew this distressed us but she kept on saying that you needed to embrace other beliefs and cultures. It started when she went to Africa on work experience. She wanted to discuss her ideas. I'm afraid I got angry with her. It was as if she was rejecting us at the same time."

A creeping chill began to dance up Tom's back. A vivid picture of Karen, heady with the African experience. Mud huts and camp fires? Or a shanty town? Erratic water supplies, poor services and avid believers in voodoo? Did the wisdom of the elders make her look at her own life as a washed-out version of faith and humanity? Embracing one faith while rejecting another? The image of Peter's Cross on a child's back came crashing into his mind. He took a long, slow breath.

"You said she studied sociology, Mr Abbott. What exactly did she do when she was in Africa?"

"She was working as a researcher. Something to do with education, I think. Not as a teacher though. I'd have remembered that. I was a teacher."

"Of?"

"English and RE."

That figures, thought Tom. Karen's upbringing must have been a wow. He checked the clock and saw that it was almost two. Seymour should be nearly there by now.

"I'll call you if I hear anything," he said. "In the meantime, there is someone you could talk to, if that would help?"

"And it will keep my mind occupied, I suppose?"

"I'm sorry but yes."

"I'll ask her to call you at the B&B," said Tom. "Her name is Alice Roberts."

"I bought one of these contraptions yesterday." Mr Abbott waved a mobile phone. "Give her this number."

Tom watched from the reception area as he walked away. Shoulders erect and head up. A passing glance would see a well-turned out, older man who knew where he was going. So many lives as an illusion, thought Tom. Anyone looking at his mother would generally see nothing other than an elderly woman with a sweet smile and unruly grey hair. Only a few would catch the increasing confusion in her eyes.

We're all layered, he mused as he went back upstairs to the CID office. Complex creatures with private and public faces. Needs and beliefs that can lead you to unimaginable things – but then what is acceptable or the norm in this multi-cultural world? He sure as hell didn't know. Maybe he'd book himself in for a counselling slot with Alice too. Her brand of psychic common sense could be very reassuring.

Tom went back to the case corner and looked at the schematic of events linked to Patrick's death. Liverpool, Africa, London, Ireland. Real mother, the Abbots. Boyfriend. Fire, ritual, scars and stones with lavender. Layers and layers reflecting the complexity of human relationships and the clashing of good and evil. Strip that down and the simple fact was that a child was killed. Who would always be more important than the why.

He continued to study the details on the board in front of him. Maybe he was refusing to accept the obvious. For example, say that Karen got interested in other beliefs and practices and felt so let down by her family and its church that she'd fully embraced them. That he could understand. But nothing made sense in terms of what happened to Patrick. Was she complicit? Why? And why was he killed anyway? Erzulie said it was to do with illness or loss of strength. Whose? Karen's? Or someone else? Karen wasn't ill until she went into hospital. Or…

He found Philip Jones' number. It answered on the third ring. Tom bothered with little preamble, just his name and the question.

"Yes," came the reply. "I was intending to call you. She is HIV positive."

Chapter 24

Karen closed her eyes and let herself sway with the rocking of the train. It almost sounded like the chanting of her friend in Benin… Martine's face swam into her mind. She was always so kind and funny. Teasing Karen's pale arms and legs. Asking her about how western women kept their men happy and introducing her to Na and her family. It all seemed so long ago now. Without Martine there would be no Mathieu and without Mathieu there would have been no Patrick.

A sob bubbled in her chest. No, she must not think of him. Not now. She would not grieve for him. Not yet. He was with Celeste. He must be with Celeste. Her fingers clenched around the strap of her handbag on her lap. No-one knew she couldn't remember. Blank days. There were so many blank days. She needed them to tell her what had happened. She had money now.

Tichun, tichun, tichun, tichun. It was as if the train was talking to her, keeping her calm. A pretty word. Patrick would like it.

The words changed as the train slowed down. Karen opened her eyes to check which station they were at and then looked up at the poster showing the stops along the line. She tried to count but for some reason her eyes wouldn't focus properly. She thought it might be six more, or maybe seven. She sat up straight and blinked furiously. She must not miss her stop. Finsbury Park. The words swam. Seven Sisters and the stop after Finsbury Park.

Her carriage was nearly empty. Two slim, Chinese girls sitting close together at the far end were giggling behind their hands at some private joke. A small man in a dark suit clutched a briefcase on his lap as if terrified of being robbed. He probably would be, if he held it like that, she thought, her mind suddenly and gloriously sharp. Keep looking and concentrating, she told herself. Not long now. She opened the top button of her coat as she watched him as he stared straight ahead, nervously licking his lips. Maybe he was getting warm, too.

She blessed Cherie for her friendship as she slipped her hand into the bag and closed her fingers around the bottle. Just a little sip would ease the cramps in her stomach. While no-one was looking.

Shit. Tom's mind raced with the knowledge. He tried to think what difference this made. Did she know? What about the child? He reached into his pocket for his mobile. With one eye on the phone and the other on the general activity in the CID office outside, he rang Seymour.

"It's Tom," he said. "Can you talk?"

"Just about to pull into Euston. Pretty full here so can't say too much. What's the story?"

Tom explained and was rewarded by a long, low whistle.

"Hang on, just getting off…" Tom heard voices and the clanking of doors. A few moments later, Seymour's voice came back on the line.

"Gives us a motive for the mother," he said. "If she was a believer or in cahoots with someone else, who had it, like the boyfriend. Well known that individuals try all sorts to rid themselves of the virus – the evil spirits of disease."

Tom closed his eyes in utter despair. For fuck's sake. It was a biological condition, caused by sex, drugs and fucking ignorance. Evil sodding spirits and child sacrifice, my arse. Jesus.

"Tom?"

He struggled to shape his mouth with the right words.

"Are you going off on one of your western, white middle-class, secular, internal rants up there?"

Tom grinned, his tension easing.

"Yes," he said. "You a bloody witch doctor or something?"

"Sod off." The words were as friendly as a fatherly slap on the back.

"Just tell me what else I should be thinking," he said. "Call me back." This because Ryan was now in front of him, waving her hand madly and mouthing something that looked like distinctly like, "Got her!" Before he had time to say anything, she was hitting him with the detail.

"A waitress served her breakfast. In a café on Warren Street. Karen left an unstamped, addressed envelope on the table, under a generous tip. Waitress put stamp on and posted same during a quick break before the lunchtime rush. Saw the bit on the news. Rang us."

Tom opened his mouth to ask the obvious.

"Rang the Met and the PO," she continued, running her hand through her short, dark hair so that she looked like she's been electrocuted. "Local police are heading to the sorting office as we speak. The waitress," she glanced at her notepad, "a Carly Holmes, thinks she can remember what it looked like so she'll be helping them find it."

"Any idea where the address was?"

Ryan grinned.

"She's working her gap year from Sydney," she said. "That's why she registered the place because she's going there at Easter. It was near Stratford-on-Avon."

Tom stared at her. Looks like Mr Abbot was in for a bit of interesting reading.

"Maybe I'll hang off calling him until we've confirmed the name and address," he said. "God knows what she was going to land on him this time."

"Don't you think you should at least let him know she seems to be okay?"

She was right of course.

"As ever," he said.

Ryan nodded and walked across to the case white board and added the latest development. Now they needed to know where Karen Abbott was heading. With any luck, it was in the letter.

Tom's mobile phone buzzed. He pressed the button to speak, his eyes focused on the board and his mind wondering how Mr Abbott would react. Probably want to be on the next train south.

"We've got something, Charles," he started before a voice cut in.

"Is that you Tom? What time will you be home for your tea? You raced off this morning without me hearing you."

He closed his eyes and took a long, quiet breath. The last time he had stayed overnight at his parents' house was just after his father died. No need to make a scene. He hadn't intended to visit today but he could.

"About half six," he said, well aware that he would get there and there was only a fifty percent chance she would be expecting him.

"It's chicken," she said, before hanging up.

Seymour was on his way to Marylebone police station to get an update on the whereabouts of the letter. He was rather non-committal, saying he reckoned they could be in for a long wait if the bags from the 12.30pm collection had been emptied already. If they were in luck, they would be able to narrow the search down to the bags picked up by the driver who worked the area around Warren Street. Couldn't be that many letters for Stratford-on-Avon. On his advice, an alert was on its way to the transport police in case Karen had any plans to take a trip on Eurostar.

Tom called Alice.

"Do you know if Karen has a passport with her?" he asked. "Could you ask Cherie?"

"And hello to you too, Tom," she said. "I'll ask, of course. I'm glad you called, though, because I've been thinking. You remember the experience I had when you first met Jane?"

How could he forget. "Go on."

"I've been going through my notes," Alice continued. "Just to see if there was anything I'd overlooked that could help you. And on that day, I could see and smell fire and acrid smoke. There was screaming. I know you said that could link to events at the house in Liverpool but there was more than one voice. More than one person calling for help."

Tom wasn't sure what she was getting at.

"So, what are you saying?"

"I don't know yet," she said. "But I have a horrible feeling that it was a premonition rather than a reflection of what happened. I can't settle."

"This isn't actually very helpful," Tom said, thinking of the time she'd been able to give them a fix on the location of a very unpleasant academic. "What we really need is a clue to Karen's whereabouts. Can you float a few crystals or whatever over a map of London?"

Alice wasn't amused. "You of all people shouldn't be sceptical," she said. "I assume you're getting overtired. I'll do my best. Any pointers?"

"Warren Street. She was seen there earlier today. Sorry."

"Apology accepted. Go and have a hot drink and a biscuit. Your blood sugar's probably down."

Tom smiled. Maybe he'd take her advice. If it achieved nothing else, it would kill some time while he was waiting to hear from Seymour.

"Before I do as I'm told," he said. "There is something you could do for me? Someone in need of a friendly chat?"

Karen felt she was burning up inside. Anxiety, she thought. It would be okay when she got back up into the fresh air. Her heart was thumping in her chest and her legs felt all at once remote and cold. Dampness crept across her top lip and forehead. Karen swallowed and looked up at the side of the train, willing her eyes to fix on the map. Two more stops. Think of the plan, she told herself. Concentrate on what she needed to do. She was nearly there. A tiny cry trembled in the back of her throat, eager to burst out of her mouth. She put a fist to her teeth and bit. Hard.

The little bottle was still in her hand but when Karen put it to her lips, no warming liquid trickled down her throat. Confused, she looked around her, wiping her hands across her coat.

The Chinese girls had gone. A lone, young man was slouched in their place but the man with the briefcase was still rigidly there. What was so precious in that bag, Karen thought. His soul? She must have spoken out loud because he suddenly turned around and looked at her with an expression of fear in his eyes. She wanted to laugh. What did he have to lose that was so important? If he only knew… she could tell him…

"He said my baby is dead," she said loudly, the words bouncing along the walls of the train. She started to giggle at the look on his face. "That somebody killed him but I think the family stole him."

"Yeah, right."

His mouth hadn't moved. Did she hear that? Did he say that? Her head tightened and she shook it to clear the words away.

"There are people down here who can help me," she announced, wanting to keep her mind focused. Only one more stop. Or was it two? She would have to stand up soon and wait by the door to make sure she didn't miss it.

"Shut up yer drunken bitch."

Who was he to say that? What did he know? He had no idea, him with his stupid briefcase.

Karen took a deep breath and ignoring the strange sensation in her head, she got slowly to her feet and made her way towards him, grabbing the rails as she tried to compete with the rocking of the train.

He stared back at her, saying nothing now but she as determined to explain. What did he know?

The train was slowing and she found it easier to keep her balance as she stopped in front of him, holding tightly onto the bar.

"You" – but she got no further before a stream of vomit poured from her mouth. Karen's eyes were closed as her insides twisted. Even in the midst of her agony, she could hear someone behind her laughing.

"I'm sorry, I'm ill," she insisted as the man in the bright yellow jacket hauled her off the tube. "He was being nasty. I don't want to get off here." Panic rose in her throat as she saw the name Finsbury Park on the wall.

"Drunk, you mean," he said, his hand tight under her elbow as he moved her towards the escalator. "You can't go round throwing up over innocent people, minding their own business. Get yourself some fresh air and a black coffee. Then when you've sobered up, do us all a favour and get a taxi."

"Please," she protested. "You don't understand…"

He propelled her firmly out of the station entrance and into the street. He stood looking at her, hands on his hips. Blinking back the water from her eyes, she looked around her, recognising nothing. She flung up her arm and licked the sourness from her lips as the taxi pulled up.

Chapter 25

It was like looking through the eyes of somebody else. Karen stared out of the window of the taxi so hard her eyeballs ached. She could see faces and buildings but her mind was refusing to make anything of them. Nothing was making sense. She was so very tired. Her heart was like a clock ticking, making her feel frightened that she would be too late. That they wouldn't wait for her. Every afternoon until 4pm. The phrase echoed in her head like a mantra. Until 4. Until 4.

"What time is it?" she said. The driver didn't answer and she wondered if she had spoken at all. Then there was a click and his voice boomed into the cab.

"Seen it?"

"No… I wanted to know the time," she said.

"Half three," he said. "Want me to turn round and go back again?"

It seemed that she had only just begun to nod her head when the taxi lurched her sideways as he took advantage of a gap in the traffic. She struggled upright and then realised that the glimmer of a memory was stirring. She held her head still, trying to maintain a focus on whatever it was. It came again.

"It was above a bookshop," she said. "Not selling them, making them. Do you know it?"

Alice opened the buttons of her second-best coat as she waited for this virtual stranger to bring her afternoon tea. She knew more about Mr Abbott from Tom that she suspected he knew about her, but even so, the first few moments of their meeting outside the department store on Deansgate were very odd. Never having been on a blind date in her life, Alice could only now appreciate the agonies some people put themselves through.

She was sitting at her favourite table in Kendals' coffee shop, in the corner and right by the window so you could see everything going on. She watched as he made his way towards the till. She admired a man who held himself properly and he certainly hadn't let himself go. Given all that had happened in his life recently, she was especially impressed.

That said, she knew what comfort there was in routine and 'putting on a brave face'. When nothing in the world mattered any more, every little detail had to be made to matter. Either that or give up completely. Like Mavis Watkins did when her Fred died. She was left with two other children but the loss of her eldest was the end of her.

Alice shook the memories out of her head before Mr Abbott reached the table. It wouldn't do for him to see her with a remote expression on her face.

"Thank you," she said, helping him to take cups, teapots, milk jugs and plates off the laden tray. The next few minutes passed companionably enough as they sorted out respective slices of cake and got their tea just as they liked it.

"So, Mrs Roberts," he said. "I must say you are not quite what I expected. Do you do this type of thing often?"

He wasn't looking at her but his tone was polite enough.

"Most weeks," Alice said and smiled at him as his head flicked upwards and their eyes met properly. "Take tea here, that is," she continued, before taking a sip of a very acceptable brew. "I've been a widow a long time, Mr Abbott, and have learned to find comfort and pleasure in the simple things."

"By talking to those such as myself in difficult times?"

"No." She shook her head and put her cup down. "But I've known Tom Ashton for a while now and worked with him before. If that puts your mind at ease a little?"

"I have to be honest with you, Mrs Roberts. Meeting with you is just helping to pass the time until we find out where Karen is."

"Passing the time is what I have done for most of the last twenty years," Alice said but without sadness. "I'm very pleased to be able to be here. And it's Alice." She took a bite of carrot cake and waited for him to speak. His aura was shaded with pink and grey. Not that she needed that. Anyone could see that this poor man loved his daughter and was filled with fear for her.

"Do you have children Mrs – Alice?"

She told him of the miscarriages and their despair. How she was always grateful that Jimmy never turned from her but accepted the situation as "the way of it". She was candid in a way she hadn't been

247

for years but when the tears formed, she blinked them away.

"Never leaves you," she said, her voice cracking just a little. "You just bury it deep."

"Then you do understand," he said softly. He looked at her with such grief in his eyes that she felt a real ache in her heart for him. "And it's Bernard."

"Tell me about her?" she said.

"We got married when I finished my teacher training," he said, cradling his cup in his hands. Alice noted that his nails were carefully trimmed.

"Sheila was keen to start for a family straight away and I figured it was better to be young with small children when you have the energy. Nothing happened. Nothing at all. I didn't want to have tests and it began to put a strain on our relationship. Sheila started going to talk to our parish priest. Well, to cut a long story short…"

Alice listened as he described the way Karen, or Mary as she was called then, came into their lives. For a fleeting moment she was jealous. It seemed almost like a film – the priest acting as a broker in the procurement of a child, with few questions asked. As he spoke, Alice grew increasingly convinced that she was right. That there was a blood link between either Sheila or Bernard and Karen's mother. It would explain why the process moved so quickly and smoothly. The waitresses were beginning to clear the tables, so there was no time to waste.

"This might seem like an odd question, Bernard, given what you've said. But did either of you know Annie Colgan?"

He shook his head but she saw the blush on his cheek. She reached across and patted his arm.

"It doesn't matter now," she said softly. "There's no need to keep it all hidden any more." He was silent, so she pressed on.

"Was she your sister? Or Sheila's?"

"Where on earth did you get that from?!" The bluster was real enough but it was based on surprise rather than annoyance.

Alice shrugged her shoulders. The whole story ran like the plot of a Catherine Cookson novel, even without the reading of the other night.

"It just seems to make more sense to me," she said. "Not being a Catholic… I suppose I have an impression of keeping things inside the circle, so to speak. Not so much secretive," she knew she had to be careful here, "but protective of the interests of the church itself as well as its own. If a woman became pregnant, out of wedlock, then the whole situation could be managed to the satisfaction of everyone, presumably."

Bernard Abbott was still quiet but his expression told her she was spot on.

"Annie didn't want to keep the child? Or was it deemed the right thing to take Karen away from her?"

"This is all water under the bridge now," he said. "No point going over it all. It won't help us find her."

Years of avoiding the truth was a hard habit to break, Alice thought.

"It might," she said. "And it might help you too."

They ignored the brisk clearing of their tea things by a wiry, young blonde girl. Alice could see the clock over by the handbag section and there was still nearly an hour to go before the shop shut, even if the café closed up earlier. Besides which, she was in no hurry to get home. She had left some dried food out for Jack before she left. Tom was so busy these days, the poor creature was thinking about moving in with her completely.

"You know," he said. "I've never told anybody this. We always swore that we would keep the secret to our graves but then we never anticipated… Patrick, Sheila's cancer, Karen's determination to meet her mother, this." He spread his arms wide to capture the nightmare.

"Annie is my cousin. On my mother's side. I don't remember her much, just the occasional holiday when I was younger. I was born here but my parents were born in Ireland. Like Sheila's. Annie was a rather ordinary girl who stupidly responded to the flattery of a local traveller. The family closed ranks while she had the baby. In fact, we didn't know any of this until Father McCardle said he would help us. It turned out Sheila started talking to him just as the whole thing was flaring up. They used to talk a lot – he said he would contact colleagues in Ireland. There were many young girls then… being helped by the church…" His voice tailed off a little. "That's how we found out about Annie. We felt it was meant to be; keeping it in the family. It was a good solution all round."

"Did you keep in touch with Annie? To let her know how her daughter was?"

"We were advised not to. She was a bit unstable; they had to put her away for a while. And, well, that suited us. We wanted to feel like a real family and we did. For a long time." He fell silent.

Alice checked the clock again. They'd have to leave soon but there was still so much to talk about. "Put away for a while?" Did he really understand what that meant? Did Karen?

She considered the options. A drink? A meal? Should she offer to make him something? Goodness, no. Maybe a drink, she decided. She began to pull on her coat. Karen's father stood in anticipation.

"Is Patrick a family name?" she said, as she fastened the buttons.

"No," he said. "We wondered if it was her father. Terrible arguments over the spelling. Karen insisted on leaving off the 'k'. Like the French."

Karen remembered the smell. Funny how smells stayed in your memory long after the sound of a voice or a face had faded. As soon as she walked into the shop and her nose and mouth filled with the leathery, chemical scent, she began to cry. Wordlessly, she pointed up at the ceiling and the old man nodded and took some keys from his pocket. He opened a door near the window and let her go through to the staircase that led to the flat above.

A waft of the softly acrid fumes stayed with her and she noticed how they merged with the fragrance of incense and spices the further she climbed. Her shoulders began to heave with the effort of carrying her burden, her boy, her darling boy. She couldn't believe that she was finally here. She'd done it. Oh, to understand, she had to understand before she could grieve. To be sure. She just didn't know how it was meant to be done.

The woman wasn't there. Gerard sat, black and beautiful on the leather sofa near the shrine. His hair looked golden in the light. Another man, much older, was standing utterly still, by the window. He looked familiar. The lights were dim and the flickering candles hurt her eyes,

"Where's Celeste?" Karen said, confused. She wanted to talk to the woman who'd looked after Patrick when Karen was struggling to care for him. Mathieu's sister. Gerard's sister. Keeping it in the family they said after Mathieu was killed. So, kind. She was looking after Patrick when he was supposed to have died. She must know.

"Where's Celeste?" she said again, looking round wildly, feeling panic rise in her chest. She couldn't bear this much longer.

"Sit down, Karen," said Gerard. "You must be tired. Did you bring the money?"

She stared at him. This wasn't going right. She didn't know what to do.

"I have to know," she said. "You promised me."

"The Pastor will speak. When you pay him."

But that meant another whole day! No, no. It had to be today.

"No!"

Gerard moved so quickly she only realised he had when the slap rang across her face. She sat, shocked and angry, her cheeks burning.

"I have money," her voice rumbled from deep within her. "Look, here…" She fumbled in her bag, her eyes struggling to focus on the contents in the gloomy light. She pulled out a bundle of notes and held it out to Gerard, her arm shaking.

He took it and with the speed of a serpent, flicked through the cash.

"This is not what we agreed," he said.

"I'll have the rest tomorrow," she pleaded, looking first at Gerard and then the Pastor. "It's all sorted. Please, tell me where she has taken Patrick?"

The two men exchanged a look and she felt the truth claw at her heart.

"Tell me!"

The office was buzzing. Talbot continued to relay the information he was getting from the caller, a Mr Braithwaite. There was a piece on Karen in the early edition of the Evening Standard. She was drunk and abusive, apparently. Forcibly ejected from the tube after being sick all over him. He decided to call the police when he read the article in the paper. He was hoping to get a name so he could sue for compensation.

For heaven's sake.

"When and where?" shouted Tom.

Talbot asked Mr Braithwaite.

"It was around three," he said. "On the Victoria Line."

"Station?" yelled Tom, almost hopping up and down on the spot with frustration. Talbot should know better than this. "And someone get a tube map."

"He's not sure." Talbot replied after a moment's discussion. "He was a little preoccupied with wiping down his suit. He was travelling to the end of the line so didn't need to keep track. But he thinks it might have been Finsbury Park."

Dean was waving Tom over to his desk, where a map of the London tube network was displayed on his computer screen. He scrolled the image to reveal the full extension of the blue Victoria Line. Tom's eyes quickly scanned the names of the stations. Victoria,

Green Park, Oxford Circus, Warren Street… right. Next, Euston, okay, St Pancras, Highbury & Islington, Finsbury Park. His heart thumped when he saw the next station on the line.

His phone was out of his pocket in an instant.

"Seen something?" Dean said.

Tom realised he still hadn't told the team about his visit to London with Seymour. They were going to be pissed. Now he couldn't remember why he felt the need to keep it quiet.

"A hunch," he said, waiting for Seymour to answer. "Something I heard when I was down at the Met. Local communities in…" He broke off as he heard DS Seymour's deep voice. "Charles," he said. "I think she's on the way to Seven Sisters Road."

Chapter 26

"Right." Tom stood with his back to the window opposite the door. He perched on the thin window ledge and waited until he had everyone's attention.

"DS Seymour is on the way to Seven Sisters' Road. There's a large Haitian and African community there. He talked to those with a knowledge of witchcraft and voodoo during Adam's case. It is possible, therefore, that Karen knows this community, has been part of it, or believes that those responsible for Patrick's death have some link there. This is all supposition but with Seymour's connections, and the local guys, we will find her. So..." He moved off the ledge and flexed his numb buttocks. "There are two parts to all this now. The first bit is finding Karen Abbott, alive and well. The second will be interviewing her about Patrick's death. We've no further leads on the boyfriend so she's all we've got. She seems to be losing it again so she's going to be visible. And that increases the likelihood of picking her up on suspicion. We'll add in trying to obtain money with menaces."

"Eh?" Dean boomed.

"Keep up, Doris," Elliott said, before holding up his hands to protect himself from a half-serious left hook. "You were out. I finally got to speak to Annie Colgan. Karen called her this morning, demanding money. Gave all the instructions for the transfer of £5,000 to her bank account. Colgan agreed at the time but now she's changed her mind, after speaking with her priest."

"Well, put it on the sodding board then," Dean grizzled.

"She certainly seems to have a purpose," observed Ryan. "Not exactly wandering around aimlessly, in a daze of ill health and booze, whatever our witness said. Maybe she's looking for revenge?"

"Or protection, "said Elliott. "What else does she want the money for?"

"Good point," someone said.

"She could be wanting it to get out of the country," said Talbot. "Make a new life."

The room was silent for a moment as the team digested the possibilities.

"What about the letter?" Dean was making sure he'd missed nothing else.

"Hopefully any time now," Tom said. He was itching to get on the first train south, to be in at the centre of things but he knew Frank wouldn't sanction it. And besides, there was (possibly) a chicken dinner waiting for him.

"I'm going to let her father know." Tom saw the slight wriggle that meant Ryan was about to make a point. "Suggest you all push off early because we're going to be dissecting every bit of evidence we've got so far to back up any prosecution. No guarantees they'll find her today. There are places to hide if you're among friends and Seven Sisters' Road stretches a bloody long way."

"Will Seymour be leading things in London?"

"Yes," said Tom, making things clear for Ryan and everyone else. "Until she's in custody. Then I will take over. There may be the opportunity for some of you there if, for whatever reason, the interviews have to be conducted in London."

"You mean if she's too fragile to be brought back to Manchester?" said Ryan. "Physically or mentally?"

Tom nodded.

"Though that has the potential to bugger up the admissible evidence, of course," he said. "Go on, clear off you lot."

After a quick call to Seymour to remind him to contact him at any time, Tom grabbed a coffee from the machine – just this once – before getting back to his desk. He called Mr Abbott but was greeted with the engaged signal. Maybe the guy was trying to get in touch with him so Tom put his phone on the desk and waited for it to ring.

He sat still for a moment, absorbing the strange peace that settles on a busy place when it is almost deserted. He didn't have to leave for his mother's for another half hour, so he eased his chair back and closed his eyes. Mr Abbott was obviously talking to someone else. He let his breathing slow and his mind immediately recognised the permission it was being granted. He quickly reached the heightened level of awareness below normal consciousness. Bliss.

Mental filing was how he looked at it. Based on traditional meditation; he'd been taught the technique by a fellow officer on the QT. Invaluable during many sleep-deprived months of training and exercises.

His body began to feel like it was rising from the chair, light and free. His breathing slowed even further and his head jerked slightly as his neck muscles relaxed.

"Fuck!"

Being catapulted from a state of near nirvana to full alert by the impertinence of the phone was never a tranquil experience. Tom's heart thudded in his chest as he grabbed his mobile. His head, disapproving of the interruption, began to ache.

"Ashton," he barked. He heard a beeping noise, followed by the unmistakable sound of a call box accepting a coin.

"You need to relax, Tom," said Alice in hushed tones. "I can't stay on long. Bernard will expect me back from the toilet soon."

Tom closed his eyes, waiting once more for enlightenment.

"Bernard?"

"Honestly, Tom. You asked me to talk to the man."

"Sorry, sorry." He sat up straight and inhaled deeply. She'd told him they were meeting for a cup of tea. It was now just past six and they were still in each other's company. Nice one Alice. "Go on."

"One thing I thought was significant," she said. "I'll give you the rest later. He said Karen spelt the boy's name without a 'k' on the end. French spelling, apparently. Does that help?"

"It does," he said. "Anything that adds to what we know is important. Can you see if you can get anything from him about her time in London? But before any of that, ask him to give me a ring. I've just tried him and his phone was engaged. Do you know who he was talking to?"

"He's not been on the phone," she said. "Oh, unless he's talking to someone now – hold on…"

Tom stood and stretched his back while he waited for her to come back on the line.

"I can just see our table from here," she said. "He's just sitting there. I'd better get back."

He thanked her with promises to catch up first thing in the morning and disconnected. He tried Mr Abbott's number again. Still engaged. Probably forgotten to lock the keypad, he decided.

He was just about to push open the rear door of the building when his phone rang again. There was enough light for him to see who was calling so he let the door close and stepped right back inside.

"Well?"

"She's been seen in London," Tom said. "We think she's heading for a place call Seven Sisters' Road. Does that mean anything to you? Did she ever talk about it?"

"I don't think so," he said. "She used to live in Tottenham. How do you mean… seen?"

Tom delicately explained the episode on the tube, glad that Mr Abbott had Alice for company.

"Oh dear lord," he cried. "She's ill! I have to get down there…"

"There are no guarantees that she won't take off again," Tom said. "You could be wandering around without news for hours or days. As soon as I hear anything, I will call you, I promise."

"You can reach me just as easily down there," came the stubborn reply. "I'm not a child. She might need me."

"In that case," Tom said, before realising the news was being relayed to Alice and the elderly couple were now engaged in a vigorous conversation. He just caught the phrase "very well", before Mr Abbott's voice came fully back into his ear.

"I will be on the first train in the morning, Detective Inspector. Unless I hear from you before then."

"There is something else you should know," said Tom and told him about the letter.

"We don't know for sure it is addressed to you yet but it's a fair chance. Do I have your permission for my colleagues to open it and fax it to me if so?"

"Of course. But… if you don't find it until I am down in London, I must read it first."

"This is a murder enquiry, Mr Abbott," Tom warned.

"And my daughter has nothing to do with that!" He was speaking quietly but the admonishment was loud and clear. "If she has written to me…" his voice broke. "Personal matters…"

"In our presence," Tom said, firmly but not without kindness. "I'm sure you understand." Before he hung up, he told Mr Abbott how to lock his phone, then strode out of the building. If he didn't step on it, he was going to be late.

"Hello, Tom!" Her face broke into a smile of delight as she saw who was knocking on her door. "What brings you here on a Wednesday night?"

He tried not to let his dismay show and smiled back.

"No reason, just thought I'd pop in." He followed her into the house and was relieved to be greeted by the smell of cooking. "That said," he continued and nodded towards the kitchen. "Got enough for two?"

His mother laughed.

"I still haven't got used to only doing for one. Chicken casserole. I was going to freeze the remainder but as you're here…" She chattered away as she walked towards the kitchen. Tom's eyes scanned the living room as he passed the open door. TV and lights on. Gas fire lit. Curtains drawn. All as it should be.

He relaxed a little. She'd only forgotten she'd called him. Everything else was okay. For now. But even as the thought drifted away, an unbidden image filled its place. His mother on her knees, with a box of matches, lighting the fire. Fire and gas. His anxiety rose as he watched as she opened the oven door to reach in for the baking hot Pyrex dish. His stomach lurched. Gas oven. What if she put it on and forgot to light it?

"Just going to wash my hands," he said. Once upstairs, he rang his home number and left himself a message.

"First thing – get some brochures. For electrical appliances."

Karen's head was aching so badly she could hardly hear what they were saying. The pastor kept saying that her spirit was dying and she needed to heal that before she could be reunited with Patrick. Gerard pushed a glass into her hand, telling her to drink. The juice was cool and slightly bitter – the way he always made it.

"I will work with you," the pastor's deep voice rumbled into her hear. "There are evil forces in you – these must be banished. We will pray together. To the mother first and then to Mahu. For strength."

The air became heavy and cloying. Gerard began to chant, softly and slowly and the wave of sound was so familiar that Karen's exhausted being longed to sink beneath it. To be back in the family.

The pastor joined in, his words riding along the surface of the melody. He spoke about seeking freedom from illness and from wickedness. Praising Mary and Mahu. Praising the purity of children and their power. Patrick's little face swam into her mind. He was smiling. He was happy.

It was the sound of clapping hands that sent Patrick scurrying back into her deepest memories. She took a deep breath and opened her eyes. Gerard and the pastor were both standing in front of the shrine, looking at her. The room was brighter now and the air was fresh.

"You will go now," the pastor said. "And return tomorrow at 3pm with the money for your healing."

She tried to open her mouth to speak but her tongue felt too large to control. Gerard took both her arms and before she knew what had happened, she was in the street outside and the door of the shop was closing behind her. She started to walk away but her feet didn't want to obey her and she fell hard onto the pavement. There was no pain. She looked at her hands spread in front of her and she began to crawl. Two feet, in boots and laces up the middle, stopped in front of her.

"Are you alright?" a woman's voice. It sounded far away, as if she was a mile high.

All Karen could manage was a grunt.

"She's hammered," came a second voice.

Karen dragged one hand from the pavement and tried to raise it up towards the owner of the boots. Off balance, she fell forwards onto her cheek.

"The cops will find her. Come on."

Chapter 27

Karen huddled trembling in a doorway. It felt like a lifetime since she left them. The streets were quieter now and she sank down, wrapping her arms around her body against the cold. She reached for sleep. One more day. That was all.

"Here."

Karen dragged open her eyes. They focused on a young girl's face so black she was almost a shadow of herself.

"We couldn't finish this. Doggie bag. You have it." She thrust a bag into Karen's lap.

"What time is it? "Karen managed to ask.

"Just before nine. Bye."

It wasn't even tomorrow yet.

"Tom? I'm at Marylebone. We've got it." Seymour's excitement was infectious. "And it is addressed to Mr Abbott. What's the plan?"

Tom put down his cup of coffee.

"Work," he mouthed at his mother's questioning glance. He got up to take the call in the hallway so he didn't interrupt any of the Poirot drama she was watching on TV.

"I've cleared it with him already. Open it and then fax a copy to the office."

Tom paced up and down the brown-flecked carpet while his colleague opened the envelope.

"Well?"

"Three pages. Handwritten, small writing, a bit of a scrawl. Hang on a sec."

Tom wanted to reach down the line and grab the thing off him. Hurry up.

"Anything about her intentions?"

"It's a rambling rant this," said Seymour. "Stuff about her mother, God, betrayal. Let me get to the end."

Tom sat on the bottom stair, quietly serenaded by the program's signature tune. His mother, taking advantage of the commercial break, came out of the living room. She waved his cup at him.

"Fresh one?"

"Not for me, thanks," he said. "Am going to have to go back into work."

"Tom?" Seymour was back. "No names or places. But she does say that she is going to find the woman who took care of Patrick when she was ill. My feeling is that this is to do with the community and anyway, we're not likely to get any joy with social services tonight. I'll fax this now and get back over to Seven Sisters."

Tom's mother was settled back in the easy chair with all her attention fixed on the screen. He kissed her on the top of her head (which smelt freshly washed).

"Bye love," she said. "Take care."

He waited until he was in the car before calling Karen's father. He arranged to pick him up on the way.

She crammed some of the food into her mouth with her fingers. The tangy mix of noodles, chicken and vegetables was still warm and she relished the heat more than the meal itself. Her raw and empty stomach heaved as it tried to manage the sudden influx. She swallowed a second mouthful and then a third. Before long, the foil container was empty, apart from some dark liquid. She lifted it to her mouth and tipped it so she got every last salty drop. Wiping her face with the back of her hand, she scrabbled round in the bag to see if there was more. No food. Just a little book of matches and a paper napkin.

Nine o'clock. Suddenly charged with nutrients, her brain began to work. She couldn't stay out here all night. She had to find a place to stay. She got shakily to her feet and the world lurched. She propped herself up against the door and waited for the sensation to pass. She still had hold of the matches so she shoved them in her pocket. Wobbly, but upright, she ineffectually brushed down her clothes, before taking a step forward to see where she was.

It could be anywhere. But she could get a taxi to take her to a cheap hotel. Yes, that's what she would do. Taking each step very slowly, she walked across the pavement to a lamp-post near the kerb and held up her arm.

She forgot about the money until the driver asked her for payment. There were just a few coins in the bottom of her purse and a patchy recollection grew of what had taken place in the flat.

"I'm sorry," she said. "I haven't got enough."

The driver swore, leaned backwards from his window and wrenched open the passenger door.

"Get out."

"Where am I?" she said as she got out.

"Use yer eyes." The taxi sped away.

Karen stood helplessly on the pavement and looked this way and that. Shops, cars, traffic lights, people. Then suddenly, she began to laugh. She was back where she started! The book-binders with a large silver car in front was just across the road. A red glow from the windows above told her they were still there. No-one could tell her that her guardian angel or her tending spirit hadn't guided her. She was meant to find her way back.

Soon she was outside, banging on the door. There was no response. She looked to each side of the shop to see if there was another entrance to the flat above. A half-glass door to the left seemed to be a possible so she banged on that until her fist ached. Standing back, she could see shadows pass behind the curtained windows. Why did nobody come?

It took almost ten minutes before she remembered she still had her mobile phone. Only for Gerard. She found it quickly and rang his number. It never occurred to her that he wouldn't answer. The least they could do was to find her somewhere to stay. Until she got the money.

He did.

"Hello, Karen," he sounded friendly enough. "Got the money already?"

"No," she surprised herself at how strong she sounded. "I need somewhere to stay until tomorrow. You owe me that."

He laughed. He carried on laughing before he said, "Until tomorrow," and then she heard a slight click.

But his voice was still there. Not talking to her but about her. She didn't understand.

The words were faint, as if he had put the phone down and walked away. She strained to hear the broken conversation.

"She's a liability. After tomorrow… no use for her. I'll have all the money I… away. By the time she… round we'll have gone."

"It would be best if she dies too."

"…anyway. She's an alcoholic. Mixed with the potions, it won't be long… accident. She's addicted. She doesn't know it. Besides which she has…" Gerard's voice faded even further and she missed what he said.

Too? The word grew and grew in her heart and she pressed the little phone even tighter to her ear. Oh, my darling Patrick. What have I done?

Then a laugh. From the pastor.

"She really thinks Celeste was looking after him, doesn't she?"

A rage, a furious, frantic, roaring rage swirled around her and she yelled down the phone. Every obscenity and curse she could think of. At some point, her tinny voice must have been heard above their cruel laughter because the line went dead. She banged and banged on the door, cursing them and crying out for their damnation.

Tom sat quietly with Mr Abbott as he read through his daughter's letter. The older man's hand shook very slightly as he held the pages close to his eyes and it was more than five minutes before he sat back in the chair and closed his eyes.

"We let her down so badly. All of us."

Tom extended his hand to take the letter from him and began to read.

There was no salutation; no 'Dear Dad' or even 'Dear Mr Abbott.'

I want to tell you this. There are lots of things you don't know and after all this is over, I'm going away and it'll be better if this is all done with before I go. Better for me and for Patrick.

"Would you mind getting me a taxi?" Mr Abbott spoke with almost a whisper and Tom realised as he looked up that she must have dealt him a real body blow. Keen as he was to read on, he could do that just as easily at home.

"I'll take you," he said. "Would you like me to make you a copy of this?"

Mr Abbott shook his head.

"Those words will be burned in my mind for the rest of my life, Detective Inspector. I just hope and pray I get the chance to make amends."

Jack was waiting for him outside the front door.

"I'm sorry boy," Tom said as he bent down to stroke the cat's head. "It's all a bit crazy at the moment. Did you get anything from Alice earlier?"

What am I doing? He thought as he pushed the key in the lock. I'm getting as bad as she is. Mind you, the day the cat answers back is when I'll really be in trouble.

His answering machine light was flashing.

"Hi, Tom. Give me a call if you're not in too late? Love you."

For the second time that evening he sat down on the stairs. She loved him. She'd just said it. On the

269

phone. He stood up and played the message again. Grinning, he waltzed into the kitchen and punched the air. Jack jumped up onto the work surface next to him, so in the absence of Lily, Tom picked Jack up and swirled him around. The expression on the cat's face due to the indignity of his position made Tom laugh out loud.

"I think a glass of merlot for me and a tasty treat for you."

Tom pulled out a balloon-shaped glass from the cupboard above the microwave and selected a bottle of wine from the rack under the counter. Whistling, he reached across to open the fridge, keeping Jack from a full assault on the contents with his right foot. Peering in, he pulled out some ham for the cat and a ripe blue-veined cheese for himself.

As he uncorked the wine, he checked the clock and decided that it would never be too late to call her and say goodnight.

She was clearly half-asleep. They made an arrangement to meet the following day and before he said goodbye, he told her he loved her. The line was quiet for a heartbeat before she answered. He could tell she was smiling.

"Me too," she said.

Norah Jones was playing softly on the CD player. His mouth was tingling from a particularly large piece of cheese and he ran his tongue around his mouth to round up any stray bits of cracker. He took a slurp of wine and sent a text to Seymour.

"Am at home now – ring any time," and added his home number for speed. Then he remembered the letter.

His home phone rang as he got into the hall where he'd left his jacket.

"Tom Ashton."

"We've got a fire. At the flat I took you to. Two bodies."

"Identity?"

"Don't know yet. Both men. But we've reports of a woman banging on the door earlier wanting to be let in. A white woman."

"Shit."

"The search has gone up a notch now, Tom," said Seymour. "This is not just about Patrick any more. It's a Met case too."

"I'm on my way," said Tom. "Keep in touch."

He shot upstairs, packed a bag and left a pile of dried food out and a bowl of water for Jack. He resealed the wine. Good job he'd only had half a glass.

"Best try Alice tomorrow, buddy," he said. Jack was standing by the front door. Judging by the way he trotted out ahead, Tom reckoned he'd already decided that for himself.

He should really tell Frank. With any luck, he'd be half-asleep too. He pulled up his boss' number on his phone as he got settled in his car.

"No, Tom," the Rodent was crystal clear. "Until they find Karen, this is not your case. DS Seymour will keep you up to speed with developments. I expect to see you in the office first thing."

Tom wanted to kick himself. He should have asked for forgiveness not permission. Now he was stuck 180 miles away from the action. Shit.

Tom thumped his way back into the house and dropped his bag on the floor. At least there was almost a whole bottle of red wine waiting for him.

Damn. He just knew the case was going to break without him.

Five minutes later, he was sitting with Jack on his lap and a large glass of wine in his hand. He took a welcome gulp. As he stroked the cat's warm back, he let his mind wander over the facts of the case. Come on Charles, he thought. Give me something.

"Ow! For heaven's sake, cat!" He tried to dislodge the animal for drilling its claws in his thighs. "I bet you don't give Alice the same treatment." She was right, he thought. When she said something terrible was stirring. Maybe this was what she had seen? That day she collapsed on the doorstep. Fire, smoke, cries, voices. Bloody hell. He took another long drink.

Burn in hell, Karen thought as she ran along the road and down into a side street. I know I will. Her feet seemed to know exactly where to take her. As she rounded the corner at the bottom of the street. She saw it. Cleansing and purifying in its silent blackness. She didn't even break stride. She ran straight over the bank and into the water.

He was awake almost as soon as the phone rang. Shallow but restful sleep was another army legacy.

"What have you got?"

"Tom, where the hell are you?"

"Travel got blocked by the DCI. I did leave you messages and a text?"

Charles Seymour grunted.

"It's a fuckin' circus down here. Get yourself up and running. We've just fished Karen Abbott out of the Thames. And she's still alive."

Chapter 28

As Tom drove along the dark and empty motorway, he thought back to Karen's letter. It still didn't make much sense to him but if they could just talk to her…

Charles was right. It was a rambling rant but it was also clear that Karen Abbott was having to deal with some pretty damaging stuff. She accused her adopted parents of lying to her and of being to blame for all that had gone wrong in her life. That they colluded with the authorities to try and take Patrick away from her. That they'd stifled her. That they had stopped her knowing who she really was.

"Why didn't you tell me?" She'd written that line four or five times throughout the letter. That she always knew there was something they weren't telling her, that she never felt quite like she belonged. The one thing she was glad of, she said, was that it gave her the chance to find herself. And what she believed in.

Two-faced, she called them. All forgiveness and turn the other cheek and church every Sunday but they still dished out disapproving horror at the thought of her 'getting into trouble'. Into trouble? The knowing glances. All made sense now. She had loved Mathieu. Patrick was wanted. Not a sin. Not a sin.

Tom checked the motorway signs. A few more exits to go. He opened his window to get a blast of cool air. His mobile phone sat mutely on the seat beside him, so presumably she was hanging on. He indicated to overtake a large container lorry and moved into the middle lane. Motorway driving should always be like this, he thought and he eased the BMW back up to a steady 80mph.

He was building a picture. A young woman, possibly with her natural mother's 'wayward' genes if there was such a thing, being brought up in a kind but claustrophobic environment. She decided to flex her wings and head off to Africa for work experience and falls in love with the excitement and colour of the place.

She learns about the traditions and community and meets a man. Story as old as time there. Maybe this Mathieu guy was even more appealing because it was all so different. Okay, then what? Parents are less than pleased. Not the supportive family homecoming she expected. Check that. When did she come back? What happened to Mathieu? Did he dump her? Maybe, maybe not – there was something in the letter about losing the man she loved. Whether he was dead or he left, she was abandoned. Then she comes home and at some point, has to deal with dying mother and the knowledge that practically the whole of her life was built on secrets and disapproval.

She found some sort of 'family' when she lived in London. She said that a few times too. 'I was finding my own family' she wrote. Better than the one she came from or the one she had. Something like that.

Angry? Yes. Bitter? Without doubt. Off the rails in more ways than one, for sure. Even so, he thought. Doesn't give the tiniest clue as to whether she was in-volved in her son's death. Maybe Abbott was right and she wasn't involved and didn't even know about it. Well, at least now, they were all going to get the opportunity to find out. Thankfully, he was going to be able to have some time with her first. Her father was following down at his own pace.

Tom knew he needed to concentrate now. The signs for the M25 told him he wasn't going to be long now. Seymour had told him the North Middlesex Hospital just off the North Circular Road. Tom vaguely knew the geography but, in his experience, it was easy to go the wrong way.

Karen lay as still as she could with eyes tightly closed. A kaleidoscope of reds and yellows played across the middle of her lids but she knew it wasn't a dream this time. She knew exactly where she was and what she had done. It was finished. Patrick was dead. Was he with Mathieu? She hoped so. Was Gerard dead? She hoped that too. But she prayed that his spirit would never be allowed to rest for what he'd done.

"I'm in the car park," said Tom. "What ward?"

I'll meet you at the main entrance," replied Sey-mour. "You'll never find her on your own. Place is a maze."

"Someone posted with her?"

"Of course."

Tom was heartily sick of hospitals. And he was desperate for the toilet. Fortunately, there was one just inside so he nipped in quickly and was just coming out as he saw the familiar long, easy stride of his colleague approaching from along the corridor.

"How's she doing?"

"More in shock than anything," Seymour reported as they walked briskly back the way he came. "Reckon she was in the water about four minutes. Cold but not as bad as it has been. Didn't need too much resuscitation so the lungs are okay. Doctors feel she's going to be fine to interview but they've taken blood samples to check for drugs and alcohol. She was rambling in the ambulance."

"Saying?" Tom wrinkled his nose. He was getting to really hate this smell.

"My lovely boy. Calling his name. That sort of thing."

"Penny's dropped then," said Tom.

DS Seymour stopped suddenly and turned to face him straight on.

"Do you really think she didn't know about it?"

"Beginning to think so," said Tom. "But then, I think she may also have created the situation that led to his death. Knowingly or otherwise."

Four days later, Tom was back with the team in the CID office. Everyone was there, apart from DS Charles Seymour. He was now fully back at the Met.

Karen Abbott was being held on remand in the hospital wing of Styal Women's Prison. She was charged with the murders of Gerard Baptiste and a Bernard Duvalier; and with being an accessory to the murder of her son Patrick Baptiste. She seemed to be suffering some sort of mental breakdown and was felt to be at further risk of self-harm but the doctors seemed to think she would soon be fit to plead. Mr Abbott was paying for her solicitor, still hoping she would agree to see him.

"From the top, Tom," said Frank Dawson. "I think we could all do with understanding what went on here. But before you start," he said as Tom opened his mouth to do just that. "I'd like to say well done to all of you for wrapping this up so quickly. This is a fine example of not only expert investigation but of teamwork and inter-force collaboration." He nodded to signal he was done.

Tom stood at the front of the room, looked around at the satisfied faces and felt the buoyancy that comes from getting a result.

"We knew we were dealing with other cultures and beliefs," he said. "But what made this case unusual (if that even approaches being the right word) is that Karen Abbott is white. How did she get into the situation where her child would be at risk from evil practices that have their roots thousands of miles away? I've managed to talk to her and we have got a pretty good picture now." He paused, conscious of the story he was about to tell.

"Okay. One piece of the jigsaw started in a small place in Ireland in 1972. Her natural mother, Annie Colgan, got pregnant. Being from good Catholic stock, the family closed ranks, put her in the care of the local convent and passed the child, Karen, to a distant cousin living in England. The local priest was the broker. No unnecessary administration required. Mr and Mrs Abbott registered the child as their own. There was no legal adoption it turns out, for all the role Mr and Mrs Abbott portrayed. Probably couldn't get away with it now. And it wasn't just any convent, mind you. This was the Good Shepherd in Limerick. One of the Magdalene Laundries."

Tom was rewarded by a collective "Aah…" as people made the connection.

"The holy sisters were not nice women by all accounts. Annie Colgan was encouraged to forget her daughter and pay the penance for her sins. She was there for three years. Seems she rose to the challenge but when she got out began using alcohol as a crutch. She never married, lived with her parents – father also a heavy drinker – until they died. She's a stalwart member of the local church."

"Karen, meanwhile," he put his hands in his pockets and relaxed his back against the wall, "was having an uneventful, if dull, upbringing in the Midlands. Bright and conscientious at school, there was no hint of any instability until she hit her teens. She was a bit of a loner, popular but with no close friends. Mr Abbott (thanks Alice, he thought), remembers that she was hard to control but he left most of that to his wife. I'd guess that anything to do with hormones clearly terrified him."

Ryan tutted at him and he threw up his hands in mock horror.

"Fast forward. Daughter does okay at school, goes to Liverpool University to study social science. No serious boyfriends as far as we know but does have a few drink problems."

"Taking after her real mother." Dean observed.

"Exactly. After drifting between jobs for a few years, she begins to get some direction and decides to do some voluntary work overseas. Mr and Mrs Abbott quite happy about this. Must almost seemed like missionary work to them. Karen ends up in Africa. In Benin. DS Seymour says that it's a part of the world where the people talk and go to the local pastor or witch doctor for advice during the week but then attend church on a Sunday. Voodoo and Christianity happily exist side-by-side. The majority of worship is decent."

Tom eased back, away from the wall and began to pace a little, hands still in his pockets. The sun was beginning to shine through the venetian blinds on the windows and the room was getting warm. It would soon be Easter.

"She met and fell in love with a man called Mathieu Baptiste. A community worker. She found out she was pregnant by him when she came back to England. They kept in touch, she says, and he was going to join her here but then he disappeared. She tried to contact him on a number of occasions but she was told via the agency she worked for that he was dead. Mr and Mrs Abbott were not supportive, in fact, they were highly critical. Now we know why. Just like her mother. Karen was by now living in a flat in Tottenham and did so until Patrick was two years old."

Tom sat on the edge of a desk.

"She's given us some of this but I think we have to colour in the rest. Okay, she's alone, drinking too much, feels she has no family to support her. She comes to the attention of social services and the child is temporarily taken into care after she was found slumped outside her own flat one afternoon. Dead drunk. Patrick was crying inside. Seems she'd been trying to get in touch with Mathieu again. Anyway, the experience gave her a jolt. Got friendly with the care worker who put her in touch with a voluntary community group nearby who might give her some support."

He paused in case there were any questions so far but none came. He pressed on.

"She goes to a place on Seven Sister's Road where she meets some people she feels she can relate to. They become her support system. At the same time, Mrs Abbott is terminally ill. Karen is told, at the age of 28, that she isn't their daughter. She is shocked and angry but feels this might explain some things that were going on in her mind. She persuades the Abbots to tell her who her mother is. Annie Colgan was easy to trace. Although the priest who arranged the whole thing died years ago, Mrs Abbott had kept some old letters from Annie and it turned out she was still living in the family home. Karen calls her and goes to visit. Mr Abbott paid for her trip to Ireland but he was loath to give her any more money, even for the boy. He didn't really like who Karen had become.

"From what the manager of the refuge told us, Karen genuinely wanted to find her 'roots'. She didn't ask for anything. Not then. But it was not a happy meeting."

"I can believe that," said Elliott. "The woman was as warm as hoar frost."

"Imagine what that felt like? Not only did her mother reject her, it was on the orders of the Catholic Church. Suffice to say, Karen Abbott turned against that particular branch of religion. And cut off contact with Mr Abbott. Not until, mind you, he had given her a substantial sum of money. Fast forward a year or so. After months of searching, Karen finds Mathieu's brother Gerard. What motivated him? Well, we can't ask him now, but certainly money, the power to manipulate and, knowing he was infected with HIV, the tool for a voodoo cure."

"And," said Mary Andrews, "DS Seymour said there was sometimes a kudos with having a white woman."

Did he now, thought Tom.

"I've heard that," said Ryan. More mutterings followed.

"So, plenty of reasons why she would be happy being embraced by this community. And to start experimenting with substances other than alcohol. Voluntarily to begin with. Gerard suggests and organises the move to Liverpool. Karen said she was happy to have a new start. And she knew the city well. Then Gerard begins to ask for money. Karen gets in touch with Mr Abbott demanding cash."

"When?" This from Talbot.

"She said she couldn't remember this at all but Mr Abbott said it was last September. She seems to have quite a few gaps. She admitted drinking a lot but often, though, she lost days from her memory which leads us to believe she was given, or took, increasingly large doses of drugs. Particularly in the run up to Patrick's murder.

"Apparently Gerard changed towards her. Not affectionate. She was worried, frightened of losing him. He seemed to resent the time she spent with Patrick. She coped the way she always did. She drank. And with that, undoubtably, she took a fine old cocktail of drugs that turned her into a zombie.

"It maybe that the other man who died in the fire was the one who conducted the ceremony. Karen has no recollection of that time. She was told by a woman called Celeste – supposedly Mathieu and Gerard's sister – that she was going to look after 'our little one' until Karen was 'better'. Karen told us she felt cherished, that she 'belonged'."

"Does she know she's HIV?"

The hard question broke across the room like a sword.

"No."

Tom stood while he tried to get the next sentence right.

"Here was a woman, desperate for her own family, searching for something. Feeling the utmost betrayal by her own faith – and kind if you like – and finding something addictively attractive in this world of her lover. And, as it transpires, her lover's brother." He sighed.

"Is this why she left him?" asked Dean.

Tom shook his head.

"He told her this was the only way she would get Patrick back. She had to get herself straight. She believed that her child was being cared for. She was trying to get her boy back. Instead, she left him vulnerable and available for what Gerard wanted. A sacrificial lamb."

"Shit." Talbot, the only father on the team, hung his head.

"I still don't understand what happened in London," said Mary Andrews.

"She didn't believe Patrick was dead. She went to find him. It seems that she was made to realise the dreadful truth so cruelly that her world crashed in. All those months of alcohol and drugs made her confused, with episodes when she was totally divorced from reality but she knew what she was doing when she set fire to that place. She knew full well who was inside."

"Suppose it's retribution of sorts," observed Elliott. "The bastards who killed the boy end up in flames. Wish we could have brought them to justice though."

Tom couldn't determine the mutterings that followed but Elliott had a point. Whilst they had answers and the men concerned couldn't do this again, it was a grim result.

"And the woman you met, Tom? What was her role?" Frank Dawson's gaze was direct and searching. He knew how Tom felt about Erzulie. Confused, admiring and anxious to believe the goodness he saw in her. Tom could see everyone else was waiting for his answer.

"We can't trace her," he said, honestly. "The Met say she is probably back in Africa."

He looked around the room and caught his friend's questioning glance. A knowing passed between them. The room was quiet as people absorbed what they'd been told.

Dean stood and waved his arms around the room.

"I propose a drink tonight – everyone up for it?"

Judging by the noise, everyone was. Tom smiled and thought that Dean's words were strangely prophetic. Quietly he went over to his computer and sent Lily a message.

"Dinner at my place tomorrow night? Am planning something special."

He'd buy the champagne on the way home tonight, knowing the timing was right.

Her reply came almost at once.

"Yes, please."

THE END

About the author

Maureen Devlin was born in Liverpool in 1957.

In 1979, she qualified as a pharmacist from the University of Leicester and, in her first professional role, turned an under-performing business into a highly successful concern. After gaining a PhD in pharmaceutical microbiology, Maureen joined Glaxo-SmithKline (GSK), originally working in research and development, before moving on to customer relations. On leaving GSK, Maureen excelled in several roles, including working for the National Prescribing Centre and as an NHS consultant.

A lifelong lover of the arts, Maureen was a talented actress and a much-respected member of the Altrincham Garrick Theatre. She also enjoyed writing and was a regular contributor to the Manchester Writers' Workshop.

Ancestral Sin is the third of a trilogy of crime novels featuring Detective Inspector Tom Ashton. Tragically, Maureen's untimely death in 2009 meant that she did not live to see its publication.

Printed in Great Britain
by Amazon

48003387R00162